FORGET ME

SYNERGY BOOK 5

MICHELLE MCCRAW

LAZY DOG BOOKS

Cover by Avery Kingston

ISBN: 978-1-7368294-9-3

BOOKS BY MICHELLE MCCRAW

Synergy Series

Work with Me

Friend Me

Trip Me Up

Boss Me

Forget Me

This book is a milestone, my fifth.
I dedicate it to my kids, Peyton and Jonah.
I know you'll never read these books—please don't!—but my wish is that pursuing my passion has shown you that you can pursue yours.
I hope that shouting my ideas, my words, into the world will give you the courage to make your voices heard, too.

1

MIMI

I'D FORGOTTEN EVERYTHING. Except his pretty eyes.

Blue and round, though the tequila had dulled the details. I couldn't recall the exact shade or if they had flecks in them. Just blue. And glasses. Clark Kent glasses. The pendant light that hung over our heads glinted off the lenses.

The shape and color of the frames were fuzzy in my memory, but I was ninety-two percent certain they weren't round and metal like Byron's. Even as drunk as I was, I'd have run the other direction.

How long had I stared into his eyes while we sat at that Divisadero Street bar? It felt like hours, but the tequila. So much tequila.

A flash of memory: blue eyes crinkled in concern and a big hand gripping my arm to steady me on the stool. And another flash, though this one flitted away from me, just out of reach. His gaze burning into me, serious and intense. Something pressed into my hand.

I looked down at my palm like it would still be there. But there was nothing except an ugly plastic ring, the light-up fake diamond as big as a walnut. When I tapped it, it flickered weakly in neon pink. As Bree's maid of honor, I'd laid down the rule: no vulgar swag at her bachelorette party. But one of Bree's other friends had brought a sack full of plastic crap. And after a couple shots of tequila, I didn't care about the rules. I wrenched the ring off my finger and dropped it onto the counter.

Damned hangover. I rubbed my temple, but that did nothing to soothe the tightness around my brain.

Although I didn't remember much about his appearance, I remembered how last night's mystery man made me feel. Interesting. Cared-for. Safe. And I'd laughed so hard my stomach muscles were still a little sore.

Actually, that might have been from the puking.

The buzz of my phone against my kitchen counter set off a new pain somewhere in the vicinity of my molars.

I plucked the cheap fuchsia sash off of it—the script on it read, "Hot Mess," and hadn't *that* turned out to be true?—and tossed it aside. I scraped the phone off the counter and squinted one eye at the display. Bree. I stabbed the answer button.

"Why are you up so early?"

She groaned, and her voice came out hoarse. "Had to hug the throne. You drank as much as me. How are you?"

"Same." How was my breath? I couldn't show up to my presentation smelling like regurgitated tequila. I cupped my hand over my mouth, breathed out, and sniffed. Minty fresh. I jammed a pod into the coffeemaker and hit the brew button.

"Mimi," my best friend whined, "wasn't this easier in our twenties?"

"The drinking part or the hangover part?"

"Both. I remember going out on Saturday night and then drinking mimosas at Sunday brunch. Now just thinking about champagne—or orange juice—makes me want to hurl."

"I guess a lot of things are different now that we're over thirty." Like the weird rash around my mouth I'd had to cover up with an extra layer of foundation. The one that looked suspiciously like beard burn, though I definitely didn't remember kissing anyone. "Hey, do you remember much from last night?"

"Ugh, not really. Especially after the third round of tequila shots."

Third round? I strained my sluggish memory, but it was a blur of Bree's head thrown back in laughter, the other girls' giggles, and those glasses framing a pair of twinkling blue eyes.

The coffeemaker light blinked off, and I picked up my mug. The bitter scent of it made my stomach seize. I set it back on the counter. "Did you have a good time?"

"Yeah. Thanks for coming out. I know you had a lot going on with your brother's engagement party yesterday."

"I wouldn't have missed your bachelorette party for the world. We've been friends too long for that." We'd been best friends since we'd met in the theater showing *The Incredibles*. Both our families had refused to watch it with us. It was the third time for me, the fifth time for her. We'd bonded over how much we identified with Violet, though we hadn't known how to express it then. As our friendship deepened, we'd obsessed over Spider-Man, Henry Cavill's Superman, and every one of the Avengers.

So even though I didn't usually waste time at parties, I'd rearranged my entire weekend to fit in both Ben's party and hers, working late on Friday night to finish up my presentation.

"Thank God we have a day to recover before we have to go back to work," she said.

I hummed and pulled my presentation out of my satchel, just to check it one last time. The crisp pie charts, the line graphs showing my projections. There was nothing for perfect Larissa to find fault with, and we were going to wow her boss, Jackson Jones. Who also happened to be an executive at Synergy, where I worked.

"Oh, no," Bree said. "That's not an I'm-going-back-to-bed *hmm*. That's an I'm-going-for-a-ten-mile-run *hmm*."

I chuckled. "You know I hate running. Actually, I have to work today."

"On a Sunday?"

"It's for the foundation. We have a brunch meeting in the Mission in half an hour, and I'm presenting next year's budget to Jackson Jones."

"Wait, you're not even getting *paid* for this?"

"No." Though someday if I copied my little brother and turned my passion into a paid job, I could have an occasional day off. "Hustle culture, you know."

"Ugh, don't give me that bullshit. You're a mensch. You're doing it for—for the kids."

I knew she'd almost said *for me*. It was true that I'd started volunteering for the foundation for my best friend. For the time I'd heard that jerk, Anthony Anker, call her Blinky Barbie on our first day of seventh grade. I'd wanted to get up in his face, try out the punch my brother had taught me the summer before, *definitely* make sure Anthony never made fun of my friend's tic again, but Bree had held me back, told me he wasn't worth getting detention over. But all these years later, I'd kept up my volunteer work because I truly loved the work the foundation did for kids with Tourette's. Kids like Bree had been.

I'd just opened my mouth to break up the tension with a joke when she said, "Did you think about what we talked about last night?"

Staring at my poster of Doctor Strange, I scanned back for a memory of anything other than tequila and screams of laughter and dancing. Dancing? "You're going to have to refresh my memory."

"You don't remember?" Shit, she sounded hurt. "We talked about how you're the last single person in our friend group. You promised to try to—"

"Doubtful." I twisted my mug on the counter until its handle was at a precise 45-degree angle. "You know how focused I am on my career now. And on the foundation. I don't have time for distractions."

"A distraction like Byron, you mean? That guy was a douche

canoe. There are tons of good guys out there, Mimi. Guys who'll help you and won't steal your promotion."

"I don't need help. I can succeed all on my own." The words came out sharper than I'd intended.

"I know, I know. All you need is smarts, drive…"

"And confidence," we finished together. My mother had said those words about a million times.

"Your mom got married," Bree said.

"She's the top environmental lawyer in the state. I'd never compare myself to her. And just because you're a week from saying 'I do' doesn't mean it's right for everyone. I want to establish myself in my career first."

"And scratch that itch with one-night stands?"

I lifted my chin even though she couldn't see me. "There's nothing wrong with my no-strings hookups. I get all the benefits, none of the arguing over whose work function we have to go to and where we spend the holidays."

"It's kind of nice to have someone to spend the holidays with, you know."

I eased a hip against the counter. I hadn't missed the way Mom's eyes had gone soft when my brother showed up at her Hanukkah party with his fiancé. They'd worn matching ugly Hanukkah sweaters. Even my cold, black heart had melted a little at how adorable they were together.

Me? I couldn't exactly ask one of my hookups to come to my parents' party after I'd slipped out of his apartment before dawn and stopped replying to his texts.

"What, you want me to show up to your wedding with a plus-one?"

"No!" Her laugh was high and strained. "We already gave the final count to the caterer. But you're deflecting. Even Ben—"

The intercom dinged, saving me from my best friend's speech about how even my little brother had finally found lasting love. She was right about all the coupling-up. A week never went by without the arrival of an invitation to a wedding or a bridal shower or an engagement party. If someone sent me a birth announcement, I was going to puke. Again.

"Sorry, Bree. Someone's at the door." It was probably Ben dropping by to check on me. Though last I'd seen him at his engagement party yesterday afternoon, he'd been pretty tipsy himself.

"Good luck with your big presentation. I know you'll rock it. Call me after?" She made a kissing sound before I disconnected.

I walked to the intercom. It was just like Ben to bring me a sack of breakfast pastries to soak up the alcohol. My stomach gurgled.

"Hey," I said into the speaker as I buzzed him up.

I opened the door a crack and headed back toward the kitchen to tuck my presentation into my satchel. Then I froze. Ben still had a key. Why would he use the buzzer?

When I whirled back around, the answer filled my doorway. Six-foot-something of tanned skin, blond hair, a clean-shaven jaw that could cut glass, and eyes the color of the Pacific Ocean on a rare sunny day. Ben's friend, and his fiancé's cousin, Mateo. I stared at his muscle-rounded shoulder where his too-tight black T-shirt clung to it. Looking at his face was like staring into the sun. Eye-searingly bright and beautiful. Too handsome to be real. And today I didn't need a distraction that came in the shape of a flirty Thor look-alike.

"Good morning, bella," he said, stepping into my apartment.

I wrinkled my nose at the faint scent of cigarette smoke that wafted in with him. I'd known Mateo long enough not to feel any flutters in my belly. Everyone in his world—male, female, old, young—got a flirtatious nickname. He was an equal-opportunity player, and it meant nothing.

Case in point: at Ben's party yesterday, he'd chatted up Marlee, Ben's work-bestie. She was the most beautiful woman I'd ever met, all smooth honey hair and fashion sense. But she was taken, and Mateo knew it. Still, I'd caught him looking at me over her head a couple of times. Like he wanted me to notice that

Marlee was the kind of person he spent time with. Never someone like me. With me, he was silent and aloof.

In fact, why had he come here this morning? He'd never been to my place, not even with Ben.

"Why are you here?" I crossed my arms. "Fresh out of swimsuit models to seduce?"

His sparkling grin drooped. He looked...hurt? "I came to check on you. Are you feeling all right this morning?"

"Fine," I said. "Though I'm actually in a—wait. What do you know about last night?"

His dark-blond eyebrows scrunched down. "Don't you remember?"

I thought back to yesterday. I'd been buzzed already when I'd dashed from Ben's engagement party to join Bree's bachelorette party in progress. Had Ben noticed and sent Mateo to watch over me? It was the kind of thing my little brother would do.

I didn't remember seeing Mateo at the first bar. Or the second one. I remembered the booth, the round table spread with shot glasses, Bree snort-laughing, sparkling plastic tiaras, holiday lights blinking around the window, and the room spinning around me as the drinks kept coming.

"No. Why? Were you there?"

The corners of his mouth turned down. "You don't remember?"

"Should I?" I'd definitely have remembered if he'd been at the bar. Bree's friends would have made him the king of their court. They'd have flattered him, touched him, flirted with him in a way that made me itch. They didn't know Mateo like I did. He might be fitness-model gorgeous, but he was about as deep as a puddle.

He seemed to deflate. Then he pasted on a shadow of his usual teasing smile and held out a white bakery bag. "I brought you breakfast."

My stomach roiled. "No, thanks. Hangover. I need coffee."

"No." He brushed past me. "You need carbs. Sugar. Do you have any ginger tea?"

I scurried to catch up with him, but his broad shoulders and the stink of cigarettes filled my entire galley kitchen. My throat burned. I didn't have time for another visit to the toilet. I waved my hand in front of my face. "Sorry, but you smell like smoke, and"—I swallowed—"I'm afraid my stomach isn't settled enough for that. Thanks for dropping by, but…"

His face fell, but he set the bag on the counter before he shoved open the kitchen window. Huh. I'd thought it was painted shut.

"Better now?" He stood beside it for a moment as if he could air himself out.

I took a deep breath of the cold, fresh air. "Better. Thanks."

"Now, for your stomach." He opened an upper cabinet. "You need something with ginger. Or prickly pear?"

Prickly pear? "No. I live in the real world where we drink coffee when we're hungover. Thanks for coming, but I need to get ready."

"Ready?" He shut the cabinet and turned toward me. "You look perfect."

"Thank you." The words came out flat, automatic. He said that kind of shit to everyone. In my oversize black sweater and jeans, I wasn't anything approaching perfect, not compared to a demigod like Mateo. Obviously, he kept up his physique with daily work-outs. He was the kind of guy who'd drink kale smoothies with his equally hot underwear-model partner. Who talked about supplements and reps and flipping prickly pear.

Not that there was anything wrong with that. It was just different. I preferred to work out my brain with spreadsheets, fueled by a bag of salt-and-vinegar chips. Hard pass on kale.

"I need to go. To a meeting. I'll eat there." I squeezed around him into the kitchen to shoo him out.

"Yes, your meeting with Larissa and Jackson. Shouldn't you eat first?"

"My—my what? How do you know about that?"

He looked down at the bag and mumbled something.

Right. Ben must have mentioned it at the party yesterday. Get a couple drinks into him, and nothing was a secret. Not that my foundation meeting was a secret, but it definitely wasn't any of Mateo's business.

"Okay, so, good chat, but I'm sure you've got some muscles that need sculpting." He didn't. They were absolutely perfect, but his ego didn't need any stroking from me. "And I've got to leave."

"You'll deal with Larissa's bullshit better if you don't show up hangry. Try these. They're delicious." He reached for the bakery bag, but when his arm brushed mine, he jolted. The bag knocked against my cup of coffee and tipped it. Dark-brown liquid gushed across the counter, straight toward my papers.

"No!" I leaped to pick them up, but Mateo's solid body blocked my way. Coffee soaked into the papers, melting my perfect pie charts and smearing my lovely line graphs. "Shit, Mateo. That's my presentation for"—I checked the clock on the wall—"for my meeting that starts in fifteen minutes!"

"Can you print new ones?" He grabbed the kitchen towel and blotted at the papers, but all that did was transfer the stain to my pristine ecru towel. Panic tightened my throat.

"Don't! Stop." When I grabbed his arm, he flinched. The wet paper ripped.

Even if I could magically dry the paper in fifteen minutes, a pie chart held together with Scotch tape wasn't going to impress anyone. My presentation, and my chance to impress Jackson Jones, was ruined.

"I—I'm sorry, Miriam."

My body heated, and my anger boiled over. "Dammit, Mateo. I'm going to be late, and now I have no presentation. Get out of my way." I tossed the papers in the trash. I didn't have time to go to the office and reprint them. I'd have to show them on screen. Except—

Horror dawning, I looked down at the coffee. It had breached my satchel. With my laptop inside. When I yanked it out, coffee dripped from the corner.

"Shit!" I snatched the ruined towel from Mateo and blotted at the edge. *Please, please,* please, *start.* I set my laptop on a dry part of the counter, flipped it open, and pressed the power button. A few pixels lit, then the screen went black.

I mashed the power button, and this time, nothing happened at all. "Goddammit!"

His face was paler than my kitchen towel. "Can I do anything?"

I ground my molars. "Get. Out."

"I—I can ask Lito—I mean Cooper—to get you a new laptop—"

"No!" He might be Mateo's favorite cousin Miguelito, but to me, he was Cooper Fallon, my boss's boss's boss. No way could he learn that I'd ruined my Synergy laptop. His temper was legendary, and even his soon-to-be sister-in-law might not be safe from one of his infamous tongue-lashings. "Just go."

"But I—"

"Go!" I pointed at the door.

He folded into himself and shuffled away. My apartment door clicked shut as I stuffed my deceased laptop into my soggy satchel.

Despairing, I glanced at the clock again. I'd definitely be late. Neither Larissa nor Jackson Jones would be impressed. And tomorrow, I'd have to ask my boss for a new laptop.

Thanks, Mateo.

2

MIMI

WE WERE MEETING at one of those fancy hipster places where the coffee was fair-trade and organic and the treats—if you could call them that—were low-carb and keto-friendly. A place that appealed to Larissa, who ate practically nothing and never missed a spin class. She belonged to the same class as our donors, always put together, never a blond hair out of place.

I wished I were like her.

But today, I was exactly the opposite. Sweaty, out of breath, and ten minutes late with no presentation to show them. Just my dead laptop in its soggy bag and an aching head full of figures.

I was sixty-three percent sure she'd fire me. Though could you fire someone from a volunteer position? Either way, she wouldn't give me the praise I craved. Not that I deserved it.

The aroma of cinnamon and nutmeg from Christmas-spiced coffee made my stomach curdle. I swallowed. Puking in front of Jackson and Larissa and the other woman at their table would be the cherry on top of my disaster sundae.

I hurried over. "Sorry I'm late."

Larissa didn't have to say a word. The arch of her eyebrows

and the flick of her straight, platinum-blond hair said it all. I remembered the last time I'd disappointed her, when I'd asked for more time to process an expense check because I was heads-down in month-end close for Synergy. She'd broken her typical sweet-as-honey front to say with steel in her tone, *We've talked about this, Miriam. I need to be able to rely on you.*

And I'd let her down again. This time, in front of her boss. The flat line of her pink lips hit me right in my squishy, people-pleasing center. My cheeks burned.

"Sit down, Miriam. Let's begin," she said coolly.

"Sorry," I mumbled, letting my laptop bag slide off my shoulder. I didn't even have a good excuse today. Nothing but a hangover and the mistake I'd made by letting Hurricane Mateo into my apartment.

"Don't worry about it." Jackson leaned back in his chair and stretched his long legs out under the table. He rolled his shoulders under his faded black Santana T-shirt. "I'm usually the late one. Feels good not to be the slacker for once. Let me introduce you to my sister, Natalie."

Being called a slacker made my chest twinge. I put on a wobbly smile and stuck out my hand. "Miriam Levy-Walters. But everyone calls me Mimi."

She stood, half a foot taller than me in her heels. She wore heels on a Sunday? Her long-sleeved magenta sheath dress showed off her slender figure. She was blond, unlike her dark-haired brother, and her golden hair coiled at her nape in an elegant bun. Their eyes were the same, though. Warm chocolate brown irises fringed with a bounty of dark lashes.

I wiped my sweaty hands on my jeans before shaking her hand. I wished I'd worn slacks instead. If I'd known Jackson's socialite sister was joining us, I'd have put more thought into my meet-up-for-coffee-on-a-Sunday attire. And worn boots instead of ballet flats. I felt like Ant-Man standing next to her.

Natalie's grip was comfortingly firm. "I've heard great things about you. I'm glad the finances are in good hands." Her forehead creased, but then she smiled. The transition was so fast I wasn't sure I'd seen her frown at all. "I'm looking forward to seeing the work you've done on the projections."

The back of my neck itched. She wouldn't be hearing great things about me today.

"Nat's joining the team to help with the gala. Coffee?" Jackson shifted his feet as if he'd spring up and fetch it. A bazillionaire like Jackson Jones getting *me* coffee.

"No, thanks. Funny story…"

"In that case"—Larissa straightened her papers—"let's get the numbers out of the way."

Larissa was a paragon in the nonprofit world, having won an award for her previous nonprofit. But apparently, numbers were her weakness. I'd volunteered every week at Jackson's brand-new foundation for neurodivergent kids ever since he started it, and one day, he'd introduced me to the new director, Larissa. He'd said she needed help to put together a balance sheet and, knowing I was an accountant at his for-profit company, asked me to help her.

Larissa needed a lot more than a balance sheet. Her book-keeping was a disaster, but I'd organized it, and I was proud of what I'd done.

Well, except for today's coffee catastrophe.

I swallowed. "I have some unfortunate news about the budget presentation. My laptop died, and the printouts got ruined."

I couldn't summon back my anger at Mateo. I was the fool who'd let him into my place to bumble around. Besides, if I hadn't taken the papers out of my bag to admire them in an overflow of hubris, they might have been saved.

"Aren't they on the server?" Jackson asked. "I can grab them. I'm logged into the VPN."

I squeezed my eyes shut as heat flooded from my face to my neck. "No. I finished them up Friday night from home. I didn't think to upload them."

"You should have emailed them to me." Larissa's voice was

sharp as a wasp's sting. It wasn't the first time she'd reminded me not to leave anything to chance. She never did. Well, except for those receipts.

I looked down at my shoe. I'd been burned before, and I'd been afraid Larissa might take credit for my work. But that was ridiculous. She might be autocratic and a slovenly record-keeper, but she was no thief. Not like Byron. If I'd sent the presentation to her, at least we'd have something to show the Joneses.

"I thought you accounting types always dotted the Is and crossed the Ts. And it was just creative types like me who fucked up." Jackson chuckled.

The cold lump in my stomach prevented me from seeing the humor in the situation. "I'm sorry."

"What's wrong with your laptop?" he asked.

"Coffee?" I winced.

"Hand it over." He cracked his knuckles. "I'll work some magic on it."

"No, I'll just…" But I couldn't refuse his beckoning fingers. I slipped the laptop out of my satchel and handed it to him. He tsked as he pulled the device from its soggy case and patted it dry with the hem of his T-shirt.

Larissa cleared her throat. "Can you at least summarize the financial projections for us?"

"Sure." I pulled out the fourth chair and sat down. Jackson already had my laptop's battery out and was drying it with a paper napkin, but he looked up when I began to speak.

I tried to paint word pictures of the beautiful charts and graphs I'd worked so hard to create. But after a few minutes, I caught Jackson yawning behind my laptop, which he'd tented upside down on the table. Larissa's gaze was on her phone. Only Natalie smiled at me encouragingly.

Finally, I wrapped up weakly, "I'll send you the presentation tomorrow. There's an older copy on the server, and when I get back to the office, I'll be able to recreate the final projections."

Larissa looked up from her phone. "We need those numbers asap."

"Of course. Sorry," I mumbled.

"Now"—Jackson rubbed his hands together—"we get to the fun stuff. I brought Nat here so she can rescue the party."

The foundation's gala was hardly a party like Ben's backyard engagement celebration yesterday. In my ruined projections, we'd planned for it to bring in half the foundation's revenue for the year. The stakes were high.

"Rescue?" I repeated.

"A minor hiccup," Larissa said, waving her hand. "The venue canceled on us. But I've got a backup."

"Canceled? We're getting the deposit back, right?" I asked. Larissa had asked for it in cash although I'd advised against it.

"Deposit? I don't think we paid a deposit." She lifted her nose.

"I—of course we did. Didn't we?" Maybe I'd approved a cash withdrawal for something else.

"I think I'd remember," she said.

"I'll check the accounts again." I glanced wistfully at my dead laptop and the spreadsheets it held hostage.

Jackson said, "Regardless, since the gala's two months away, it's all hands on deck. That's why I brought in Nat."

"I've helped my mother with dozens of these things," Natalie said. "We'll pull it together."

"But my gala's going to be special, right?" Jackson asked. "Not one of her cookie-cutter black-tie galas."

"Sure." She laid a hand on her brother's arm. "We'll make it something you can be proud of."

"I'll help, too," I said, scrambling for anything that would make up for my mistakes. "I was my school's prom committee chair."

Larissa snorted. "A high-school prom is hardly a million-dollar fundraising event."

I winced. She was right. Our budget had been a hundredth of a percent of that.

"Still, we can use you. Thanks, Mimi," Jackson said.

"We need all the help we can get," Natalie said. "With a brand-new venue and no food, we don't have much time to pivot."

Oh, wow. I'd forgotten that the original venue, a hotel, had included catering from the onsite restaurant. The donors expected fancy food for two thousand dollars a plate.

"It's going to be a blast. You'll see, Mimi." Jackson wedged a corner of a napkin into a crevice of my laptop. "The planning committee needs to be out front to represent the foundation. I'm good, but I can't do it all." He flashed us a dazzling smile, and if I'd had any cash in my wallet, I'd have whipped it out and given it to him. For the kids.

"Parties aren't really my thing." I almost wished I'd opted out of last night's party. Then my head wouldn't pound like Larissa had beaten it with my dead laptop.

Jackson leaned forward. "But my parties are everyone's scene. Right, Nat?"

She rolled her eyes. "Hardly. I'll make sure you feel comfortable at this gala, Mimi. Promise." And her smile was so kind I nodded.

I'd always preferred the planning and behind-the-scenes work to actually attending events. At parties, I hung awkwardly at the fringes. Not like Mateo, who was always at the center of the action.

Plus, what was I going to wear? Ugh, clothes were even worse than parties. I'd worry about that later. First, I needed to focus on why I was at the meeting. "I'll draw up a revised budget with the new venue. You'll get me the invoices, Larissa?"

Larissa waved her elegantly pale hand. "Jackson's paying for it out of pocket. You don't need invoices."

"But"—I cocked my head at Jackson—"you'll be writing off the expenses on your taxes. Surely you want to track them?"

"Well, I…" He shrugged and shot a quick glance at Larissa. "Larissa said she'd take care of it."

I widened my eyes to keep from rolling them. Larissa lost half the receipts before she got them to me. If she tried to take care of anything to do with money, she'd be sure to screw it up and then ask me to fix it. "I'll help her."

But Larissa didn't look like she appreciated the help. She pursed her lips again. "Really, I—"

"Hey!" Jackson cut in. "Speaking of help, what about promoting Mimi to that open assistant director position? Her financial skills are a good complement to your nonprofit experience."

My skin buzzed, and my breath stuttered in my chest. There was an available paid position at the foundation? One Jackson Jones thought I was qualified for? Assistant director sounded like a lot. And I'd hardly call it a promotion since I was currently an unpaid volunteer, but I wasn't about to contradict the guy in charge.

Larissa smiled, but it didn't reach her cool blue eyes. "I thought you said I could select the candidate."

"Oh." Jackson shifted in his chair. "Yeah, of course."

The buzz on my skin turned to painful tingles. Sometimes it felt like the thing Larissa liked best about me was that my labor was free. This morning's presentation fiasco hadn't raised my value in her eyes.

"I'm looking for someone with nonprofit experience. Though I suppose I could consider Miriam."

Mom's voice sounded in my head. *Speak up for yourself. Ask for what you want.* "I'd love that. I've already done a ton of research—"

"We'll talk about it later." She didn't look at me, but her smile for Jackson was lemonade-sweet. "Thanks for the idea."

"Have we covered everything?" Jackson asked. "Nat and I need to pick up Alicia and the kids for the family brunch."

Larissa scanned her paper. "That's all that was on my list. We'll meet again in a couple of weeks, after the holidays. Natalie, if you'll send me your ideas for the gala with projected costs, I'll send it to Miriam for tracking."

"I will." Natalie stood and brushed the wrinkles from her dress. "Mimi, I'm looking forward to working on the gala with you. Happy holidays."

"Happy holidays," I said, even though Hanukkah had been over for weeks. "I'm looking forward to it, too." It sounded like a lot of extra volunteer work, but if I did well, Jackson and his sister would notice. Larissa wouldn't have a choice but to consider me for the assistant director position. I could finally get paid for my work at the foundation, quit my job at Synergy, and have some free time. Maybe I'd even humor Bree and find time to date.

Jackson handed back my laptop and the battery. "Leave it out of the case for a few more hours, put the battery back in, and give it a try."

"Thanks." I tried to infuse the word with my full gratitude, not only for the laptop help but for speaking up for me about the assistant director position.

He winked and turned to escort Natalie out of the café.

Larissa hit me with a steely glare she must have been holding in for the last hour.

"Look, I'm really sorry," I began.

She checked that the Joneses had exited the building. In a frosty voice, she said, "If you want to be considered for the assistant director role, you have to up your game, Miriam. Humiliate me again, and I'll have to let you go."

"But I—"

She leaned closer, and her voice dropped to a whisper. "I'll warn every nonprofit in the Bay Area about you. Not even the animal shelter will let you scoop cat shit. Understand?"

I blinked at her uncharacteristic crudeness. "I—of course. It was truly an accident."

She flashed me a chilly smile. "Women like us can't afford screw-ups like today. Take my advice: whatever caused this one, cut it out of your life."

"Absolutely." I nodded. I could promise her that.

She swept out of the café in a cloud of expensive perfume and a click of red-soled heels.

I stared down at the coffee-stained napkins Jackson had left piled around my laptop.

A server scurried over to me. "That'll be nine ninety."

"Nine ninety?" I hadn't had so much as a black coffee or a gluten-free biscotti. Still, I reached for my wallet.

"That blond chick didn't pay for her skinny latte."

I handed over a ten, then a couple of singles.

"Thanks." The server swept the empty mugs and napkins onto her tray and whirled away.

It figured that Larissa was too concerned with the management of a multimillion-dollar foundation to concern herself with the minutiae of ten-dollar lattes. The next time I saw her, I wouldn't say a word about it. I'd call it an investment in the assistant-director position.

Which I wanted. Badly.

Nothing would prevent me from nailing this gala and proving to her and to Jackson Jones that I was assistant-director material.

I picked up my coffee-scented laptop.

Not even Mateo Rivera would stop me.

3

MATEO

I SHOWED my ID to Bernard at the entrance to my tía's gated community.

"Got identification for your friend?" the guard joked.

"This guy?" I pointed with my thumb at the eight-foot plastic snowman poking through the back window of my Jeep. "He doesn't need ID. He's Frosty the Snowman. A fucking celebrity!"

While Bernard chuckled, I slowly pulled my Jeep inside the gate and up the hill to tía's place.

My security guy wasn't in his SUV outside like he was supposed to be. They never were.

So I hauled Frosty out myself and weaved among the other decorations on her football pitch–sized lawn, an orange extension cord looped over my shoulder. I passed the giant inflatables, a Santa who could "ho, ho, ho" and a snow globe with a festive palm tree inside. I patted the nose of one of the plastic reindeer pulling a second Santa's sleigh. Finally, I trudged past the one I was sure her neighbors were the most thrilled about, a life-sized, floodlit crèche, complete with a pair of resin goats, a cow, a donkey, two lying-down sheep, and one standing. The Magi still waited on the other side of the lawn for Epiphany in January.

When I found the bare spot she'd complained about last week, I set Frosty down and tethered him with a couple of stakes. Then I plugged in his cord and found an empty receptacle on the over-taxed outdoor electrical box. I clutched the gold cross around my neck and sent up a silent prayer before I plugged the cord into the outlet. I said a silent thank-you when light-up Frosty didn't brown out the entire neighborhood. No, her yard full of Christmas shit glowed brighter than ever.

You're welcome, rich neighbors.

Dusting off my hands, I hopped up her porch steps and rang the bell.

Carlo answered the door, crumbs trailing down his black fleece. He didn't even bother looking apologetic, not like he would if it had been my cousin who'd found him inside the house instead of outside, watching for her cabrón of an ex.

"Hey, boss."

"Spice cookies?" I asked, pointing at the crumbs.

The tops of his cheeks went dark as he carefully brushed them into his palm. "They're my favorite."

"Mine, too. She in the kitchen?"

"Yeah. Smoke?" He dug in the pocket of his fleece for his pack.

"Nah. Thanks."

When he set the cigarette to his lips and raised his eyebrows, I shook my head again, though my fingers itched to snatch it from him and take a pull. I'd seen the way Mimi's nose wrinkled when I walked into her place yesterday. How she'd almost puked.

I'd let my nerves get the better of me and taken three quick puffs outside her apartment. Quitting was fucking hard when each drag brought back a dozen rosy memories of hanging with my papá in his tabacaria.

I shoved one hand in my pocket and set the other on the front door.

"I'll just do a perimeter check." Carlo slid outside, and I locked the door behind him even though I was going right back out. My cousin's orders.

I followed the scents of vanilla, cloves, and cinnamon into the kitchen. It reminded me of tía Camelia's place on the island at Christmastime. She always used to send treats home with Papá and me. My body jolted with the reminder that I wouldn't be spending Christmas with my extended family back on the island.

But tía Rosa was family, too, and I pasted a smile on my face for her. She transferred cookies from a baking sheet to a length of parchment paper on her counter.

"Hola, tía." Forcing a careless sway into my hips, I sauntered to her side and kissed her cheek.

"Mateo." Buttery warmth filled her voice. "I'm glad you came by. Don't let me forget to send you home with some of these."

I nabbed one from the counter and crunched into it. "Wouldn't dream of it. Want to see what I brought you?"

"You brought me something?" Her brown eyes sparkling, she wiped her hands on a towel.

"An early Christmas present."

I got her a coat from her closet and helped her into the sleeves. Outside, her gaze arrowed to the snowman.

"He's perfect!" She clapped her hands like she was six and not sixty.

"You need to see him from the street." I extended my elbow, she looped her arm through it, and we descended the steps and strolled to the end of the sidewalk.

While she admired the fresh addition to her Christmas menagerie, I glanced at the houses on either side. Military-straight lines of clear bulbs outlined the roof gables, windows, and porches. Both of their doors were decorated with lush evergreen wreaths that had to cost more than my monthly grocery bill. Not an inflatable or plastic lawn ornament in sight.

But they wouldn't dare call the homeowners' association on Cooper Fallon's mother.

"Gracias, hijo." She pulled on my sleeve, and I bent down for her kiss.

"It's nothing," I muttered.

"It's not nothing." She put her hands on my cheeks so I looked her in the eye. "You're a good boy, Mateo."

But I couldn't meet her gaze. Not after what I'd done to Mimi's presentation earlier today. My fingers went to twist the ring on my right hand, but it wasn't there.

She clutched my hand. "I wish you could see yourself the way I do. The way Miguelito does."

"Miguelito?" I snorted. "He thinks I'm a fu—ah, un tonto."

"If he thought you were un tonto, he wouldn't have brought you here and made you my head of security."

"We both know you don't need security."

"Ah." She winked. "We do. My son doesn't. So he pays you, you hang out with your favorite tía. It's what he would call a win-win."

I tried to flash her a smile, but tía always saw through my bullshit.

She clicked her tongue. "Let's go inside. I'll make some coffee to go with the cookies, and you'll tell me what's bothering you."

In her kitchen, my tía stirred sugar into a cup of strong, black coffee. "What happened with Miriam last night? She looked like she'd had a few too many at the party. Lito and Ben were worried about her."

"They asked me to follow her." I set down the cookie I'd been about to inhale. "Did you know she was going to a bachelorette party?" If I'd known, I'd have brought more than my bare knuckles to defend her from all the leering guys.

She shook her head, frowning.

"A despedida de soltera. Her friend Breina is getting married next weekend. Ben and Miguelito are going." I'd only remembered when I saw Breina shove the glittering plastic tiara into Mimi's dark curls and drape the sash across her gorgeous tits. I smiled, remembering the way Miriam had hugged her friend, her usual formality dropping away as she'd landed a sloppy kiss on her cheek. What I wouldn't give to have that directed at me. And I had, for a short time last night.

"They got pretty drunk, but they were together, and they were okay. Until their men showed up." A growl roughened my voice. "They took her friends home and left Mimi alone. And the assholes who'd been circling all night converged."

"But you were there." Beaming, tía clapped her hands. "You rescued her like un caballero."

"I don't know about that." I ducked my head, remembering how I'd hidden behind a newspaper until Mimi's friends left. "I had on my glasses, not armor."

"Oh." Her face fell. "But even wearing those lentes feos, no one can resist you."

"No one except Mimi." Though for a little while last night, her sparkling eyes and that unexpectedly bright smile had been all for me. She'd seemed to see past my smooth exterior to the essence of who I was. And she liked what she saw. We'd talked about everything: how she loved volunteering at the foundation, how she admired the director. Though from what Mimi said, Larissa seemed like a conniving, gaslighting bitch. She'd even talked about her uneasiness at being the last one of her friend group uncoupled.

I'd hoped to do something about that last one. But when I showed up this morning with my hopeful sack of buñuelos, it hadn't taken me long to figure out that she had a Mateo-sized gap in her drunken memories. And after I'd ruined her presentation, she hated me even more than she had before.

"She didn't remember. That's me. Forgettable," I mumbled.

"Forgettable? Never, cariño." Tía laid a soft hand on my arm. "I'm just glad that when the alcohol loosened that stick up her ass, she finally saw how wonderful you are."

"Tía!" I yelped.

"It's true. That girl needs to loosen up. I know, I know." She waved off my protests. "You like her. But you have to admit she's a little…uptight."

"Driven."

She shook her head. "Ambitious."

"She volunteers at Jackson Jones's foundation. She's more like Ben than she seems."

My aunt didn't look convinced. "Sometimes I think Ben got all the heart in that family."

My fingers tingling, I jumped up and grabbed the baking sheets. I ran soapy water into her sink and scrubbed at the greasy residue and crusted-on cookie crumbs. No, Mimi had shown all kinds of heart last night, especially when she…

"Do you think I should tell her? About the—the kiss?" I almost didn't believe it had happened. But I'd seen the proof this morning in the beard burn she'd tried to cover up with makeup. How had she forgotten? I'd never forget the way she pleaded my name just before her soft lips landed on mine. The taste of her— tequila, sweetness, and cinnamon—when I opened to her. The shape of her in my arms, all soft curves I wanted to trace with my hands and my tongue.

"Shouldn't you?" Tía stepped up next to me at the sink and laid a hand on my back.

"No. Especially not after today. After I ruined her presentation." The anger flashing in her eyes had cowed me. Angry Miriam Levy-Walters was fearsomely beautiful.

"You should make it up to her. Then you can tell her about last night." She rubbed a circle on my back. "You've had so much sadness in your life, hijo. You deserve to find happiness. And if it's Mimi you want, go for it. No one can resist your charm."

"Mimi can," I grumbled at a sticky spot on the last baking sheet.

"Turn it up a notch, then."

"I can't. Whenever I try, I fuck it up." Like when I'd ripped her paper.

"Remember, she's human, too. Not some saint above an altar."

"Is she?" And I wasn't completely kidding. "She works full time, plus she volunteers at the foundation. And she's the smartest woman I've ever met."

"You're smart, too. You don't have to have a fancy college degree to prove it. You take care of Miguelito and me."

I snorted. "Lito can take care of himself. And Ben, too. And of course I take care of you. You're my favorite tía." And the closest thing to a parent I had left, I didn't say. She knew.

"You're a good boy. Worthy of her. Show her. Help her the way you help everyone else. So it didn't go well today." She shrugged. "Try again."

I supposed I owed Mimi that after fucking up her presentation. "Okay. I will. Can I have some extra cookies, please?"

She reached into the drawer for a plastic container. "That's my boy. Woo her with food."

4

MIMI

BY THE TIME the photographer finished with us bridesmaids, my cheeks ached from the rigid smile I'd pasted on my face.

Bree and Josh, who had to stay behind for even more pictures, looked just as fresh as they had when they saw each other for the first time this afternoon, when he peeked under her veil and they couldn't stop laughing. Now they gazed into each other's eyes, sharing secrets while the shutter snapped. Their happiness was indecent, really.

Not that I was jealous.

I had a great job and an even better opportunity with the foundation if I could impress Larissa with my work on the gala. I wished she could see Bree's wedding reception at the Conservatory of Flowers. Bree and Josh had wanted something in an outdoor garden, but it would be too cold at their late-December wedding. So I'd suggested the conservatory. The greenhouses were warm and overflowing with color and fragrance.

It was my best event idea since I'd asked our prom queen's mom, a wannabe social media influencer, to decorate the school gym as a showcase and promised that every attendee would tag and repost. We had the most blinged-out prom ever.

We'd used the freed-up decorations budget to rent a chocolate fountain. Not my idea—I was allergic to chocolate—but I'd approved it. And in the end, I regretted it. A bunch of drunk high-schoolers and molten chocolate aren't a great combination. As the prom committee chair, I personally received dozens of dry-cleaning bills from angry parents.

My stomach growled. I hadn't eaten anything since a cup of coffee and a mouthful of pastry while we had our hair done this morning. I passed up a waiter's offer of a glass of champagne and started toward the appetizer buffet.

Before I could snatch as much as a cheese tartlet, the too-familiar smell of Paco Rabanne overpowered the earthy, leafy smell of the greenhouse and turned my stomach inside out. I froze, six feet away from the buffet table, wishing the potted palm to my right was thick enough to hide behind. But it was a spindly little thing, and its soft fronds provided neither cover nor defense. I turned, knowing who'd be there.

I used to think his smile was cute, but now it looked smarmy, a flash of whitened teeth. He looked impeccable as always, his suit pressed and his tie knotted in its usual half Windsor.

He straightened his round glasses and settled his arm around a woman's waist. She was petite, probably a hundred pounds dripping wet, with a button nose and silky-smooth hair. It was like Byron had deliberately chosen my exact opposite.

"Mimi. Funny seeing you here," he said, pulling himself up straight to look me in the eye. In my heels, I was the same height as him.

I swallowed to coax some moisture into my mouth. I wished I hadn't passed up the champagne.

"I'm in the wedding party." I gestured at my navy-blue satin bridesmaid gown like he didn't already know. "What are you doing here?"

He tucked the woman into his side. "This is Tanya. She's Josh's cousin. Small world."

"Small world," I echoed.

Tanya smiled uncertainly.

None of this was her fault, and now she was Bree's family. I stuck out my hand. "Nice to meet you, Tanya. I'm Mimi. Bree and I have been best friends since we were eleven."

Her hand was limp in mine, and I suddenly felt too much. Too forceful, too big, too loud. The uncertainty that had flattened me after Byron had stolen that job from me crept back into my heart, cold and prickly. He'd never cared about me. I'd been a fool to think he could.

"We miss you at SquawkClip," he said. "No one can close out the month as quickly as you did."

The prickles subsided. "Tha—"

"You should have stayed on the team. I'd have made you my assistant."

"Wait. What?" I blinked so hard my fake eyelashes tangled. "Your assistant?"

"You could be my right-hand person. I have seven people reporting to me now."

My chest heaved with all the words I wanted to say. To yell. I deserved that job. Even Byron had told me I did. But he'd drawn on his network behind my back and taken it for himself.

I held it all in. I couldn't make a scene at Bree's wedding. Not in front of Tanya, who was part of her family now.

"I'm happy where I am. I'm a senior accountant on a fantastic team. And I believe in Synergy's mission."

"SquawkClip is the hottest, most exclusive social media video site out there. Everyone wants an invitation."

"I know." I'd watched it rise in popularity and media mentions since I'd left. But I'd always felt like a hypocrite working at a company that promoted invitation-only curated video feeds from beautiful people. My teenage self would have consumed those videos like potato chips and felt just as queasy afterward.

Byron shrugged. "Too bad your volunteer work always distracted you from your paying job. You'll rise higher if you keep your eye on the ball. It's ironic that as an accountant, you're so careless with your own time and money."

I pressed my lips together to keep the angry words inside. *Be nice for Bree.* I glanced at Tanya.

He pushed his glasses up his nose. "If you change your mind and want to come back, give me a call."

The thought of working for Byron or for the company that chose him over me lit a fire in my gut. Still, I smiled. "Sure."

"Hey," Ben slid up to me on his dress shoes, a little breathless. He must have run when he spotted me talking to my ex. His lip curled. "Byron."

"Ben." Byron dipped his chin. Even though they were about the same height, he managed to look down his nose. When we dated, he'd never been brave enough to say anything, but it was obvious he sneered at Ben's lack of a college degree and professional job.

He didn't know Ben had both a degree and a great career now. Neither my brother nor I would bother to educate him. Byron wasn't worth the trouble.

He looked between us. "You're here with your brother?"

I bit my lip to keep from grimacing. "No, I—"

Cooper strode up to us, two glasses of champagne in his hands. He handed one to Ben and offered the other to me. I took it, grateful for something to grip that wasn't Byron's neck.

Ben's face glowed. "Babe, meet Byron, Mimi's ex. And...?"

"Tanya," I said.

Cooper shook their hands. "Nice to meet you. I'm Cooper."

Byron's jaw dropped. "Cooper *Fallon?*"

Cooper gave him a tight-lipped smile and tangled his fingers with my brother's. Yeah, I'd been surprised, too, when Ben got together with his billionaire boss, who was featured in the financial news every other week.

Byron blinked. "So who are you here with, Mimi?"

The cold prickles came back, even in the warm greenhouse. Why hadn't I thought to bring someone, anyone? My last one-night-stand, that guy I'd met in the frozen-entrée aisle one night after work back in November. What was his name? Van? Vin? I'd tossed his number in the trash.

If only I hadn't been so drunk last weekend I'd missed my chance with my mystery man. I set the glass of champagne behind a red-tipped bromeliad.

"I'm here by myself," I said.

At the same time, Ben said, "She's here with us," and jutted out his jaw. "You'll leave her alone if you know what's good for you."

That was my brother, always leading with his heart. "Ben—"

"Is he bothering you, Mimi?" Cooper asked.

"N-no," Byron said. "I just wanted to say hello."

"You've done that," Ben said, edging in front of me. "Now step off."

Byron straightened his glasses and glared at me like my brother's overprotectiveness was my fault. Then he turned on his loafer and walked away, dragging Tanya behind him.

"That wasn't—" I began.

"Are you okay, honey?" Ben asked. "You got so pale I was worried."

"I'm fine. He surprised me. That's all."

"Good. He's not worth it."

I glanced between Ben and his fiancé. "Are you two having a good time?"

Cooper flashed a quick smile. "Of course."

"He's lying." Ben threaded his arm through Cooper's. "Watch out for Mom. She's been talking to Bree's mom, and now she's got wedding fever. She tried to pressure us into setting a date." Ben's smile was forced. "We're not ready for that yet."

I'd have to ask him later why he looked like someone had made him eat one of the bridesmaids' bouquets. "She won't bother me. She's always said I should establish my career first. Besides, you guys are practically married."

"I think my getting engaged might have knocked something loose in her. She was asking where Bree got her dress."

I swallowed. The warm greenhouse and the scent of lilies overpowered my senses. "I need some air."

"Want us to come with?" My brother took a step toward me.

I held up my hands. "No. All I need is a minute to myself."

I turned on my pinchy pumps and weaved through the beaming guests, the hand-holding pairs celebrating couplehood, toward the exit. I wasn't ready to get married yet. Though maybe Bree was right. Maybe I wasn't happily single anymore. It sure would've been nice to have someone to wrap an arm around when Byron confronted me. Someone to hold me up in the face of his scorn.

Someone kind and caring like my Mystery Man.

Somehow I'd screwed that up. There was no new number in my phone. I'd ransacked my apartment and found nothing but a neon-green, penis-shaped straw and a condom still in its "Bad decisions make great stories" wrapper.

I shoved open the door and stepped outside to fill my lungs with cool, fresh air.

But the air wasn't fresh. A man stood twenty feet away in the designated area, a cigarette pinched at his lips.

His broad shoulders and black tee were heart-sinkingly, couldn't-pretend-I-didn't-know-him familiar.

There went my get-myself-together-time.

5

MATEO

BACK IN THE days when I used to work at my papá's shop, I could always tell when someone was about to try to steal a carton or a cigar from the box by the cash register. Even if my back was turned, my hairline would prickle.

I felt that now.

Slowly, I turned from where I'd been admiring the camellias. I plucked the cigarette from my lips and blew out a long stream of blue smoke.

Mimi stood at the door to the conservatory, shivering. Her sleeveless gown was the color of midnight on a moonless night back home on the island.

I lunged for the cigarette receptacle, almost knocking it over in my haste. "H-hello."

She scrunched up her nose. "Are you stalking me?"

"Um." I steadied the urn and flicked the butt into the slot. "Ah, no. I'm driving Ben and Miguelito."

She crossed her arms over her chest, which was a shame. The sweetheart neckline made her breasts look amazing. Though I had a better chance of saying something intelligent if I wasn't gazing at her gorgeous tits.

"I thought you were security, not a chauffeur."

I shrugged. "I do what my cousin asks."

She looked away, and I noticed her fingers trembled. They did that the other morning when she refused to eat the buñuelos I'd brought.

"Are you all right?" I asked. "Have you had anything to eat? Or—or are you cold?" Shit, why had I left my jacket in the car? I took a few steps toward her. I yearned to wrap her in my arms the way she'd let me that night at the bar.

"I'm fine." She held up her hands in front of herself as if to ward off an evil spirit.

I must have reeked like an ashtray. I took a step back.

Her shoulders lowered. "Thanks for the spice cookies you sent with Ben. They were delicious."

"Of course. My tía is the best cook I know."

When she shivered again, I said, "You should go inside where it's warm. Unless you'd like to borrow my jacket? It's in the car."

She shook her head.

"Are you hungry? I'll fetch you a plate." I tipped my chin at the doors behind her.

She snorted. "You'd never make it out alive. Not looking like that." She circled her hand at the black T-shirt I wore whenever I worked for my cousin.

I smoothed my hand over it like I could magically transform it into a suit and tie. Maybe then she'd respect me. She'd look at me the way she had last Saturday night.

No, I'd fucked that up. I'd been what I always was. A fun way to pass the time. Forgettable. Not worth keeping.

"Sorry I'm underdressed. I didn't expect—"

"No, I meant..." She pressed her lips together. "I meant the way your muscles look in that shirt."

I couldn't help it. I flexed. It was as automatic as breathing.

But Mimi didn't react the way people usually did. She never had.

"I need a few minutes alone," she said, looking vulnerable in a way I'd never seen her. "You know?"

"Not really. I hate being alone." I turned up my lips in a wry smile. But I'd give her the one thing she asked for. "I understand. I'll go sit in the car."

Her dark eyebrows tightened, but I did what I'd said. I turned and walked back to the SUV. I closed myself inside and tried not to watch her as she stood, shivering, enjoying being alone more than she enjoyed my company.

6

MIMI

BEN'S FRUSTRATION showed in the fluttering of his hands before he grabbed my shoulders and kissed my cheek. "Thanks for coming."

I hugged him. "Anything for you, Benny."

A week after Bree's wedding, I'd dropped my Sunday-morning apartment-cleaning ritual to answer his SOS text, and he met me under the dripping overhang outside the community center where he often volunteered.

"This is a lot, Mimi. Deep breath."

I didn't know if he meant his last words for himself or me, but I sucked in cold air as he flung open the double metal doors to the gym with a dramatic flourish.

Inside the gym, it sounded like a Warriors game was in progress. Shouts and sneaker-squeaks echoed off the wood floors and cinder-block walls. Some teenagers—the quieter ones—screamed at each other in groups. One set was engaged in chicken fights, smaller-framed kids riding on their friends' shoulders and whacking each other with pool noodles. Weaving among them all, both a pickup basketball game and a soccer game were in simultaneous progress.

In the far corner, Mateo wedged his broad shoulders into an ominous-looking circle growing around some disturbance.

"I was supposed to have five volunteers," Ben shouted in my ear.

"They all stayed in bed?" I shouted back. I was starting to wish I had.

"Stomach flu. They all went to the same party on Christmas Eve. Thank God you and Mateo are here."

I reached into my raincoat pocket for my keyring with the safety whistle on it, but I came up with something else round and metallic. I slipped it onto my thumb for safekeeping and reached into my other pocket.

When I put the whistle to my lips, Ben knew to stand back. The kids closest to us didn't. I let out a piercing blast, and they clapped their hands over their ears.

"Hey!" I had to shout it a few times and punctuate it with a couple more shrieks from my whistle, but the ball games stopped. Mateo finally settled the fight in the corner, and fifty teenagers' faces turned my way.

When I had their attention, I bellowed, "Listen to Ben. He's in charge."

Ben wisely got Mateo and the ballplayers to help him organize the kids into teams for silly relay races. I went to the other end of the gym where the introverts had peeled off and gently encouraged them to team up. If not for my brother, I'd have been tempted to join them on the bleachers and pull up my favorite Steve-and-Bucky fanfiction on my phone, but this was Ben's day. He'd ensure everyone had fun.

It was hours later, when the kids had burned off their initial energy and had formed into groups to work on a craft and talk, that I finally leaned against a gym mat hooked to the wall. The afternoon sunlight speared through the high windows and flashed on my thumb, reminding me of the ring's presence.

Because that's what it was, a ring. A scratched-up gold band that looked like it had seen some years.

What the hell was it doing in my pocket?

I squinted at it, and the way it caught the light creaked something open in my brain like a crowbar on a painted-shut window. My Mystery Man, his blue eyes darkly serious behind his glasses, pressing the warm circle into my palm.

"Keep it safe," he'd said. "For me."

I stroked it with my fingertip. I'd done a crap job of keeping it safe, forgetting it in my coat pocket. At least I still had it. But how was I supposed to get it back to my Mystery Man? I'd checked the contacts on my phone a hundred times. There was no entry for *Man, Mystery* or *Stranger, Blue-Eyed,* or even *Kent, Clark.*

"Hello."

I jumped and reflexively covered my thumb and the ring with my fingers. If Mateo knew what had happened at Bree's bachelorette party, he'd go all security-specialist on me and give me a lecture on meeting men in bars when I was tipsy.

I squinted up at him, trying to mask my irritation. Fantasizing about my Mystery Man was even better than the raciest Stucky fanfic, and he'd interrupted it.

"Why are you talking to me?" I curled my lip. "At least five of those girls are over eighteen and old enough to flirt with. Don't let me stop you."

His blue eyes creased like I'd punched him, and guilt twinged in my belly. Why was I always such a jerk around him? He didn't deserve it. Not always, anyway.

He gave me a tight-lipped smile. "I came to thank you for helping Ben today. I was worried about him with all these punks."

"Punks?" I bristled. "They're just kids. They've been out of school for a week and a half for the holidays, and they're climbing the walls. Same as you and me at that age."

"Hey." He took a step back and put his hands in front of his chest. "I meant no offense. I was a punk like this once. I know exactly how out of hand the situation could have gotten."

"Oh. Sure." It wasn't hard to imagine a teenage version of Mateo. His boyish good looks, easy flirting, and loose movements made him seem younger than he was.

Like I'd said it out loud, he reddened. "I—ah. Thanks for bringing your whistle and being the voice of authority they needed."

"No problem. Ben knows he can call on me whenever he needs me."

Mateo nodded, and suddenly, his face lost its boyishness. Those blue eyes bored into me in a way that reminded me of… something. Probably his cousin's laser glare. My skin prickled from my scalp all the way to my toes. I shoved my hand with the ring into my jeans pocket.

"Mateo!" Ben shouted from across the gym. "Little help?"

I tore my eyes off Mateo. Ben stood next to a rack of basketballs, but a couple of kids played keep-away with the last one. It looked like they'd done it in fun, but I was glad Mateo was there to even out Ben's side.

"Excuse me," Mateo said, "but I've got a couple boneheads to set straight."

He jogged off, his sneakers squeaking out a warning. The kids handed the ball to Ben as soon as they saw beefy Mateo approach.

After the kids left and Mateo went to fetch the car, Ben plopped down next to me on the gym floor.

"Tired? I know today was a lot."

"No, I'm good." I rolled my shoulders. "What can I help you with?"

"Nothing." He waved at the empty gym, the balls and hula hoops and ancient scooters stored neatly in their racks. "Come to our place for dinner?"

Dinner with Cooper and probably Mateo sounded painful. "How about a restaurant? Just the two of us?"

"A place with a heated patio so I can bring Coco?"

Thinking of Ben's dog—and his fur—made my eyes prickle.

"I helped you all day. No patio. No dog."

Ben gasped dramatically. "Coco is a sweet, sweet boy. The only reason he's not your best friend is that you're allergic."

"Let me tell you, I haven't missed the allergy-med fog since you moved out." I froze. Allergy medicine.

"I think I roofied myself," I said.

"What? Today?" Ben peered into my eyes.

"That night of your party. I took my allergy meds before I went to your party, then I went to Bree's bachelorette party. I think the meds amplified the effects of the booze. I got pretty wasted, and I—I don't remember much."

He paled. "Do you think something happened?"

"I woke up alone at my place, still in my clothes. Nothing seemed…amiss."

He blew out a breath, then he smirked. "Nothing amiss? I *guess* that's a good thing. Though you could use more *amiss* in your life."

"Says you." I crossed my arms. "I like my orderly life."

Ben grumbled something that sounded suspiciously like *boring life.*

"Hey, you're practically married to the most orderly person I've ever met. There's nothing wrong with orderly."

His eyes sparkled wickedly. "Not when it goes with a killer bod and a tongue that—"

"Boss's boss's boss," I reminded him, cringing. "Where do you want to go?"

"Greasy burger place," he said without hesitation. "I never get to eat that when Cooper's here. You know, his body is a temple and all that. I mean, it *is.*" A dreamy look came over his face. "And I worship there like a Baptist on Sunday."

I shook my head. "Wait, where is Cooper?"

"He had to go to Singapore." Ben sighed.

"The week after Christmas?"

He shrugged. "He's a captain of industry, you know. Capitalism doesn't take holidays."

"How was your first Christmas together?"

"Good." He grinned. "We went to Rosa's, and she made the most amazing food. I couldn't even tell you what half of it was, but it was delicious." He rubbed his belly. "Mateo made this to-die-for bread pudding. I don't even like bread pudding. Pudín de pan, they called it."

"Mateo," I grumbled. He was everywhere. At Bree's wedding when I needed a minute alone. At my apartment when I needed to prep my presentation. Heat rushed from my chest up my neck. I hadn't yet made up the ground I'd lost with Larissa from my botched presentation. When I'd sent the updated financials to her, her response was terse. And made no mention of the assistant director position.

"I don't understand why you don't like him. He's hot, witty, and about the nicest guy you'll ever meet."

"Witty?" I snorted. I checked the gym doors, but we were still alone. "Dude is a meathead who can hardly string two sentences together."

"I don't know what you're talking about. He told jokes at Rosa's and had us all rolling on the floor."

I shook my head. "I guess I'll have to take your word for it. Besides, the guy hates me."

"Hates you? He wouldn't stop talking about you. About how beautiful you were, all dolled up at Bree's wedding. About how smart you are."

I snorted. "You must've had too much Christmas punch. No way he talked about me like that. He thinks I'm a giant nerd."

The first time I'd met Mateo, soon after he'd moved to San Francisco to head up Cooper's security detail, I'd been so over-whelmed—I had no idea people that gorgeous existed outside of superhero movies and fitness magazines—I'd let loose one of my dorky math jokes, the one about the infinite mathematicians.

He'd stared at me open-mouthed for a second, and then he'd said something about the weather. It had reminded me—painfully —of Byron. How he'd always frowned at my math puns. He'd said they made me sound ridiculous, like I was trying too hard.

And Mateo thought the same thing. That I was a Poindexter. An unattractive one. I always caught him staring at the parts of me Byron hated—my butt, my thick thighs. Byron had gotten me a set of exercise bands for my birthday one year. *Booty Busters,* said the label.

Muscle-bound Mateo must have judged my booty in need of busting, too.

But I was done talking about Mateo. Something niggled at the back of my brain whenever I thought about him. "Remind me when you're starting your new job."

"It's really just a continuation of the internship I was doing. But my official, full-time start date is the fourth."

"Look at you, Mr. Mature," I teased him. "A degree and a grown-up job."

"Hey, being an executive assistant is a grown-up job!"

Not according to Mom. But I didn't say it. She never pressured Ben the way she did me. She knew women had it harder than men. As she'd told me a hundred times, because I didn't pee standing up, I had to work harder to prove myself, to earn what they were given without a thought. Even my brother Ben had turned a spotty work history, the world's longest bachelor's degree, and a little help from his billionaire boyfriend into a great job at a foundation, doing exactly what he wanted. While I'd worked for free for a year, giving up my evenings and weekends, and was struggling to convince Larissa I was worthy to bring on staff.

"What about you?" he asked. "Any developments on the job front?"

"Actually..." I chewed my lip. "There's a full-time position opening up at Jackson's foundation."

"With all your volunteer work, plus your financial experience, you should be a shoo-in."

"I don't know. I haven't made the best impression on Larissa. Or Jackson. And it's an assistant director position. I'm just a senior accountant at Synergy."

"Want me to talk to some people? I could ask Cooper to talk to Jackson. Or I could do it myself. We see him and his family all the time."

I scanned Ben from his button-down to his jeans. Was that a *crease?* Even his sneakers were scuff-free. Ben had a laundry person who took care of his clothes. And a real job at a foundation that helped at-risk kids. It was larger and better established than Jackson's, so it wasn't an assistant director position like I was going for. Yet. Still, in many ways, my little brother had surpassed me.

I couldn't take advantage of his connections to advance. No, I wouldn't lie to myself. I was too proud to take the help he offered. Too proud to admit I needed my younger brother's help.

"No, thanks. I'll do it on my own."

"You're sure? It wouldn't be any trouble. People in that circle do it all the time."

"Ben." I chuckled. "You're part of that circle now. But I've got it, thanks. I'll figure out how to impress Larissa and earn that job all on my own."

"I know you can do it. And I'm so proud of you for making this change. It would've been easy to keep rising through the ranks at Synergy. It takes guts to be honest with yourself about what you want out of your career."

"Some days it feels like a bad idea. You know, we accountants are a pretty conservative bunch." I tried to laugh, but the sound was trapped in my stomach.

"You've got this," he said. "And if anyone deserves to be happy, it's you."

Tell that to Larissa. And to the Mystery Man who'd disappeared from my life as quickly as he'd entered it.

I stroked the ring on my thumb. A clue. Though I was too much of a realist to think even my Mystery Man could make me happy forever.

But the job at the foundation? If I secured that, I'd prove my worth to Mom. To everyone.

And then I'd be satisfied.

———

I'D HUNG my Mystery Man's gold ring on a chain around my neck. It was for safekeeping, just like I'd promised, not because I liked the warm weight of it nestled against my heart.

At five thirty on the first workday of the new year, I stroked it where it lay under my oversized black blouse as Larissa scanned Synergy's first-floor conference room and sighed.

"I wish we could find a permanent office space for the foundation. But every building I've looked at is so unassuming and drab."

"I'm sure you'll find something you like. Eventually." Though she'd been looking for a year, and I was starting to think her standards were too high. "Until then, I can get space at Synergy whenever I want. And the coffee's free."

Her nostrils flared like she smelled the burned-at-the-end-of-the-day coffee, but she said, "You're doing the best you can."

It sounded almost like praise, but it wasn't enough for my greedy, affirmation-seeking self. I opened my mouth to offer to bring her a soda or whatever I could scavenge from the break-room, but she interrupted me.

"Miriam, I think I may have accidentally left the café the other day without paying. Did you cover my tab?"

The ten-dollar latte. "I did, but it was no big deal," I lied.

"I pay my debts. Text me your PayMo username, and I'll pay you back."

"Okay, sure. But speaking of reimbursements, I still need the receipt from—"

"Hey, sorry I'm late." Natalie scurried in, looking impeccable as always in a white—white!—wool blazer and trousers. She was built like a model, taller than me and slender, and she looked like she'd just walked off a runway. A vibrant red Prada satchel swung from her shoulder.

"No problem at all." Larissa's smile for Natalie was warm and sticky like a sweet roll. "We're so glad you could join us."

Natalie shook Larissa's hand, then mine. Her grin was infectious. "Good to see you again, Mimi. Jackson sent me your budget projections. The detail was impressive."

A warm glow started just below the ring at my breastbone and spread through my chest. It wasn't like the time one of the popular girls had discovered I was good at math and acted like my friend so I'd help her with trigonometry. It was nothing like Larissa's blink-and-you'd-miss-it gratitude. Natalie's heartfelt praise pushed my cheeks up into a smile.

She plunked her satchel on the conference table and pulled out some papers. "I came prepared with some thoughts about the gala. And a budget proposal." She shot me another quick, conspiratorial smile.

Larissa sat at the head of the table. "Miriam, can you bring me a bottle of water? Do you want anything, Natalie?"

"Oh." Natalie scrunched her forehead. "No, thanks. I'll wait to start until you get back, Mimi."

Larissa fluttered her hand. "Don't worry about it. We'll catch her up later. Miriam's a quick study."

My fists balled. Reminding myself I'd been about to offer to get her something, I shook out my fingers. Besides, she'd just complimented me.

"Be right back," I said. I jogged to the break room and grabbed three water bottles from the stash in the fridge. I supposed in a lean organization like the foundation, an assistant director might also act as an all-purpose assistant. But when I'd gotten my accounting degree and sat for the CPA test, I hadn't envisioned wanting a job where I fetched water. And now I was doing it for free. A chill flowed across my skin.

When I walked back in, Natalie and Larissa had their heads together, peering at something on Larissa's laptop screen.

"See? I told you the country club would work," Larissa said. "It's got all the space we need."

"Sure. It's a little generic, but we can dress it up with flowers. Great job getting something on such short notice," Natalie said.

Larissa's lips pinched, but she nodded. "We can update our contract with the florist. Miriam will take care of that. She excels at administrative tasks."

I shouldn't have minded. After all, I was just the financial volunteer for the foundation and, by extension, the gala. And I'd do whatever it took to pull off the gala. Still, my chest tightened.

Natalie glanced at me. "I bet you'd like some of the creative parts, too, Mimi. Want to help me pick out the food? It'll be tough to find a caterer on such short notice, but the sampling part will be fun."

Warmth reignited inside me. Finally, a chance to contribute something meaningful. "Sure. Do you have any ideas?"

She slid a paper to me. "I have quotes from five caterers. Are these in the right range?"

I glanced at the numbers. All but one were within my projected budget. "The first one is a bit high, but the rest look okay."

One corner of her mouth quirked up into a lopsided smile, making her look like her brother. "I think I can sweet-talk them into the right number if we like them the best. I'd rather not eliminate them yet."

"That's fair. I know we need to put on a quality party, but we also need to keep expenses down so the money goes to the kids."

Natalie grinned. "Well-fed donors are happy. And generous."

"Is their generosity positively correlated to the amount of food?" My math joke landed with a splat. Both women looked at me blankly. "I mean, if we double the food order, maybe they'd be doubly generous."

Natalie flashed me a weak smile. "Actually, people spend more time networking at these things than eating. But they like the food to be pretty."

"Okay. I don't know how good I am at picking out pretty food for rich people to ignore, but I'll try it."

Larissa's ash-blond eyebrows pinched together. "I need you to take this seriously, Miriam. This gala is important to the foundation."

"Of course!" I tried to gather words. "I'll give it one hundred percent of my attention." Which wasn't absolutely true. I needed at least one percent of my attention to stand up and move around. Another five percent to eat and maintain hygiene. And at least forty percent for my actual job upstairs. But Larissa didn't seem to understand numbers.

Which was why she needed me. Even if she wished she didn't.

Maybe I shouldn't have been so hasty to be one of the deckhands Jackson had called for. I stood a better chance of advancing if I kept my head down and churned out numbers.

Working on the gala was a risk. If it was a success, Jackson would know I'd helped. And with his support, Larissa would have a hard time denying my application to the assistant director position. But if we screwed up the gala, Larissa would make me her scapegoat, and it would be easy for her to carry through her threat of ensuring I'd be turned away from work at any other charitable foundation.

Risk wasn't my thing. It was why I'd become an accountant in the first place. Every company needed accountants. The money was good, and employment was stable.

But stable wasn't enough anymore. I wanted something more. Fulfillment. A sense of doing good in the world. Of helping kids.

I glanced at Larissa again. Her forehead still pinched. Then I caught Natalie's hopeful smile, so much like her brother's.

"I won't let you down," I promised.

Natalie hugged me. "It's going to be great. With your money smarts and my eye for design and Larissa's"—she swallowed—"leadership, we can't fail."

"Members of the committee will have responsibilities the night of the gala. Miriam, you'll need to dress...appropriately." Larissa's cold blue gaze tracked from my end-of-the-workday frizzy hair to my billowing black tunic and shapeless black slacks.

"I'm sure she has something to wear," Natalie said in a rush. "Or...or I can take you shopping! That'll be so much fun!"

Designer clothing and handbags weren't my thing—accountant, remember?—but I knew for a fact the bag Natalie had slung so carelessly onto the table cost in the four figures. A shopping trip with Natalie Jones sounded spendy and humiliating.

"I've got something to wear," I lied. Ben would help me. He was always offering to make me over. I wouldn't let him do that, but he could help me find an evening gown that didn't cost more than my rent.

"Great!" Natalie clapped her hands. Her phone buzzed on the table, and she scanned it. "Anything else we need to go over today? My brother's here to pick me up."

"Jackson?" That was an odd way to put it since he'd been working in the building all day.

"No, my other brother, Andrew. I'm taking him to dinner."

"Speaking of dinner, don't forget to give me the name of your plus-one for the gala, ladies," Larissa said.

"A plus-one?" This sounded like the kind of math I didn't like. The ring seemed to burn against my skin.

"Someone to sit with at dinner. The committee are going to be scattered at various tables so the donors have access to us. Surely you want a friendly face next to you."

I didn't have time to date anyone, much less find someone to bring to a function. Would Ben go with me? But how pathetic would bringing my brother be?

Not quite as pathetic as showing up alone, like I'd done at Bree's wedding.

"I—I'm not seeing anyone."

"You don't have to be seeing someone to bring a date." She pursed her lips. "Tempt them with free food."

My cheeks went cold. Sure, I liked a free meal just as much as anyone did, but was *that* what she thought of me? Because I didn't belong in her rich-girl world, she looked down on me. Was that why she didn't want to work with me?

"I can find you a date," Natalie said. "I know lots of guys. Or...girls?"

The warmth rushed back into my face. "Thanks." As kind as it was of her to offer, the men Natalie knew would probably look down their noses at me even more than Larissa did. "Give me a few days to work my network"—and by "network," I meant the few numbers I'd kept from my one-night stands—"and I'll let you know if I need help."

"Sure, no rush." Natalie grinned.

"The gala is in six weeks. Valentine's Day. Don't wait too long, or all the best ones will be snapped up." Larissa chuckled.

Great. I knew in the back of my mind we were planning the event on February 14, but until she pointed it out, I hadn't thought about asking someone out on Valentine's Day. Any man in his right mind would run the opposite direction. And normally, I'd encourage a guy to beware the desperate single woman on a Hallmark holiday.

But this time, the desperate single woman was me.

7

MATEO

WOO HER WITH FOOD.

Leaning against the bank of mail slots in the tiny lobby of Mimi's building, I clutched the tote bag my tía had given me to my chest, hoping to keep it warm. It wouldn't be nearly as woo-worthy after a spin in the microwave, but we were definitely approaching the window where tía's famous pollo guisado would be cold.

A pair of cute hipsters had let me into the building. I could have used the key Ben had loaned me to let myself in and start the food warming in the oven. Back on the island, we did things like that all the time. But Mimi had built tall walls around herself, and I had to respect her boundaries as much as possible.

Jesus, I wanted a smoke. I stared longingly out the glass door. It'd be so easy to step outside and light one up, calm my trembling fingers. But I'd smell like cigarettes, and Mimi would hate that. Besides, I'd promised myself I'd quit. I was strong enough to do it, too, even after all these years.

Where was she? My cousin was a driven executive at Synergy,

and he was usually home by seven. I'd talk with him about how hard his company worked Mimi.

Though I doubted she'd appreciate that.

The street door opened, and she breezed in, her dark curls falling into her face and her coat flopping open. The tip of her nose was red, but her skin glowed. She was a sunbeam spearing through the ever-present clouds.

I peeled myself off the wall and hugged the bag tighter. "Good evening. How was work?"

"Mateo?" Her beautiful brown eyes flicked wide. "What are you doing here? Is Ben okay?" Her eyes were red-rimmed with fatigue. I'd definitely talk to my cousin.

"He's fine. I came for you. I brought you dinner. My tía made it."

Her stomach growled, and she put a hand over it. "Wow, that sounds great." She sniffed. "Smells good, too. What is it?"

"Ah-ah," I teased. "It's a surprise. Can I bring it up for you?"

The tiny frown line she got between her eyebrows whenever she looked at me appeared. "I guess. But why didn't you text first?"

I grimaced. Miguelito said the same thing even though I lived just across the driveway from him and Ben. "Sorry. I never had to text anyone back home. In the small town where I lived, people just showed up on each other's doorsteps."

"Well, we don't do that in San Francisco. Next time, use your phone."

Those tiny phone keyboards weren't made for my big fingers. My texts were always full of typos that the autocorrect mangled, and without my glasses, I sometimes missed it. But for Mimi, I'd try. "Anything for you, bella."

When she scowled, I deflated. Usually, my teasing made people smile. But Mimi saw through my flirtation. Nothing worked on her. Nothing I tried, anyway.

I trudged behind her to the stairs, and we climbed to the

second floor. I waited while she inserted her key into the lock and flipped on the lights.

Her apartment looked the same as the last time I'd been there, the morning I'd come to check on her after her night of drinking. But since I'd just come from my tía's house, with her riot of candles and crèches and Santas, it looked barren. Even I had put up a string of discount-store multicolored lights over the fireplace in my tiny house. But Ben told me their family was Jewish, and I'd watched him light the menorah at his and Miguelito's place weeks ago.

Her place was neat and bland, not a book or knickknack out of place. The furnishings were much more frugal than the ones in Miguelito's guesthouse. The only color in the place came from the superhero posters stuck to her walls—Wonder Woman, Doctor Strange, Thor, and others.

I set the food on the kitchen counter. "Mind if I heat it up?"

"No. Here, I'll show you where things are."

"Don't worry about it. I can find my way around a kitchen. Unless you keep kosher? I wouldn't want to mix up your meat and dairy dishes."

Her tired eyes flared for a second and then narrowed. "No. I don't eat pork, but I don't keep two sets of dishes. Use whatever you like. I'll go change."

She left, and I breathed out. Before the holidays, she'd yelled at me. Maybe I'd been granted my Christmas wish.

I wasn't going to screw up the Christmas miracle. I got out a pot for the stew and set it on the stove, then I found a casserole and put the rice in the oven to reheat. The pudín de pan also went into the oven. We'd start with the green salad I'd made.

I found her plates and cutlery and set the table, folding the napkins into sharp rectangles the way I imagined Mimi liked them. I placed the forks and knives precisely parallel. Just as I was arranging the bouquet I'd brought into a vase, Mimi stepped into the kitchen.

"Wow," she said. She wore slippers, the kind that made a

scuffing sound when you walked, plus gray leggings and an oversized UCSF sweatshirt. Her hair was tied up into a loose fountain of curls on the top of her head.

Jesus, she looked ready to tuck into bed. I wished I had the right to do it.

"Wow," I echoed.

"Oh, uh, sorry." Her freshly washed cheeks reddened. "Habit. It's been a long day." She crossed her arms over her chest. Had she taken off her bra?

I held a potholder in front of myself to hide the erection stiffening against my thigh. *Woo her with food, tonto.*

"Everything's ready. Sit down, and I'll plate it up."

"Thanks." She tilted her head like she was trying to figure me out, but she scuffed over to the table and sat.

I scooped rice and stew onto two plates and brought them to the table. "It's chicken, not pork," I said.

"Thank you." She leaned back into the stiff wooden chair. "It smells fantastic."

"My tía is a great cook. Almost as good as my father was." I sat in the chair across from her.

"Was?" She didn't pick up her fork but inhaled over the steaming plate.

Shit, why had I mentioned him? Food always brought him to the front of my mind. "He died."

"I'm sorry." She did that thing that people did, pity softening her eyes.

I didn't want her pity. Though I wanted everything else from her. "It was a long time ago. Ten years. And I was grown when it happened. How was work?"

She blinked, then her lips turned down. "Fine." She picked up her fork and scooped up a bite of rice and stew.

"Really? You don't look like it was fine. And you stayed so late."

"Work was fine. It was the foundation meeting after that wasn't great." She closed her lips over the bite of food, and her eyes rolled up. She chewed and swallowed. "God, that's delicious."

"What happened at the foundation meeting? It wasn't about your presentation again, was it?"

"No, no." She chewed another bite of stew and hummed. "We have this big gala coming up. You know, a fancy-dress party. I volunteered to be part of the planning committee. It's, um, kind of a big deal for the foundation. Plus, I have to actually go to the gala. Like, dressed-up." She rubbed at the frayed cuff of her sweatshirt.

"You don't want to go?"

"No. I mean, yes, I do. It'll be great for networking. Jackson Jones will be there, and I want to impress him. There's this job I could get. A full-time one with his foundation, and I think he's in favor of giving it to me."

"A job with more money?" San Francisco was expensive. Everyone needed more money. Except my cousin and his billionaire friends.

She sipped her water and smiled, her lips sparkling with moisture. I rocketed my gaze up to her eyes, but they were just as distracting with their droopy, sleepy lids that reminded me of the night at the bar, when she'd kissed the hell out of me.

"It's probably the same money I'm making at Synergy. But it's a job that matters. The foundation helps kids. Neurodivergent kids. I had a friend growing up... Anyway, I want to be part of it. I want to succeed, but I also want my work to help people."

Warmth bubbled in my chest. I'd fallen for Mimi's beauty and her sharp mind, but now I learned she had a soft heart, too. She was an angel.

"But..." She picked up her fork and separated a chunk of potato from the stew but didn't spear it. "Not only is it formal attire—and I don't wear formal dresses—but I'm supposed to bring a plus-one."

"Clothes are easy, especially in a city like San Francisco."

"Not when you're shaped like me." She waved at her baggy sweatshirt.

"You were stunning at your friend's wedding. You have a gorgeous shape. Like a woman, not a toothpick."

Her cheeks went as red as the roses in the vase. "Um...thanks. But shopping can be a challenge."

I puffed out my chest. "I'll take you shopping. I'll find you a store with dresses you'll love."

She raised an eyebrow. Clearly, I'd vaulted over the protective wall she kept around herself.

"I...I mean, if you like. Or I can ask my aunt."

She twitched her lips to the side. A maybe. I could work with that. What I wouldn't give to see her in formfitting silk.

"And!" The thought flashed into my brain too fast to hold it in. "I'll go with you. To the gala."

Her eyes widened. I'd gone too far. I'd smashed through that wall like a sledgehammer. "I mean, as your date. A friend."

She bit her lip, and I could not. Stop. Staring. I remembered how she'd nibbled my lip that night. How she'd tasted. But she didn't remember any of that. I had to claw my way back to it somehow, and my gut told me the gala was the key.

"I don't know..."

"I have a tux." I didn't, but my cousin had a whole rack of them in his closet, and we were the same size. "And I'm great with people."

Both of her dark eyebrows shot up. It was the absolute truth although I was nothing but awkward around Mimi.

"And!" If I let her say the word *no*, it'd all be over. I had to keep talking so she didn't have a chance to say it. "I'm a fantastic dancer."

She released her lip, and it popped back red and shiny. She narrowed her eyes at me. "Is that a euphemism?"

I fought to bring a sexy smirk to my lips, but it probably ended up looking pained. "Do you want it to be?"

"No. No." Her cheeks went red, not blotchy like when Ben

blushed, but a smooth wash of magenta across her cheeks and forehead. "But dancing? Do you think we need to dance at this thing?"

"Need to? No. Should we? Absolutely." There was nothing I wanted more than to hold her in my arms, her face so close it was out of focus. I'd want to pull out my glasses to study her features like I'd done at the bar.

"I don't dance."

One corner of my mouth kicked up, and the words flowed out like water. "Hermosa, I'll make you look good."

Her gaze flicked to my mouth. She licked her lips. Then, surprising me, she grinned. "Am I supposed to take your word for it?"

Gracias a Dios. My flirting skills were back online. I raised my eyebrows. "Care for a demonstration?"

"Here? Now?" Her eyes darted around the tiny kitchen.

"Anytime you want. Ben can vouch for me. We danced on the island."

Her mouth rounded into an O. "You're gay?"

"Bisexual. But I promise, I never kissed your brother." I'd thought about it the first time I'd met him, but I quickly found that although he and Miguelito weren't together yet, my cousin already considered him his. And when I met Mimi, I discovered Ben was nothing more than a pale shadow of his vibrant sister. In an instant, I fell for her lush curves, her full, coral lips, the intelligent snap of her deep brown eyes.

She narrowed her eyes at me. What else could I offer her?

"I'll bring you food. Whenever you want." I gestured at her almost-empty plate. "And…and I'll stop smoking."

"Just so I'll take you to this gala?" She tilted her head. "What's in it for you?"

I had to use care in the minefield she'd set up inside her walls. "A chance to dress up, talk to people, and spend time with you. Besides, eating with a friend is better than eating alone."

She was silent for a few seconds. Then a few more. Finally, she said, "Okay. It's on Valentine's Day. But that doesn't mean anything. Understand? We're just two people, dressing up for a free meal. A work-related free meal."

"Friends," I said, extending my hand across the table.

She nestled her small, soft hand in mine. I fought the urge to bring her fingers to my lips and, instead, pumped her hand once.

"Deal," she said.

Reluctantly, I released her hand and blanked my face to hide the joy that wanted to stretch it into a goofy grin. "Deal."

8

MIMI

I WAS SETTING out copies of the gala budget when Natalie stomped in, ten minutes early, her knee-high boots clomping on the wood floors of Synergy's first-floor conference room. I'd have looked like a little girl playing dress-up in them—if they even made a wide-calf size—but Natalie looked impossibly tall and elegant.

"Bring it in," she said, waggling her fingers. "I need a hug."

I wished I could hate her, but I couldn't.

"Hi, Natalie." I straightened the copy of the budget at Larissa's seat and reached up to hug her. She wasn't as bony as she looked, and the hug felt good. I hadn't realized how much I missed Ben and his generous hugs since he'd moved out.

Natalie gripped me tight and then relaxed. After a few seconds, she released me, and we stepped apart. With what seemed like a lot of effort, she smiled. "Good afternoon."

"Is something wrong?"

"Just my pigheaded brother. He...never mind."

"Who, Jackson?"

"Of course. Andrew is the sweetest, most reasonable guy

you'll ever meet. Well, except for his disaster of a love life. My brother Jackson, on the other hand, makes me want to scream sometimes."

"Is it about the gala? Do we need to make a change?" I snatched up the copy of the budget. It wouldn't do to anger the founder with a wrong choice. I was doubly exposed. He could take it out on me at my actual job and at the one I hoped to get. Not that I thought Jackson was vindictive. So far, he'd been nothing but supportive of me.

Byron had been like that, too, though, until he'd bit me like a snake.

Natalie shook out her hands. "No, there's nothing we need to do. It was something I wanted him to do. But it's fine. We'll work it out."

"Okay. If you're sure." I laid the papers back at Larissa's place.

"Here you are." A deep voice came from the hall outside. Mateo filled the doorway with his broad shoulders and impossible height. He held a brown paper shopping bag in each hand, the tendons taut in his exposed forearms.

Why the hell was I looking at his forearms? The danger was with his mouth. What would he say to embarrass me in front of Natalie?

Looking at his mouth was a mistake, too, as I'd learned last week in my kitchen, the night I'd agreed to take him to the gala as my date. His lips were full and lush, and when he'd flashed me that sexy, tilted grin, my sensible brain had gone offline. Instead of remembering all the reasons it was a bad idea, I'd focused on his lips and whether they'd feel soft as they looked if I reached out a fingertip to touch them.

When they curled up into a smile, I blinked away. No looking at his mouth! When I gazed at the crushed paper in my hand, I remembered what we were there for: a gala committee meeting. And Mateo didn't belong.

"What are you doing here?"

He lifted the bags, his arms flexing. A delicious smell wafted into the conference room. "Ben said you had a meeting tonight. I brought food."

Having a one-on-one dinner with Mateo was one thing, but exposing Larissa, who already didn't like me, to Mateo's bumbling was a terrible idea. No matter how kind he'd been the other night.

I set a hand on the sleeve of his painted-on black compression tee and nudged him back outside the door. God, his arm was like a rock. A lickable one.

"We talked about this," I hissed. "You were supposed to text me."

"I did," he rumbled.

I snatched my phone out of my pocket. "You texted me, *In being sonnet*. What the hell did that mean?"

He grimaced. "Autocorrect and I don't get along. I meant to say, 'I'm bringing dinner,' but—"

"No. We're fine. Thank you. I'm sure you can take that to Cooper and Ben. I'm not hungry." As I moved toward him to escort him out of the building, my stomach protested with a growl so loud everyone on the floor had to hear it.

"Ah. But you don't know what I brought. And you don't want to be hangry at your meeting." He shook the bags slightly, and the smell of onions and peppers beckoned to me.

My stomach growled again, but I cut it off with a fist pressed to my middle. I wished he wasn't so tall and I didn't have to bend back my neck so far to look him in the eye. "I'm not hangry."

"Aren't you?" he said softly. "Or is something else the matter?"

That soft tone in his voice, so inviting, so unassuming, made me want to tell him all my problems. About how exhausted I was from balancing a full-time job with volunteer work. How hard I tried to please Larissa while getting so little in return. Why did he have to be so...so *nice?*

"What's this?" I hadn't noticed Larissa come up behind Mateo.

Crap. Now Larissa would have to meet Mateo and see how

awkward he was. She'd probably ban him from all future foundation events, especially the gala. I had to get him out of there. I laid
a hand on his chest and pushed. But I was like a mosquito trying
to move a mammoth.

"Lover's quarrel." Natalie crossed her arms over her chest as
she leaned against the conference room doorway.

"What?" I whipped my head around to look at her. What had
she heard?

"Hi, Mimi's hunky boyfriend." She smirked.

"He's not—"

"I'm Natalie Jones." Ignoring my protest, she stuck out her
hand.

Mateo set down one of the bags and clasped her hand. "Mateo
Rivera." He turned to Larissa and shook her hand. "And you
must be the Larissa I've heard so much about."

Larissa's cheeks turned pink, and she seemed to wilt. And
then she made a sound I'd never heard come out of her perfectly
lined mouth. She tittered, her hand lingering in his. "Larissa
Lane."

What. The. Hell. I had to get this situation back under control.
And that meant getting rid of Mateo. "Mateo was just leaving. I'll
see you later, Mateo."

"What are you talking about?" Natalie put a hand on Mateo's
forearm, and for some reason, that made my back teeth crunch
together. "He brought us dinner. I'm not letting anything that
delicious walk out."

Mateo tugged his hand out of Larissa's grasp and turned back
to Natalie, one corner of his mouth quirking up and an honest-to-
God dimple denting his cheek.

"This deliciousness isn't going anywhere," he said.

Whoa. Even the second-hand sparkle was a lot.

Larissa squeezed around him into the conference room, and
when she took the position of authority at the back of the room,
her cool mask was back. Cocking a hip, she rested her hands on

her hips in a power pose. She arched an eyebrow. "You're with Miriam?"

I heard the disbelief in her tone, and for a second, I wanted to claim him, to show her that just because I preferred to fit into the background and do good work and be recognized for it, it didn't mean I couldn't attract a man. Though who was I kidding? Mateo was all kinds of wrong for me. I didn't believe we'd work together. Larissa, who was both insightful and successful, would never buy it.

Just as I opened my mouth to say *no,* Mateo said, "I am. We're going to the gala together."

Larissa cocked her head as if she didn't quite buy it. But she said, "Good. I'm glad you were able to find someone, Miriam."

Before I could get *we're just friends* out of my mouth, Natalie spoke.

"And he brought food. What did you bring us, Mateo?"

"Empanadas from a great Colombian restaurant near here. I brought beef, chicken, potato, and cheese. No pork." He shot a swift glance at me.

My stomach gave a hopeful gurgle. I'd have eaten treif if it smelled that good.

"What are we waiting for?" Natalie asked. "Let's eat while we meet."

This situation had gotten out of hand. And that made my teeth itch. I ground them together. We were supposed to be meeting about the gala budget. I had three pristine copies of it. A dinner meeting with Larissa and Mateo was eighty-five percent sure to be a disaster. But there was nothing to be done as Mateo set the bags on the credenza and started pulling out cartons of food.

Natalie oohed and aahed at each selection. Even Larissa peered into the aluminum trays. Mateo made them each a plate of food to their specifications. The delicious aroma filled the conference room, and I swallowed.

Natalie and Larissa sat down with their food, and before I figured out how to wrangle the meeting back under control,

Mateo presented me a plate. "Sit down," he said. "Eat. And then talk."

I sat in my customary spot on Larissa's left. Mateo placed bottles of water in front of each of us, then ensured we had a packet of cutlery and a napkin.

"I'll leave you ladies to it," he said.

"No, stay," Natalie said. "Pull up a chair. And a plate. You can't just drop off food and go. Spend a few minutes with us. Right, Mimi?"

"Um, sure." I was seventy-one percent certain this would end in disaster, but I wasn't enough of a monster to eat the food he'd brought and send him away with none.

He raised an eyebrow at me, and when I didn't object, he made himself a plate of food and sat in the chair to my left.

I stared down at my plate. It looked absolutely gorgeous, a pair of empanadas at six o'clock, rice and beans at ten and two. A cup of green salsa nestled in the center.

"O.M.G. This is delicious." Natalie took another bite and rolled her eyes. "Who made this, and do they cater large events?"

Mateo chuckled. "Tres Hermanas in the Tenderloin. And, yes, they cater. My tía said they do weddings at her church all the time. She knows the owners."

"We need to get them. Don't you think so, Mimi?" Natalie said.

"But—but—we already selected a caterer." She and I had stuffed ourselves in back-to-back appointments over the weekend, and she'd even haggled the expensive one down to fit into our budget. "I cut a check for the deposit."

Larissa said, "I haven't given it to them yet."

"You haven't?" I asked. "I gave you the check on Monday."

She fluttered a hand like a five-figure check didn't mean anything. "I think we should talk to these people. Latin American food will be unique and a more memorable experience. We can plan the decorations around it. I'm thinking paper flowers, piñatas, maracas…"

"Or—"

Mateo's voice from my other side startled me, and I knocked over my water bottle. Fortunately, I righted it before it spilled more than a few drops on my copy of the budget. Which was now out of date. I blotted it with my napkin.

"You could decorate with orchids. Or, if those are too expensive, carnations and roses in bright colors. That will give it a fresh, tropical feel without being too over-the top."

I sucked in a breath. "We've already budgeted for the decorations and flowers, too."

Larissa waved off my protest. "We can figure it out with the decorator. Right, Natalie?"

"No problem. Gina's reacted to enough whims of my mother's that she can roll with this." She turned back to me. "I'm sure we can fit it into the same budget. It won't be too much extra work for you, I promise."

"I need people who are creative and flexible," Larissa said, her voice stinging. "I think Mateo might be better suited to the gala committee than you are, Miriam."

"Wait," he said. "I'm not trying to take over anything."

My stomach contracted. The situation was all too familiar. A man sweeping in and taking a job I'd worked hard to earn. Maybe Mateo hadn't meant to do it, but here we were. Again. I stared down at my plate. The food had tasted wonderful at first, but now bitterness filled my mouth.

I pushed my plate away. "I didn't mean—I'll handle it." Renegotiating the contracts and updating the budget would take time I hadn't planned for, but with Larissa's approval hanging by a thread, I'd work twenty-four-seven if I had to.

Slowly, as Larissa and Natalie cleaned their plates, the three of them undid the planning we'd done over the past week and the budget I'd painstakingly put together.

The absolute last straw was when Mateo said, "I know a fantastic bachata band. A guy I work with, Carlo, plays trumpet with them in his spare time."

"We definitely paid the deposit on the jazz band," I said.

"We can get out of it," Larissa said. "Losing the deposit would be worth it to create an authentic experience."

"But that's five hundred dollars the kids won't get."

"Miriam." Larissa gave me a flat look. "It's a tiny fraction of the overall gala budget. I'm always telling you that you need to look at the big picture. That's what I need in an assistant director."

I cringed. Crap, it wasn't Mateo who'd sunk me. I'd done it myself.

"Attention to detail is important," Mateo said. "I'm sure you need that, also."

I whipped my head around to look at him, and the broad smile he'd been flashing at Larissa faltered.

"Isn't it?" he said, his gaze not leaving mine.

"I suppose so," Larissa said. But neither of us bothered to turn to her. His blue eyes sparked with something warm, like a clear blue-sky day in September. My memory flashed back to another set of blue eyes that listened to me, acknowledged me. My Mystery Man. I wished for the dozenth time that I hadn't lost him. That he was here beside me instead of Mateo.

Mateo was just another man like Byron, thinking only of himself with no regard for what I wanted. I didn't understand Mateo's agenda yet, but it was getting in the way of mine. My Mystery Man would never have barged in here and dismantled all my plans.

He cleared his throat. "Carlo's band is looking for their big break. They'd probably give you a good deal. For the exposure. I could talk to them?"

"Yes, please." The command was back in Larissa's voice. "Remind me to give you my card, Mateo."

"Of course." With what seemed like an immense effort, he dragged his gaze off me to Larissa.

"And you'll sit at my table at the gala," she said.

"As long as it's the same table as Miriam's," he said. "Remember, I'm her date."

The silence stretched long enough that I looked back at Larissa. Her lips pinched together in a way that usually spelled trouble for me.

Then she gave Mateo—not me—a smile that looked painful. "We can arrange that."

Shit. Mateo and Larissa at the same table at the gala? Warning lights flashed in my brain. "But you said—"

Her eyes narrowed ominously. "We can arrange it, Miriam."

Mateo's muscles bunched at my side. "I should leave you lovely ladies to your planning."

Over Natalie's and Larissa's protests, he collected the empty plates and my half-full one. He packed up the leftovers and promised to leave them in the breakroom's refrigerator for Larissa to take home.

I didn't miss her flirty smile as she tucked her card into his hand.

With one last cryptic glance at me, Mateo strode out, taking the smell of the delicious food I hadn't been able to eat with him.

When he left, the fluorescent lights buzzed in a way that hollowed me out. It must have been exhaustion that made me feel dull and flat.

"So." Mischief danced in Natalie's blue eyes. "You and Mateo."

"I thought you weren't seeing anyone," Larissa said.

"I'm not. I mean, Mateo's my date to the gala, but..." But what were we? We'd said we were friends, but we weren't even that.

"It's new!" Natalie clapped her hands. "I love that new-relationship feeling. The buzz you get in your stomach, the wild sex—"

"Sex? There's no sex! We're just—"

Natalie snorted. "You two were practically having sex against the wall outside. If you haven't slept together yet, you can't be more than one date away."

No. No, no, no. I'd been down this road before. With Byron. Before I'd learned that dating someone I worked with ended in heartbreak and betrayal. And now Mateo and I were working together on the committee. Which I hoped to grow into a permanent job at the foundation. "One date? We—"

Larissa cut me off. "We could use his help now that we're going with a Latin American theme."

"But Mateo's not Latin American. He's—"

"Does it matter?" Larissa said. "It's all the same. We need him, Miriam. Don't botch this."

Well, shit. Our gala friends-date had somehow exploded into something that could make or break the job I so desperately wanted. I couldn't afford to screw it up.

9

MATEO

I WAVED at Carlo on my tía's front porch as I stepped out of my
Jeep. He raised a steaming mug at me, one of the cheery red ones
from her kitchen.

Good. I'd share last night's news with him in person.

"Hola, Carlo," I said as I stepped up onto the porch.

While we shot the shit, he lit up a cigarette and offered me
another from his pack. It was easy to refuse. I wouldn't smell like
smoke when I visited Mimi at the office this evening to tell her
Carlo's band was on board.

Last night when I'd walked into her meeting, I'd caught her
looking at my lips. This gala date would bring us closer. My
awkwardness around her was starting to melt away. I could
finally sweep her off her feet like I'd wanted to do since I'd first
met her.

I could kiss those lips again.

But we weren't there yet. Everything between us was as fragile
as the fancy figurines in my tía's china cabinet.

Especially since I had a sinking feeling I'd pissed her off at her
meeting last night. Since she never ate enough, I'd wanted to feed

her. But I'd overreached, and the situation had gone off the rails. I hadn't intended to suggest they change the food, the decorations, and the entertainment. And I definitely hadn't meant to end up as part of the committee. But the hard glitter in Larissa's eyes told me if I backed out now, things would only get worse for Mimi.

This was my chance to impress her, to prove I wasn't the fuck-up she thought I was. To make up for the disaster I'd made of her presentation. To rebuild the connection she'd forgotten.

When Carlo stubbed out his cigarette, I asked, "So what are you doing for Valentine's Day?"

He flashed me a shit-eating grin and batted his eyelashes at me. "Are you asking me out?"

I snorted and gestured at his grizzled hair and beer gut. "You are so not my type."

He put his hand over his heart. "You wound me."

"Fuck off. So. Your band—"

"We have a gig that night. We're opening for Banda Reina del Lirio at The Fillmore."

"No, no, no. Cancel it. I have a gig for you."

"Cancel it?" His heavy-lidded eyes went wide. "We booked this gig last year."

"Look, I'll pay whatever penalty. But I need you to do this for me. Play the Jones Foundation event. It's a benefit for neurodivergent kids. Don't you have a nephew with dyslexia?"

He rolled his eyes. "Fuck, Mateo. Way to hit me where it hurts. I'll have to talk to the guys."

"Really? After I got you this cushy job? Where tía brings you her special hot chocolate?" I smelled the cinnamon, even over the lingering smoke from his cigarette.

"Fine." He heaved a sigh. "I'll get the guys to go along. It pays well, yes?"

"About that." I winced. "You're going to have to make it look like a good deal. I'll make up the difference. Promise." It was a good thing Cooper put me up in his guesthouse rent-free. This favor to Mimi was going to cost me.

"¡Dios mío! You're killing me, bro. But"—he held out his palms—"I'll do it. And now we're even. Got it?"

"Claro. Now get out of here. You're off duty. Everything quiet last night?"

"As the grave, man. Not that I don't appreciate the job, but don't you think the neighborhood guard and the security system will keep him out?" Carlo tipped his chin at the camera pointed at the front door.

"From what I hear, Rosa's ex is one persistent cabrón. Showed up at Cooper's office last summer."

"Ah. Better not show his ugly mug while I'm on duty." He cracked his knuckles ominously. "No one messes with our Rosa."

I nodded. "Go home. And take your butt with you. Wouldn't want Cooper to see it." With my luck, Miguelito would think it was mine, and he'd never let it go.

He pulled a napkin out of his pocket and scooped up the end of his cigarette. Then he handed me the mug and trotted to his truck.

I rapped on the front door and then let myself in with my key, calling out, "¡Hola, tía!"

"Mateo?" Her voice was high and strained, coming from the kitchen.

Fuck, had she fallen? I blinked away a horrifying memory of my father lying on the floor of his bedroom the first time the tumor had zapped his brain.

I sprinted to the kitchen and scanned all four corners, but my tía wasn't stretched out on the tile. She stood on her tiptoes on her step-stool, reaching into an upper cabinet.

My heart slowed its frenzied rhythm even as I rushed to her side. "Get down from there, tía. You'll fall."

Only when she had both feet safely on the ground did I breathe again. "Why would you do that? You should've called for Carlo or me."

"I put it up there. I should be able to get it down."

"What do you need?" I peered into the cabinet.

"The molcajete. I'm making chicken with mole poblano."

I found the stone bowl and set it down on the counter, my mouth already watering. "You're making it today?"

She reached up to pat my cheek. "It's your favorite, isn't it?"

"It sure is." I grinned. It wasn't a dish I'd ever eaten growing up, but tía had learned the recipe from one of her Latina friends here in California, and I'd quickly become addicted. "We have something to celebrate. I have a date with Mimi."

"You do? ¡Que fantástico! Of course you do. She'd be a fool to turn you down. I want to hear all about it. Was it the food I sent?"

"Well, that and her boss. Though is she really her boss if it's a volunteer position? Anyway, she's working on this big party, and I accidentally crashed one of their meetings. One thing led to another, and now not only am I hooking them up with a caterer and Carlo's band—"

"Ah!" She clapped her hands. "You charmed them, didn't you?"

"Well, yeah, I guess."

"That's my boy, un caballero encantador." She patted my cheek. "So what's the problem?"

I'd lingered outside the conference room door. Although Mimi looked up to Larissa, I didn't trust her, and I wanted to be sure she behaved herself. "They...they think we're dating. Like, not just going to the one party together as friends like we said, but dating."

Tía's eyebrows shot up. "Miriam went along with this?"

It had shocked me, too. "She did. Which is the strangest part. She got so...so *meek* in front of Larissa. She's never meek."

"Hmm." She plucked lint off my sweater. "Sometimes people can behave differently with different people. People they think have authority over them."

I caught her wrist. No way was I going to let her feel embarrassed about putting up with Mick Fallon's abuse all those years. "Tía."

"What the *absolute fuck* is going on here?" Miguelito's voice thundered behind me, making me yelp.

"The fuck, Lito," I wheezed. My heart had lodged itself in my Adam's apple.

"Don't swear around my mother." He bent and kissed her cheek. "You okay, Mamá?"

"Of course I am." She slapped his chest. "You about gave us both a heart attack. What's the matter?"

"This cabrón forgot to lock the front door."

"I called him as soon as he opened the door. He thought I was in trouble."

"Were you in trouble?"

"Of course not."

He scowled at me. "How many times have I told you—"

"Always lock the door. I know, I know." I rubbed the spot over my galloping heart. Why hadn't I locked it? I knew better than to risk my tía's safety.

"He was right here with me," she argued. "He'd have defended me."

"What if he brought his gang with him, hmm? Mateo alone couldn't protect you then."

"I'd try," I grumbled.

"He'd defend me. And I'd call 911."

My cousin narrowed his eyes, and the darkness of his gaze erased the pretty blue. "No more mistakes."

I gusted out my breath. "Understood."

She tugged on his coat sleeve. "Why are you here on a work-day, Lito?"

"I wanted to ask you—" He glared at me. "Mateo, check the house to make sure no one got in."

"But, Lito, he's family. What do you have to hide from him?"

As if she hadn't spoken, he said, "Then patrol the perimeter."

I squared my shoulders. "Got it, boss." Though, as I walked away, I speculated under my breath about what had crawled up his tight ass.

But as I poked into the rosebushes with my weapon of choice, an aluminum bat, I had to admit he'd been right to criticize me. If I could've brought back my father, I'd have guarded him with my last breath. And if I had a dangerous man to protect him from like my cousin did, I'd probably have been just as obsessed with safety.

I'd fucked up. My cousin was right not to trust me. I'd known since I was little there was something wrong with me. I wasn't as smart as the other kids, for one. For another...

I flicked away the thought. What did it matter, anyway? Rationally, I knew it wasn't my fault, but a dark whisper in my subconscious reminded me if I were worth staying for, my mother wouldn't have left us.

I hefted the bat and tapped my left palm with it. I wasn't that broken little boy anymore. I'd grown into a charmer, just like my tía said. People liked me now. And maybe, just maybe, Mimi could grow to like me, too.

10

MIMI

WE'D JUST REACHED the last item on the gala committee meeting agenda—entertainment—when Larissa frowned at me. "Where's Mateo?"

"M-Mateo?" I hadn't seen him since our last meeting. I liked it better that way. Not being around him meant I was in no danger of falling for his fake charm. Plus, I hadn't had a chance to tell him Larissa and Natalie thought we were dating. I was forty-three percent sure it would all blow over and I'd never need to tell him. Forty-three rounded up to fifty if we were using only one significant digit. And fifty percent certainty was good enough for the weather forecasters.

"He's supposed to give us a status on the mariachi band," Larissa said.

Natalie spoke up. "I didn't think it was a mariachi band."

"It's not? Mateo said it was an authentic Latin group. We need a band, Miriam. What's the status? You are dating him, aren't you?"

Despite the crushing weight of disappointing her, of potentially losing my chance at that assistant director job, at least now I could end the misunderstanding. "Actually—"

"Evening, ladies." Mateo sauntered into the conference room. "Sorry I'm late. I just got off work and had to book it here from the west side. What did I miss?"

He winked at Larissa, whose cheeks pinked. Hell, some of the residual sparkle must have hit me because I got a little warm. Or maybe it was the black wool sweater I'd worn. I plucked it away from my chest.

"We were—" Larissa cleared the breathiness out of her voice. "We're ready to hear your report on the band."

He leaned a hip against the conference table. "They're in."

"Great. And they're a mariachi band?"

"No. They play bachata. You'll love it. It's like they're making love to your ears. The dancing is sensual, like salsa." He stood and demonstrated a swaying side-to-side motion, rolling his hips.

Instantly, I felt the phantom touch of his pelvis nudging mine. His powerful hand at the curve of my back. The rough abrasion of his thigh pressing between my legs. The whisper of his breath on my overheated neck. I let my sweater flutter back against my sticky skin.

Larissa leaned back in her chair, blinking. "Okay, then."

"Yay! Mimi and Mateo can lead the dancing." Natalie clapped her hands.

"What?" I whipped my head to face her. Mateo had said we should dance, but I'd hoped he was wrong about it.

"Get it started. It'll be fun when everyone joins in."

Fun? "But I don't dance."

"Of course you will." Larissa's voice allowed for no disagreement. "Jackson will be impressed, won't he, Natalie?"

She grinned. "He does love to dance."

"Though, if you're not up to it, you could work behind the scenes. Mateo can take your place on the committee." Larissa arched her blond eyebrows.

I knew what *behind the scenes* meant. While it might be what I naturally preferred, it also meant no exposure to Jackson Jones. My last chance at the assistant director job would float away like a puff of Mateo's cigarette smoke.

"You need her on the committee," Mateo growled. "Mimi and I are dating. If she's out, I'm out. And I take the caterer and the band with me."

What? Why had he said that? My forty-three percent certainty dropped to zero. My stomach squeezed.

Larissa's eyes went wide. "No need for that. Miriam will dance, won't you, Miriam?"

"Of—of course." For the assistant director position, for a chance to work for kids all day every day, I'd struggle into a spangled leotard and high-kick like the Rockettes.

Mateo's voice remained low. "I don't like it when Mimi is threatened. Remember, we're a package deal."

A heavy silence blanketed the conference room until Natalie said, "Hear that? It was my ovaries exploding. Mimi, if you and Mateo ever break up, I'm burning my copy of the girl code. He's mine."

"Ah, but that's never happening," Mateo said, a grin cracking his serious expression. His big hand landed on my shoulder and squeezed it right where a knot of tension had formed. "I knew from the first time I saw her that Mimi would be my forever love."

I blinked up at him. Why was he doing this for me? What did he have to gain from taking on the additional responsibility of the gala planning? From telling that lie about his *forever love* to keep me in the running for the foundation job?

"Wow," Natalie said. "I think that's the most romantic thing I've ever heard outside of a movie."

Her phone buzzed on the table, and she picked it up. She frowned at it. "Nine-one-one text from my brother Andrew. I've got to go. But I think we were done?" She raised her eyebrows at Larissa, and when she didn't object, straightened her papers then shoved them into her tote.

Larissa frowned. "But we were going to the driving range tonight."

"Sorry. My low-maintenance brother is having some high-maintenance issues. I have to keep him from doing something he'll regret." Natalie strode to the door. "See you next time."

I wished I had the confidence to tell Larissa no. To turn my back on her like Natalie did. But I needed Larissa more than she needed me. I couldn't refuse her anything if I wanted to be considered for the assistant director job.

Larissa pasted on a smile as false as her lashes. "What about you two? I've got the station reserved already. Why don't you join me? My treat to show there are no hard feelings."

I didn't buy her repentant expression for a minute. Besides, she'd definitely see through the pretense of our relationship if she watched Mateo and me interact one-on-one. She'd know that once the contracts with the band and the caterer were signed, she could boot both Mateo and me from the committee without any repercussions.

"I don't play," I said.

Mateo splayed his hands. "I don't, either."

My shoulders eased down in relief. I'd been half-afraid Mateo would want to go with Larissa. Now he and I would go our separate ways. After we talked through the *forever love* nonsense.

Larissa rose from her chair. "You don't have to know how to play golf to hit at a driving range. Come on, it'll be fun. And, Miriam, golf is a skill you should learn if you ever want to succeed in business."

"Wha—why?" Communication skills, I understood. Accounting, marketing, operations knowledge, I got. But why was knowing how to hit a little white ball a prerequisite for career advancement?

She raised an eyebrow. "You and I don't have Jackson and Natalie's privilege of having doors open because of our names. We have to find more subtle ways of influencing people. People make more deals on golf courses than in boardrooms."

"That doesn't seem right." *Or fair.*

She shrugged. "It is what it is. Your mother's a lawyer, right?"

"How did you know that?"

"I make it my business to learn about the people I work with. I bet she plays golf."

I wrinkled my nose. "Actually, she does." Did Mom believe what Larissa said? Did she enjoy golf not for the sport but for the influence it gave her? I'd have to ask her on Friday at dinner.

"Now come on. I'll show you everything you need to know."

Her gaze lingered on Mateo, and even though we weren't actually dating, my hands curled into fists. Then I flattened them against my black slacks and stood. He could flirt with anyone he wanted. Whatever was going on between us wasn't real.

Besides, I had a bigger problem: golf. I wasn't going to influence anyone positively by making an idiot of myself at the driving range. But if my best attempt at hitting a golf ball would smooth the way to the job I wanted at the foundation, I'd even wear one of those silly tam hats with a pom-pom.

Mateo probably would, too. He'd make it look sexy.

———

IN THE PARKING GARAGE, Mateo opened the door of his Jeep for me and helped me clamber up.

Pausing at the back of the vehicle, he lifted his phone to his ear. He spoke briefly into it, listened for a moment, and ran his hand through his hair. His lips moved again, then he disconnected the call. Was he canceling his plans? Did he have a date tonight?

He opened the driver-side door and stepped effortlessly into the tall vehicle.

"Look, I—I'm sorry about this." I twisted my fingers in my lap. "It's probably going to be miserable."

"Eh." He shrugged while he backed out of the space. "Like Larissa said, it is what it is."

"Well, um, thanks for doing it. Are you sure you didn't have anything else to do tonight? A date?"

He turned to look at me, narrowing his eyes. "No."

I sagged back into the seat. "And I'm sorry they got the wrong impression about us. Natalie somehow got the idea that we were dating, and I didn't correct her. And then you—you went with it. Why?"

He focused on making a sharp turn toward the exit. When he straightened out the Jeep, his eyes swiveled left and right, checking for cars pulling out unexpectedly. Finally, he said, "I want to help you, Mimi. Supporting you on the planning committee, making more of our friendship and our date, whatever you need."

"Is this about that day you spilled coffee on my presentation?"

Pulling to a stop at the garage exit, he glanced at me. "Perhaps."

Ah, guilt. I was thankful my mother hadn't baked that into me. "Don't worry about it. Really. And you don't have to pretend for me."

He kept his gaze on the road, but his lips twisted up on one side. "It's no hardship."

"Really? Because it seems like a lot." I wouldn't have done it for him. Or anyone other than Bree or Ben.

He shrugged. "If all I have to do is pretend we're sleeping together, it's not so bad."

"Sleeping together?" I squeaked. Suddenly, there wasn't enough oxygen in the car. I directed the air vents toward my flaming cheeks. "Do we have to be sleeping together? Maybe we should get our story straight."

There went that crooked smile again. "Bella, if you're dating me, we're sleeping together."

The deep rumble of his voice set off a throb between my legs. I squeezed my thighs together. "No. We're so new that I'm not ready yet. We're just dating."

He glanced at me. "But I've kissed you, right?"

"I—I guess." Kissing was pretty innocuous.

"What about making out? Have we done that?"

"Like, are you asking what base we're on? Are we in high school?"

His big shoulders tensed. "No, I was just checking to see how much I should touch you."

Touch me? I reached for the air conditioning knob and cranked it all the way into the blue. "Touching isn't necessary."

"Why? Are you sensitive about touching?"

The sibilance of his question ghosted across my skin like a warm breath, setting off tingles inside me. I hit the window control to lower it until icy air blasted over my cheeks. "Sensitive?"

"I mean, does it bother you?"

"Not—not especially."

"Then hand-holding wouldn't be a problem for you? I think they'd expect us to hold hands."

"I guess that's fine."

"Maybe a touch of your shoulder, or your cheek?"

I was tempted to hang my head out the window like a dog. Showing up to the driving range sweaty was not a good look. But neither was windblown hair. I cleared my throat. "Also fine, I think."

"Good." He grinned. "I can work with that."

Cool relief flooded into me when he turned into the parking lot of a venue I knew well: Pine Hills Golf Club, where we were hosting the gala because of Larissa's connections.

I might be unfamiliar with golf, but it had to be easier than riding in a car with Mateo and talking about touching.

We parked next to Larissa's BMW, and Mateo made a big show of helping me out of his Jeep like an actual boyfriend might. For my part, I tried. I clutched the hand he offered and smiled up at him. "Thanks."

"Of course. Babe."

I winced at the endearment. It sounded so wrong coming from him to me.

Larissa popped her trunk. "Mateo, help me with my clubs?"

With one powerful movement, Mateo lifted the blush-pink bag from her car and slung it over his shoulder like it weighed nothing.

She led the way into the Spanish Revival–style white stucco mansion that served as the clubhouse. "Since we'll be discussing the gala, the foundation will cover your club rental."

"Oh, no," I said. "I couldn't ask the foundation to pay for this."

"We'll write it off. No big deal."

"But nonprofits don't pay taxes. There's nothing to write off."

"It's for a legitimate business purpose, Miriam. It's like the breakfast meetings we have."

"But—" I bit my lip. When I hosted the foundation meetings, I did it at Synergy since it was free and offered coffee and snacks at no charge.

Larissa was in charge of both the foundation and of the job I wanted, so I remained silent.

Still, I refused to let the foundation pay for the club rental, so I handed my credit card to the woman at the desk. It cost more than I thought it would—or should—but I'd cut back on takeout to balance my budget.

While we picked our clubs, Larissa went to the locker room. She emerged in a short golf skirt and spiked shoes. Her long, blond hair was pulled back into a jaunty ponytail over a white visor. With our clubs and a bucket of balls, Mateo and I trailed her to the long stretch of green grass. Trees lined the sides and marked the far end. A row of golfers, mostly men, lined up in spaces marked by mesh dividers.

At the square of torn-up grass where she stopped, a handsome, blond man with razor-sharp cheekbones greeted her with a two-cheek kiss.

"Look who's here!" Larissa linked her arm with his as she

turned to face us. "Flavio, this is Miriam from the foundation and her boyfriend, Mateo. Guys, this is Flavio, my fiancé."

Mateo shook Flavio's hand. Like Mateo, he was tall and fit and blond, but the planes of his face were harder, sharper. His blue eyes weren't soft or kind but glittering and hard as sapphires. Though when he spoke, he had an Italian accent I had to admit was sexy.

When I shook his hand, his cologne's scent hit me like a garbage truck. I sneezed. Larissa gave me a steely glare, and I sniffled and moved farther away from her fiancé.

While Flavio set up at the tee and Larissa posed next to him, Mateo tugged me aside behind another set of golfers. "You didn't have to pay for my clubs. I could have paid my way. Or I'd have paid for both of us."

"No. It's my fault you even have to be here, when you could be doing something"—someone?—"else. I should pay for it."

"You made a face"—Mateo twisted his lips and furrowed his brow in a reflection of what my face must have done—"when Larissa said the foundation would pay for it. Why?"

I scraped my ballet flat across the turf. "Every dollar the foundation brings in should go to the kids. For anti-bullying programs. Or summer camps. Not golf. I don't want to take money away from their programs."

"And yet you want a paid position at the foundation?"

"That's different. The foundation needs employees to run. It can't run solely on volunteers."

"Most volunteers aren't as diligent as you are."

Heat rose to my cheeks. "I believe in the foundation's mission. And I like to do a good job."

He nodded. "In everything you do."

I squinted up at him. He spoke like he knew me. Like he saw me.

"Come on, you guys," Larissa said. "Mateo, I'll show you first."

Mateo let her position his feet at the tee. Then she adjusted his grip on the club, standing well within his personal space. I checked Flavio's reaction. He leaned casually on his club, occasionally waving at the other golfers. Not the jealous type, then.

Finally, Larissa stood in front of Mateo and demonstrated a swing. Was waggling her ass like that strictly necessary?

But Mateo wasn't watching her. He kept his eye on the ball, reared back in a smooth movement of his powerful shoulders, and swung through. The ball sailed through the air, hanging longer than I thought possible, and bounced straight down the center of the green.

Larissa shielded her eyes and followed the ball's trajectory. "Impressive."

Mateo grinned. "Your demonstration was successful."

She preened for a moment. "Get up here, Miriam. You're next."

In a much more businesslike way, she coached me on my stance and my grip. Still, everything felt awkward, and when I pulled back the club, she shrieked, "No, no, keep your left arm straight!"

I froze and looked at my left arm, which had bent back on the upswing. I lowered the club and tried again. This time, I focused on keeping my elbows straight as I swung through. But I missed the ball completely. It remained on the tee.

My cheeks burned as Larissa cracked up. "I'm not laughing at you," she said, blotting tears under her eyes. "It's happened to everyone."

"Seems like you're laughing at me," I muttered under my breath. Great. I'd taken a risk by coming out to try golf with the person I hoped would be my boss, and I looked ridiculous. Would she hold it against me if I was a disappointment at golf? Would the failure taint everything else I did? Frustrated tears prickled behind my eyes. I blinked them away. I should stick to accounting and leave sports to everyone else.

"If I may." Mateo stepped up behind me and braced my shoulders with his big hands. "Maybe another amateur can help."

He nudged my feet a little wider and had me point my left toes out. Then he asked me to rotate my hips to the right as I pulled the club back. My body felt one hundred percent awkward.

Still standing behind me, he placed his hands over mine on the club. Together, we pulled it back again, then it seemed like gravity took over, pulling the club down toward the ball and through. The ball sailed off onto the green, not as far as Mateo's had gone, but it passed other balls sitting on the grass.

"I did it! We did it!" He still had his hands on my arms, so I turned and hugged him, and it seemed like the most natural thing in the world when his arms came around my back, too.

"Thank you," I murmured in his ear. "Sorry, I should have asked before I hugged you. Is hugging okay?"

"Of course." His soft whisper in my ear contrasted with the prickle of his stubble against my jaw, and I shivered.

"You said you don't play," I whispered back.

"I don't golf anymore, but I played a time or two on the island. Weekends, I worked as a caddie at the club."

"A ringer!" Somehow, my fingers had gotten tangled in the waves at the back of his head. They were soft and thick, cushioning my fingers. "You're not a newbie at all, are you?"

He chuckled. "I let Larissa believe in her own assumption."

I frowned and pulled back a little to see his face. His blue eyes crinkled at the corners in a soft expression. Had I done that, too, about Mateo? Assumed he was a big, thick himbo and let that guide my behavior?

He'd let me do it. Let us both do it. He'd concealed his abilities, his real self, behind a flirty mask. What else was he hiding? And why did he feel he needed to do it? Defensive anger, like when that jerk, Anthony, made fun of Bree in seventh grade, bubbled hot inside my chest. I gripped Mateo's hair like I'd shake him for trying to be less than he was.

"No PDA, please." Larissa's voice startled me. I'd forgotten for a moment we weren't alone. "Not on the course."

Shit. I'd forgotten where we were, and I was holding him with my hands tangled in his hair like we were about to kiss. Kissing was definitely not allowed in our fake relationship. Or on the golf course. "Sorry," I mumbled.

Mateo did the opposite. He turned me easily in his arms so my back nestled against his chest. His arms banded around my belly. "Do you blame me? Flavio, you must be on my side."

Flavio looked up from his phone long enough to smirk at us.

It was ridiculous to enjoy being cuddled in Mateo's arms. Everything we were doing—from riding together in Mateo's car to his pretended ignorance—was fake for Larissa. Not real. Besides, our PDA in front of people at her club might embarrass her.

I squirmed out of his grasp. "Larissa's right. We're supposed to be, um, hitting."

"All right." Mateo strolled a few steps away and crossed his arms. "Hit. I'll enjoy the view."

I repositioned myself at the tee and looked out across the green. It wasn't much of a view. A long, flat grassy area bordered by some scrubby evergreens. What was he talking about? I turned my head to look over my shoulder at him.

His gaze was glued to my backside in my stretchy black work pants.

I cleared my throat.

His gaze traveled lazily up the curve of my spine to my face. His grin was obscene and all for Larissa and Flavio. "Don't worry, babe. They understand."

My cheeks burning, I turned my attention back to the ball. It was all pretend, his *babe* had reminded me. He didn't actually like the way I looked or want to hold me in his arms. I didn't want that, either.

While I whacked away at my allotment of golf balls, Larissa said, "So tell me, Mateo. How did you and Miriam get together?"

I missed the ball again. Shit, we hadn't agreed on a backstory of our relationship. I opened my mouth to make something up, but he beat me to it.

"I think you know that my cousin and her brother are together?" He waited for her nod before continuing. "It was Ben's birthday, and there was a family gathering. My aunt, Mimi's parents, some of Ben and Mimi's cousins. A few friends. Jackson Jones was there with his wife and their kids."

I remembered it. Ben's birthday was in July. Mateo had just come over from the island to lead Cooper's security detail. Billionaires—and their boyfriends—needed security, I supposed.

"So Ben, who I knew from his visit to the island where I'm from, introduced me to his sister. She was so radiant that day, the sun shining on her dark hair like fire."

I rolled my eyes before I drew back the club to swing. That was Mateo, romanticizing everything. My hair had been windblown that day, and I'd forgotten to put an elastic on my wrist to pull it back.

"So I did my usual thing. Small talk. A little flirting. She even told me a joke."

"A joke? Mimi?" Larissa laughed.

"I still remember it. I had to look it up because I didn't get it at the time. Want to hear?"

"Definitely."

"Mimi, do you want to tell it?" he asked.

I leaned on the club. He remembered? "No, you tell it."

"Okay. So an infinite number of mathematicians walk into a bar. The first mathematician says to the bartender, 'I'll have a beer.' The second says, 'Half a beer, please.' The third asks for a quarter beer. This is the part I didn't get. Why would you ask for a part of a beer?" He chuckled. "But the barman gets it. He sets two beers in front of all of them. And all the mathematicians—remember, there's an infinite number of them—go, 'That's all you're giving us?' The bartender says, 'Come on, guys. Know your limit.'"

Larissa, just like I'd expected, stood there with her mouth open. Flavio had wandered off completely.

"Later, I asked my smart cousin what it meant. He said it's a calculus function. And I searched for it later and learned about limits of functions. I never got to calculus in school. Still, I knew it was a joke. So I countered with one of my own—a pun."

"A pun?" Larissa asked with half a laugh.

"I said it would be hard to fog-get my first time in San Francisco."

She groaned. "That's terrible!"

I grimaced, not at the pun, but at the memory. I'd thought he was making fun of my nerdy joke. Snob that I was, I hadn't realized he hadn't had the same academic opportunities as his cousin.

Mateo winked at me. "I may have suggested I needed someone to keep me warm. My usual bullshit."

I'd assumed he was mocking me with his fake flirting. I'd been curvy since puberty, and my desk job packed a little extra padding onto my butt. Guys who looked like Mateo didn't flirt with women who looked like me. Or with women who told calculus jokes. He was an Adonis, and I was...just your regular corporate accountant.

"So that was it?" Larissa asked. "You've been together ever since?"

"No." I sensed his bluster deflating a little behind me. "She shut me down. She told me to buy a better jacket."

"I was serious about that. You were wearing a long-sleeved shirt as a jacket." I whacked the ball, and it bounced down the green.

"It was July! But that's my Mimi. Sensible as always. After that, I couldn't think of anything to say to her. Everything that came out was painfully awkward. She broke me."

I turned. "I didn't break you."

He spread his hands. "You did. Don't you remember how ridiculous I was around you after that?"

"Not really." I'd assumed he found me unworthy of his flirting or his notice.

He clutched his hands over his heart like I'd shot him. "You thought I was always like that?"

I shrugged.

"Mimi, Mimi." Shaking his head, he sauntered to me, slung one arm around my shoulders, and after a brief hesitation, brushed a kiss to my temple. "You are my kryptonite. Only you."

Larissa flashed us an arch smile. "I guess it's a classic case of opposites-attract."

I looked up into Mateo's face. We were opposites, all right. He was tall and gorgeous. I was short and normal-looking. I'd assumed he thought I was a geek, beneath his notice, but maybe I'd been wrong about that.

And now he'd saved my bacon by pretending to be my boyfriend and even added on an over-the-top story that made Larissa swoon. I was going to owe him—massively—when all this was over.

11

MATEO

A COUPLE DAYS after I'd managed not to embarrass Mimi in front of Larissa at the golfing range, I was, as my cousin Lito might say, cautiously optimistic.

Fuck that.

I bounced like a kid on his way to a birthday party as I rode up in the glass-walled elevator to Mimi's floor in the Synergy building, carrying my precious bundle. As chief of security for the CEO, Cooper Fallon—or, as I called him, my cousin Lito—I had a Synergy badge, and I didn't need an escort to surprise my girl with food.

I'd won points with the pollo guisado and the empanadas, so I was going back to the food well with a guaranteed winner in my tote bag: my tía's chicken mole.

She'd be hungry. She never remembered to eat. She'd give me one of those cautious smiles like she had at the golf course when I showed her how to hit the ball. She might even let me kiss her again. I'd done it as a nice touch for Larissa, and, frankly, a little for myself since Mimi hadn't been so prickly that night. Then, when my lips had touched the smooth skin at her temple, it had felt so right I'd wanted to kiss right down her neck.

Obviously, I hadn't done it. That would've been too far for Mimi. And definitely too much in front of her boss.

But today, maybe I could get away with a peck on the cheek, another hit of that vanilla scent her skin carried. Squashing my cigarette cravings had been easy; every time my fingers trembled for a smoke, I'd recalled her warm spiciness, and it had washed away. All I wanted was another chance to get close to her. A brush of my hand on her hip. Jesus, I couldn't wait to dance with her at the gala.

The elevator doors opened, and I stepped out onto Mimi's floor. Heads turned as I walked past the low-walled cubicles, and each worker I passed gave a hopeful sniff. By the time I made it to Mimi's desk, every eye on the floor peered at me from behind ferns and around the sides of computer monitors.

"Hey," I said softly so I wouldn't startle her.

She jumped anyway, whacking her knee on the underside of her desk. Rubbing it over her black slacks, she rotated to face me. Her eyes widened.

"What are you doing here?" she whispered.

"I brought you lunch." I lifted the tote bag to her eye level.

Her gaze flicked to the time in the corner of her screen. "It's two o'clock."

"Have you eaten yet?"

Her stomach growled, and she laid her hand over her baggy gray sweater. "No."

I clicked my tongue. "This is why you're so—" I clamped my jaw shut.

She sat in squinty-eyed silence for a second. Then she surged out of her cube and beckoned me toward the employee break-room. In the small white kitchen, she whirled on me. "Why I'm so *what*, exactly?"

I was not about to use the word *hangry* again around her. Not when she was snarling at me like a ravenous lioness.

"Smart?" I said. "To wait for me to bring you lunch?"

She scrubbed a hand over her face. "That's not what you were going to say." She inhaled and swallowed. "What did you bring?"

"Ah." I'd won her over again with food. Three for three. "Tía's special chicken mole."

"Mole?" She took a step back as if I'd said I brought her a live tarantula. "What's in it?"

I chuckled, bringing out the plastic container. "I thought you were an adventurous eater. You didn't ask me what was in the pollo guisado."

"That's because I didn't think it had chocolate in it. And I'm allergic to chocolate. Does your aunt put chocolate in her mole?"

"I...I don't know. I haven't seen her make it. I never thought about it."

"People with food allergies always have to think about what's in their food," she snapped.

Fuck, Ben had warned me she was allergic to chocolate, but it hadn't crossed my mind that she might have a reaction to the mole. The dish was absolutely magical. But I stuffed it back into the sack. Poisoning Mimi would lose all the points I'd gained.

"I'm sorry. I'll go get you something else. What would you like?"

"Nothing. I'm fine."

"You're not fine. You're—" I bit my tongue before the word *hangry* slipped out.

Her eyebrows disappeared into her curly bangs. She put her hands on her hips. "I'm going out for drinks with my friend Bree tonight. I'll eat something then."

"Oh. Ah." Words tripped over each other on my tongue. What could I say that wouldn't hit that hair trigger of hers? "Are you sure that's a good idea?"

"What, going out with my friend?"

I'd seen for myself what a good *friend* Bree had been. When her fiancé picked her up, she stumbled out without a thought for Mimi, who'd been practically passed out on the bar. I couldn't bear to think about what could have happened to her, alone in a bar full of guys who'd have gladly taken advantage of a woman as beautiful—and as drunk—as Mimi.

But I'd been there, and I'd protected her from those guys. We'd talked the way we'd never talked before. Or since. I'd gotten to know her. I'd fallen a tiny bit in love that night. And she'd seemed to like me, too, for once.

Jesus Christ, how I wished she remembered the connection we had. But I'd be a fool to tell her about it. She'd never believe me. She had to remember it for herself.

"Be careful, okay? Be sure you eat something first. And drink plenty of water."

"What the hell, Mateo? I'm a big girl. I can take care of myself."

"Not when you're drinking." My vision hazed as I remembered how that one guy at the bar had reached a hand toward her shoulder. I'd wanted to snap it off. "You can't hold your liquor," I snarled.

Her eyes went wide, and she stared over my shoulder as she squeaked, "Hey, Monique. Almost time for our meeting?"

"It is." A tall Black woman with a square jaw narrowed her eyes at us. "I just came in to top off my coffee."

"I'll be right there." *That's my boss,* she mouthed at me.

Shit! I'd fucked up her life again. But I couldn't think of a single thing to say to make it right.

"I guess I'll go." I tucked the bag with the poison food under my arm.

"I think you should," she said darkly.

As I tucked my tail and scurried from the building, my face burned even in the chilly San Francisco afternoon. She'd never forgive me for calling her a drunk in front of her boss.

I didn't deserve to be forgiven. I didn't deserve her.

All I could do was the one thing I was good at: protecting her.

12

MIMI

"SO WHAT, exactly, do you remember from your bachelorette party?" I swirled the wine in my glass. It was the first time I'd seen Bree since her honeymoon, and we were at our favorite booth by the window at our usual Wednesday-night bar, the one that served half-price appetizers until seven. The Sharks game blared on the televisions over the bar, and the place was packed with turquoise jerseys.

Bree's eyes widened, then she blinked. "Oh, everything. We had so much fun! We were all here, except you. You were late. And you came in buzzed. Remember?"

"Oh, I remember that." Though I hadn't realized exactly how drunk I was. "I came from my brother's engagement party."

"That's right!" Bree pointed at me, then sipped her martini. "Then we had some drinks, then someone said we should go to the other bar."

That was one of Bree's work friends. So we'd all piled into a couple of ride-shares and ridden to Divisadero Street. I remembered that. That was where I'd met up with the Mystery Man.

"That bar was fire," she said, "but then it got late and people started leaving." She pouted.

"You left," I pointed out. I picked up a sad, cold mozzarella stick, but I'd already stuffed myself with chicken wings and fried mushrooms. My stomach couldn't hold another thing. I dropped it back onto the plate.

"Yeah, Josh came in and hauled my drunk ass home." She giggled. "You didn't go home?"

"Not then. This guy came over and talked to me. He had glasses. I *think* he was super-hot. You don't remember him?"

"I might be married, but I have eyes. There was this one cute guy here that night. No glasses, though." She tapped the table, then her eyes went wide. "I remember! He showed up at the second bar a few minutes after we did. But he didn't come over. He just sat in a corner with a newspaper. God, I wished he'd come over."

"You're married, remember?" Could her cute guy have been my Mystery Man? I didn't remember much about his face—except the glasses—but I remembered how he made me feel. He listened when I told him how much I wanted to be like Larissa. He told me he had a boss he thought the world of, too. We made a connection.

"So, did you go home with this Mystery Man?"

"I don't think so. I woke up alone at my place. In my clothes. But I had this." I tugged on the chain around my neck and pulled out the ring I'd found in my pocket. The plain gold band was scarred like it had been worn a long time. But I remembered the Mystery Man was young, about my age.

"A wedding ring?" Bree's eyes widened. "What the hell, Mimi! Are you Vegas-married?"

I laughed. "I don't think we had time to go to Vegas. And no matter what happens in rom-coms, I'm pretty sure they won't let you get married if you're blackout-drunk. Even in Vegas. I think he gave it to me for safekeeping. To—to..." His words dangled just out of my reach.

I slipped the ring onto my thumb and spun it. Clearly a man's ring, it was way too big to fit any of my fingers.

"Wow. And now you have to find him and give it back. It's like Cinderella's slipper!" She tipped back her glass and drained the last drops of alcohol. "Then you have to marry him."

I snorted.

"I'm serious. It's, like, fate or something."

"I think you've been watching too many romance-channel Christmas movies."

"Yeah," she said dreamily. "But it's always the guy who's the buttoned-up accountant and doesn't have any Christmas spirit."

"I don't have to have Christmas spirit. I'm Jewish."

"Not too many Jewish folks in those movies."

"Nope."

"But…" She drew out the word, the way I knew meant she'd just had a terrible idea. The way she had in high school when she'd asked me to run interference while she ripped the promo sticker off the window at Taco Bell and ran out with it. *Why* had she wanted it so badly? She'd finally given up trying to explain it to me and walked out without the window cling. Fifteen years later, I still didn't understand the point.

"But?" I prompted her.

"It doesn't matter that we're Jewish. We can still like those romantic movies. Where the woman wants the holiday festival to go off without a hitch, and the man wants to bulldoze the whole thing to build a ski resort, and they fall in love anyway and in the last scene they take their kids to the holiday festival."

I wrinkled my nose. "That sounds awful. Wouldn't a ski resort be better for the town's economy? They could take their kids skiing."

She gasped. "I thought you were ditching the dark side and turning your volunteer work into a job! Becoming one of us!"

I gave her half a smile. "Not everyone can be a pediatric nurse and save lives every day. The world needs accountants, too."

"You can be an accountant and still see the romance in the world."

"Can you?" I brushed a hand over the sad-looking tinsel garland that hung below the window, and a few tarnished silver strands dropped onto the table. Five of the bulbs had gone dark on the strand of multicolored lights that lined the window. Why hadn't they taken all this shit down three weeks ago?

Bree picked up the dropped strands and arranged them in a six-pointed star on the table. "I think there's hope for you. Once we find your Mystery Man, he'll turn on your romance switch."

"Is that a euphemism?"

She grinned. "Why, yes, it is. I'm sure your Mystery Man is a very talented—"

"Bree!" I glanced at the next table of sixty-something ladies. One of them wore red-framed glasses, a plastic tiara, and a hot-pink feather boa. Like Bree and me, they weren't paying attention to the game on the television.

"—conversationalist, I was going to say."

"That's not what you were going to say."

She shrugged. "Same difference. They both start with C. Want another drink?"

I glanced at my mostly full glass. Why did Mateo have to be right? The thought of drinking more wine made my stomach curdle.

"Wait! That's him! That's the cute guy!" Bree pointed behind me.

I spun in my chair to look, but the Sharks must have done something exciting because half the bar stood and cheered. I scanned the shouting faces for guys with glasses, but none of them was my Mystery Man. When the room had settled, I asked, "Do you still see him?"

"No, I lost him when the Sharks scored. I don't see him now. Sorry."

"What did he look like?"

"Tall, built, blondish. A jaw that could cut glass." She sighed.

In California, that could have been anyone. From some random actor to Cooper Fallon to Larissa's fiancé. "Was he wearing glasses?"

"No. I told you, my cute guy didn't have glasses." She glanced down at her phone. "Speaking of which, Josh is on his way. Want a ride home?"

"Yes, please." If she'd seen my Mystery Man, I'd have stayed. But he wasn't here.

"How am I supposed to find him and give this back?" I pulled the ring off my thumb and tucked it safely back between my boobs. If I found him, he could be my date to the gala. My memories were fuzzy, but I had a suspicion he'd been a smooth talker. He'd have never called me an alcoholic in front of my boss.

"You should post a Missed Connections on Craigslist."

I raised my eyebrows. "That's not still a thing."

"It totally is! Though some of the posts are kind of disturbing." She grimaced.

"Bree, what the hell? Why are you perusing the Missed Connections?"

"It's how I met Josh. Didn't I tell you?"

"You said you saw him at the grocery store and then bumped into him at a coffee shop. It was fate, you said."

Her cheeks pinked. "I may have posted after the grocery store. And the coffee shop might have been our first date."

"Oh. My. God. I have to say, that's a little creepy and not nearly as romantic as fated love."

"Hey, I just took the advice your mom always used to give us. Go for what you want. Anyway, think about it. The Missed Connections post."

I snorted.

Bree signaled for the check. "This guy is worth a shot, right?"

I sighed, remembering that magical night. Well, not exactly remembering. But I recalled the warm feeling he'd given me. Of being seen and understood. For a few hours, we'd been the center of each other's world.

Shit. Bree's romanticism was finally rubbing off on me after all these years.

I scanned the bar one last time. The only glasses were on the grandma next to us.

But the ring on its chain was hope. A promise. My Mystery Man and I would find each other. Maybe in time for the gala.

Mateo was a flirt, not a romantic. He flitted from person to person, using his honey tongue on each one. No matter what he'd said at the driving range in front of Larissa, no matter how many meals he brought me, his heart wasn't engaged, and he certainly wasn't committed to our fake relationship. He'd understand if I ditched our date.

He'd find someone else to flirt with, to bring food to, before the end of the day.

And that would be okay. Because I'd have my Mystery Man.

13

MATEO

I PULLED open the door to the wine bar and scanned the place for the gala planning committee. Mimi's back was to me, but I'd have known her dark curls anywhere. Seeing them made my heart hammer against my ribs. Why was I putting myself through this? Why had I let Larissa pull me into a situation where I had to see Mimi three times a week, when every disapproving stare was like a knife in my chest?

Larissa waved at me, and I trudged toward their table.

I did it because Mimi wanted this job at the foundation more than anything. Because she wanted to spend all her time, not just her after-work hours, helping kids.

And because I'd do anything for her.

If my friends back on the island could see me now, following a woman around like a puppy, they'd laugh at me. *The sailfish has been hooked at last,* they'd hoot. Hell, I'd have laughed a year ago if you'd told me I'd be standing in a chichi wine bar planning a party I didn't give a shit about and could never afford to attend, all for a woman.

But my heart didn't care.

"Mateo!" Larissa stood and pecked my cheek. Well, it should have been a peck, but her lips lingered a second too long, long enough for her hand to drift from my shoulder to my chest. She squeezed my pec.

I gripped her hand and pulled it off my body, gently returning it to her side. "Hello, Larissa. Natalie. Mimi."

"You're late," Larissa said, a slight pout to her pink lips. "We chose the flowers without you."

"You brilliant ladies don't need me to choose flowers." They didn't need me for anything, but I'd go along if Larissa, who held Mimi's job in her hands, thought they did. I glanced down at her, but Mimi had her eyes on the spreadsheet lighting up her laptop screen. "And no flowers are as lovely as the three of you."

Larissa batted her eyelashes. "Too bad I have to go now. I have an appointment at the salon." She shook out her mane of straight blond hair, an obvious plea for another compliment.

I obliged her. "You're perfect. No salon could make you more beautiful."

She smiled, satisfied, and laid her hand on my arm. "You're so sweet. Thank you."

I peeled her hand off my biceps and turned it into a handshake. "Good night, Larissa."

"Bye, girls. See you Monday." With a toss of her hair, she was gone.

"Didn't she say she was engaged?" Natalie stared at my arm where Larissa had squeezed it.

Mimi glared at her spreadsheet. "Mm-hmm. We met her fiancé."

Was she jealous? She didn't even like me. Or did she?

Jealousy over a fake date could be my foot in the door. I rested my hand on her shoulder. "Don't be jealous, baby. You know my heart beats only for you."

She stared at my hand like she wanted to shake it off. With Larissa gone, would she drop our pretense? I hoped not. I wasn't ready to stop touching her.

"The night is young, ladies. Should we have another drink?" I tugged Larissa's chair closer to Mimi and eased into it. I let my hand trail from her shoulder to her back until it rested on the sexy curve of her waist.

When she let it stay, my heart skipped in my chest.

"I have a better idea." Natalie leaned forward on her elbows. "Dancing."

Mimi stiffened under my hand. "Dancing? I don't dance."

"But we have to learn. For the gala. Bachata." Natalie waggled her shoulders. "I watched a video online, but it's not the same as having a teacher."

As much as I wanted to, I didn't dare squeeze her waist. But I'd be free, even expected, to put my hands on her when we danced. "What do you say, Mimi? Should we get in some practice tonight?"

She frowned. "You can't dance with both of us. Why don't you and Natalie—"

"My brother Andrew's picking me up," Natalie bounced in her chair. "I'll ask him to come with us. Dancing with us is better than moping around in his condo."

"Perfect," I said. "I know a club in the Mission."

"Great. And here's Andrew!" Natalie jumped up and flung her arms around a blond guy about my height but slender. The pants of his expensive wool suit were creased at the hips like he'd been sitting at a desk all day. His pale skin looked like he hadn't seen daylight in a month. Finance, I guessed.

"Mateo, Mimi, meet Andrew."

I stood to shake her brother's hand. His grip was firm and dry, and he held my gaze with his full attention. His lips were full and sensual like his brother's, but his long-lashed blue eyes were the shape of Natalie's. A pretty boy, totally my type. But no one was my type with Mimi around.

"Mateo," he said. "Nat's talked about you."

"She has?" I grinned. "Good things, I hope?"

"She says you've been a champ about this gala project. And

that you and Mimi are hashtag-couple-goals." He made air quotes, then extended his hand to Mimi.

I watched them together. Andrew was probably Mimi's ideal man. Smart, rich, worked in her field. But their handshake was brief, and he turned to his sister.

"Ready to go?" he asked.

"So ready. But you're not taking me home. We're going dancing!"

"Dancing?" His sandy-blond eyebrows flew up.

"It'll be fun. It'll get your mind off—"

He tugged her into a half-hug and rubbed his knuckles in her hair. "None of that, Nutter Butter."

"O.M.G., Andrew. I'm twenty-five, not twelve." She pulled away from him and ran her fingers through her tousled hair. Her cheeks were pink and her eyebrows scrunched in a pretense of annoyance, but her smile was bright as sunshine.

I never had a sibling, but my cousin Sara and I teased each other like that. A wave of homesickness crashed through me. Dancing was exactly what I needed.

I rubbed my hands together. "Let's go. I'll drive Mimi, and you take Natalie, Andrew?"

I gave Natalie the name of the club, and her thumbs flew over her phone. "Meet you there!"

Outside on the sidewalk, Mimi trudged by my side. "You really don't have to do this. I can tell Natalie I'm not feeling up to it."

"Do you not feel well?" I glanced at her as we crossed the street to my Jeep. Like Andrew, she looked like she could've used a day outside.

"No, I'm fine. It's just…"

"What is it?" I opened her door and offered my hand to assist her into the high seat.

She gripped it and hoisted herself up onto the running board. How did she not tingle with the energy that coursed between us? But she only settled into the seat and captured my gaze. "I never meant for this to get so out of control. All I wanted was a chance to prove myself to Larissa. Not to drag you into a fake relationship with a side of party planning. And dancing. I'm sure you're tired from work."

"So are you." I wanted to trace her delicate jaw, to feel her cheek curve up into a smile. But we were alone, and there was no one to pretend for. "I want to do this. Dancing will be fun. You'll see. Besides, we need to practice for the gala."

Her eyes pinched like she was in pain. "Do we have to dance in front of all those people?"

"Don't worry. You'll look good. I promise." I closed her door. I'd always been good at physical stuff: baseball, surfing, dancing. I'd never regretted my weakness in other things, like school. Not until Mimi.

She was quiet on the ride to the club, so I played some music to get the rhythm flowing through us. When I looked over, she tapped her fingers to the beat on the armrest. Good. I swayed my shoulders.

The club was one Carlo played sometimes, but there was no live band tonight, only a DJ. Hot pink and yellow lights flashed across the stage where she shimmied to the music behind her mixer. A couple whirled beside her, skilled beyond my level. Below the stage, lines of people practiced their steps in an open space in the middle of the dance floor. More adventurous couples spun around the edges.

We found Andrew and Natalie at the bar. Natalie handed us two shots of something dark red and disturbingly familiar.

"What is this?" Mimi eyed it with a wise level of suspicion.

"The Thursday-night special. The bartender called it Mama Juana."

I laughed. Back home, we called it liquid Viagra. My aunt Camelia made a version from red wine, local honey, and herbs she grew in her garden, and she swore I'd been conceived after she served it at a family pig roast. I raised my eyebrows at Andrew. "Be careful. It's, ah, potent."

"What?" he shouted over the music.

"Don't be a baby. Drink up." Natalie elbowed him in the side and downed her drink. He followed.

I clinked my glass to Mimi's. "Salud."

Her smile was nervous. "L'chaim."

We tossed back the bittersweet shots.

"That's revolting. Like cough syrup."

It wasn't as good as tía Camelia's. The bottle behind the bar had a ridiculous straw hat for a cap. But its high alcohol content might loosen Mimi up.

"Another?" Natalie grimaced.

"I'll teach you the steps first." Loose Mimi would be good, but I didn't want to have to carry her out of another bar.

Taking Mimi's hand, I weaved through the dancing couples to the line dancers in the center of the floor. We stood behind the one at the back and watched for a moment.

"Okay, see, it's one-two-three-tap, then go right, five-six-seven-tap. Small steps, and keep your feet low."

I placed myself between Mimi and Natalie. Taking small, exaggerated steps, I demonstrated the footwork, and by the time I'd finished the first set, Natalie swayed at my side. Mimi and Andrew hung off the ends, watching.

"Let's go," I shouted. Taking Mimi's hand, I shuffled toward her, urging her to move her feet. Hesitantly, she took up the movement. "Good, good," I praised her.

Following the line in front, I showed them how to dance forward, then I taught them the turns. Natalie picked up the pattern like a natural.

Mimi did not. She forgot to tap, missed the change in direction, and bumped my shoulder. She stomped her feet in frustration. "I told you I don't dance!"

"It's okay." I pivoted, turning my back on the other lines, and faced her. I put out my palms and nodded at her to lay her hands on mine.

"To the left," I said, moving to my right to mirror her.

She watched her feet and mine for a few sets.

Finally, when her body moved in rhythm, I squeezed her hands. "Eyes up."

Her gorgeous brown eyes reflected the pink lights above the stage. Her lips moved, silently counting the steps. We'd work on that later.

"You're doing great. When I squeeze your hands, come forward." When I sensed the line behind me shift, I tightened my grip on her and as I backed up, I tugged her toward me.

"Now back." We reversed the movement. Soon, we moved in step with the block of dancers. Side to side, front to back, turn, turn.

She was no Carmen Miranda or even JLo, but her footwork didn't falter, and her hips rocked in a way that tightened my pants. Or maybe that was the Mama Juana.

When the music changed, I pulled her out of the line toward the dancing couples.

"Wait, what are you doing?"

"You've been called up," I said. "You're ready for the big leagues."

"No, I'm not! I'm still a guppy."

"Now you're mixing swimming and baseball. This is dancing, and you're ready."

We started with a simple back and forth, and I was back on mi abuela's porch, dancing with my cousins. The fug of the club was nothing like the ocean breeze back home. Still, I sang along with the music under my breath and watched Mimi under half-closed eyelids.

Her gaze hovered below my chin. I supposed that was where it ought to be since I signaled our turns with my shoulders and spins with a shift of my palm against hers. But I wanted her gaze on my face, in my eyes, so I could tell what she was thinking, how she liked dancing with me.

She said something, but the music was too loud. I leaned closer. "What did you say?"

Her cheeks reddened. "I said you're a really good dancer."

"Ah, thank you. But I'm not as good as them." I tipped my chin toward the couple on stage. He spun his partner under his arm, then he twirled under their joined hands. They moved together like they shared a mind, like two parts of the same body.

"Maybe not," she said in my ear, "but you make me feel safe. Confident."

I warmed inside. "That's how it should be. I'm the vine, supporting you. You're the flower, beautiful and fragrant."

She wrinkled her nose. "Beautiful? Hardly."

"You're an orchid. Exotic and delicate." I inhaled the vanilla scent of her hair.

"You're the beautiful one," she said. "Everyone's watching you."

I didn't bother to look. "No, Mimi, they're watching you. You're hypnotic."

Her gaze locked with mine, golden sparkles lighting up the dark depths like moonlight over the ocean.

"Why are you so nice to me?" Her gaze slipped from mine. "Nice to...to everyone."

I tugged her out of the way of an oncoming, spinning couple. "Which is it, Mimi? Am I nice to everyone, or to you?"

"Both. But especially me?"

I chuckled, then put my lips by her ear so she'd be sure to hear. "I'm glad you finally noticed."

"But I don't understand. What's in it for you? What's your angle?"

"Angle?" I reared back. "I only want..." Was she ready to hear the answer? That I wanted *her* and nothing else?

Her steps faltered. Lost in her eyes, I stepped on something soft. When I looked down, I saw I'd squashed the toe of her ballet flat. I hopped away, but Mimi's eyes squeezed shut in pain.

I stopped moving and ran my hands up her shoulders. "Sorry! Sorry I'm so clumsy. Are you all right?"

"I'm fine." But she kept her weight off the foot I'd smashed like an oaf.

"Let's take a break," I said. "Can you walk?"

She squared her chin. "Of course I can."

Still, I kept my arm around her as I guided her off the dance floor. I helped her perch on a stool next to a high-top table.

"Can I get you a drink?"

"Just water, please."

When I returned to the table with two ice-cold bottles of water, she had her phone out. "My ride's almost here."

"Your ride? I'm your ride."

"No, I called a rideshare. I've taken up too much of your evening. I have to work tomorrow."

"No, Mimi. I'll take you home."

"No. Stay if you like. I'm sure you can find a better dance partner than me. Thanks for bringing us. It was…" She stood without finishing the sentence.

"Mimi, I'm so sorry. Can I get you an ice pack? Some aspirin?"

"No, thank you." She rested her hand on mine for a moment, light and cool as the San Francisco drizzle. Then she was gone, leaving me in the dark club, sweat chilling my skin.

We'd had a connection on the dance floor. I knew we had. She'd looked into my eyes like she saw me, like she valued me.

And then I'd fucked it up. I'd chickened out when I should have told her how I felt. What I wanted.

Her. Only her.

14

MIMI

I LOVED HAVING Ben at Shabbat dinner. Not only did it remind me of so many Friday nights growing up, but I could rely on him for a deflection or two when Mom got to be too much.

His fiancé, Cooper, on the other hand? I kind of wished he had to go to Singapore again. Then he wouldn't be sitting across my parents' dining room table from me, his blond hair, blue eyes, and broad shoulders reminding me too forcefully of his cousin.

The one I'd run away from last night.

I'd thought I understood Mateo. I thought he was one of those guys whose pretty was an inch deep. That underneath the gorgeous exterior was nothing but bland emptiness. Or, like Byron, heartless cruelty.

But he'd shaken me to my core.

He'd lulled me into saying more than I intended. I told him he made me feel safe.

He countered by calling me beautiful. Byron had called me that, too, but as it turned out, he'd used his soft words to take, take, take from me until he'd used me up.

What did Mateo want? His stare on the dance floor had been hungry. And confusing.

"Mimi, may I pour you some wine?" Cooper's voice startled me. I blinked. Mom would kill me if she knew I wasn't entertaining our guest while she, Dad, and Ben finished up the dinner preparations in the kitchen.

Though the thought of entertaining my boss's boss's boss was pretty intimidating.

"Half a glass, please." What would Cooper think of the sweet Kosher wine and our family's Friday-night traditions? Although he and Ben had been together for over six months, tonight was the first time Ben had subjected Cooper to a Levy-Walters Shabbat dinner. Usually on Friday nights, Cooper had just returned from a trip and was tired, they were going out on a date, or Ben came by himself.

This was a big night for my brother and his fiancé.

Cooper filled my glass halfway. It was only then I noticed he was drinking sparkling water. Now that I thought about it, the champagne he'd drunk at their engagement party had looked clearer than what was in Ben's glass. And I hadn't seen him drink anything at all at Bree and Josh's wedding.

Was it possible to get through one of my family's dinners without alcohol?

"Jackson Jones told me something the other day," he said.

"He did?" Had his best friend and business partner told him about the assistant director position? Or had he told Cooper I'd screwed up my budget presentation earlier that month? Had Monique told him I was a drunk? I gulped the wine, wishing it were something stronger.

"He said you're dating my cousin Mateo."

Oh. Shit. Why had I deluded myself that our lie would stay inside the gala committee? And if Cooper knew, that meant Ben knew. And it would only be a matter of time before—

Mom gasped behind me. "Mimi, you're dating someone? Why didn't you mention it when we talked this week?"

Oh, only because it was totally fake, and I hoped she'd never find out. But if I admitted the lie, would Cooper set Jackson straight? Then Jackson would tell Natalie, who might let it slip in front of Larissa. If Larissa found out, I'd be off the gala committee—and out of the running for the full-time job—in an instant.

I grimaced. "It's…it's new."

"Tell me all about it." Mom plunked down the challah platter and sank into a chair.

"Ah." I glanced at Cooper, who had the grace to look guilty. I considered telling her the truth, that it was all a ruse. I probably should have gone with that. But her rounded brown eyes were so hopeful, and her smile had an anticipatory happiness I didn't have the heart to crush. I'd have to do it eventually. But tonight, I'd let her live in the excitement that had her leaning forward on her elbows.

"Cooper's cousin Mateo and I are seeing each other. Casually. Not a big deal."

"You mean, like, casual sex? Friends with benefits? Fuckbudd—"

"No! God, no, Mom." I squeezed my eyes shut so I wouldn't have to look at her or Cooper. My boss's boss's boss.

"Then…" I knew that tone. There was no escaping the inquisition now.

"We went golfing the other day with Larissa and her boyfriend. Dancing the other night. And we're going to the gala together next month. No big deal."

Though for a moment on the dance floor, it had felt like a very big deal. Until I remembered we were not a thing and freaked out. I was glad he'd stepped on my foot. The pain reminded me we were oil and water. A pair of magnets with the same polarization. Ones and zeroes.

"Golfing, dancing, and a gala? These are not things you usually do, Mimi. Are you sure it's not a big deal?"

"Positive. I promise it won't get in the way of my career. Not like—" I clicked my teeth shut. I did *not* want to hash through my last failed relationship. Definitely not in front of Cooper.

"Ah, Mimi. Seeing your brother so happy with Cooper has given me a new perspective."

Behind me, Ben snorted. He circled the table and set down two bowls of soup. "More like Bree's wedding has given you ideas. Visions of tulle and white roses and dancing the horah. Admit it."

Mom pursed her lips. "I want both my children to be happy. I ran into Breina's mother at services last week. She said they're trying for a baby."

"Bree and I just went out for drinks this week!" I said. "No way are they trying to get pregnant."

"She's over thirty. They'll need to start soon."

"Mom!"

"What? I thought both you girls wanted children."

"Someday. Not now before I settle into my career."

She eyed my midsection like it had an expiration date stamped on it. "You know I want the best for you. Now tell me about Mateo."

Ben laughed. "Cats and dogs, those two."

Cooper snatched my brother's hand and stopped him with a look full of silent meaning. "No, sweetheart. They're dating."

"What?" He perched on Cooper's knee. "You and Mateo?"

Cooper studied my face. Why hadn't he talked to Mateo about this? He could have set his cousin straight. And then I wouldn't be talking about my fake relationship with my mother, who'd never let it go. If Cooper weren't my boss's boss's boss, I'd jump over the table and strangle him. I never lied to my brother.

But now I had to keep going. "Yes."

"It's *new* and *casual.*" Mom said. "Whatever that means."

"Oh." Ben's lips turned down. He didn't have to say a word. I knew he was thinking about the bowl of condoms next to my bed and the casual hookups that cycled through my apartment every few weeks. He actually liked Mateo, and that *Oh* meant he thought Mateo was one of the guys I'd bring home when I was horny and boot out before sunrise.

But I couldn't do that with Mateo. He was part of my brother's life. His family.

Shit, why hadn't I thought of this before? Why had I let it happen?

Goddamn Larissa and her party planning and her lady boner for Mateo and his Latin American gala theme.

Ben and Mom didn't see it, but Cooper mouthed, *Sorry,* at me. Out loud, he said, "Speaking of the gala, Jackson says you're doing a fantastic job on the planning committee."

The tightness in my belly loosened a notch. "That's nice of him to say. His sister Natalie is doing most of the work, and I'm helping her. Plus the usual financial stuff."

"I understand there's an opening for an assistant director at the foundation, and your name has been discussed," he said.

Cooper had heard that? Did it mean Larissa was seriously considering me? "I'd heard that, too."

"What's this?" My mother's dark eyebrows disappeared under her blown-out bangs. "A director?"

I hadn't meant for her to hear about it until I'd gotten the position, but it was worth the distraction from the Mateo line of questioning. *"Assistant* director. And it's not a done deal. Far from it. But there is a position, and I told Larissa I was interested."

"Does it pay more than what you earn at Synergy?" Her gaze was sharp.

I definitely didn't want to have this conversation in front of Cooper. "Um, I—" I cringed and shot a glance at Cooper.

"We'd be sorry to lose you," he said, his expression unreadable. "But we understand that our employees need to pursue their passions, and sometimes that's outside of Synergy. Though I like to think Jackson's foundation is still in the Synergy family."

The tension left the back of my neck. "Thank you. Though, like I said, they're still considering. Larissa brought in an outside candidate for an interview last week. I have to wow her with my work on the gala."

"Are you sure a nonprofit is the right direction?" Mom asked. "It could take you out of the private sector. Stunt your career growth."

I rubbed at the new pinch in my chest. "This is what I want. In a few years, once I've got more experience, I could move up to director."

"But you're a senior accountant now, ready to move into management. And Synergy is an excellent company. Stable." She smiled at Cooper.

"I know, and it's been great to me. But I think my passion is in nonprofits. Specifically, helping kids. The foundation does great work with kids who have Tourette's and other neurological differences."

Mom nodded slowly. She remembered how I'd come home from school trembling with rage whenever some kid made fun of Bree.

"It's a fantastic opportunity." Ben stood. "You'll do great."

I smiled at him. Our passions were similar, and his work at a foundation he cared about had inspired me to think about my own life goals. To reevaluate them. To be a better version of myself.

"I'll help Dad bring in the rest of the food," Ben said, circling the table toward the kitchen.

I pushed back my chair, grateful for an opportunity to escape. "I'll help you."

"No. Stay. You could use the rest," he said with a fond grin. "You've been running yourself ragged between work and volunteering."

I smiled back. My brother was the sweetest. Even though space had been tight and I'd had no privacy, I missed him now that he'd moved off my couch and into Cooper's fancy mansion.

"Let me help." Cooper pushed back his chair and stood.

"No, you're our guest." Mom fluttered her hand at her future son-in-law. "Besides, we're almost done."

"Can't get good help around here," Dad grumbled as he carried in the roast.

"Sorry, Dad," Ben said, returning to the kitchen.

Mom said, "We got carried away talking about Mimi's new job. And the fact that she's seeing Cooper's cousin Mateo."

"You're seeing someone?" He set down the roast.

My cheeks went hot. "It's—"

"New." Mom rolled her eyes. "And *casual.*"

"Does he treat you right?" Dad asked.

Except for trying to set off my chocolate allergy. He'd been surprisingly sweet about golfing and about the gala. "He does."

He shot me a quick smile. "Then I'm happy for you."

"Thanks, Dad."

"And what's this about a new job?"

"Dad." My cheeks went even hotter. Why did we have to talk about this in front of Cooper? "It's just a possibility."

He pointed an oven mitt at me. "I want to hear more about this *possibility* when we all sit down. Jeannie, let's finish bringing in the dishes." He and my mother disappeared into the kitchen. Ben followed them.

"Sorry I brought it up," Cooper said. "I didn't know you hadn't talked to them about it."

"It's fine. They worry about me, you know?" He probably didn't know. What would Cooper Fallon's parents have to worry about? He led a hot Fortune 1000 company and was engaged to a man he loved.

"I get it. They want to protect you."

I chuckled. "More like push me. Mom taught me early that women have to have the tools to protect themselves."

"That's right." Mom bustled in with a dish of boiled potatoes. "Smarts, drive, and confidence. That's what it takes to succeed in a man's world." She pierced Cooper with a challenging stare.

"Absolutely. I know I have a lot of privilege, and I try to help others who don't."

"He does." Ben carried in the peas and carrots. He set down the bowl, then kissed Cooper's cheek. "He supports every women's shelter in the Bay Area."

That had to be a story. I watched Cooper's face, but it betrayed nothing but love for my brother.

Dad brought in the salad. "Let's eat."

"Prayers first," Mom reminded him.

Not even the Shabbat songs and prayers distracted Mom from her line of questioning. After we'd blessed the Challah and everyone had eaten a piece, she locked onto me from across the table. "Adam, Mimi's thinking of leaving her job in accounting to work for a nonprofit."

"Mom, I'm not really leaving accounting. I'm taking my skills to the nonprofit."

"You'll keep up your CPA?" Dad asked. "You worked so hard for it."

"Of course I will." I shuddered at the thought of retaking the exam. "I'm just adding on more responsibilities."

"It's a good career move." Cooper pushed his glass of wine toward Ben. He'd taken only a sip after the Kiddush. "Mimi can grow into other areas—operations, management, development— that she wouldn't normally be exposed to at a bigger company like Synergy."

"But at Synergy she has stability," Mom said. "A defined career path."

"Mom," Ben interjected. "Things are different now. It's not like when you were starting your career. When you moved up the ladder. People today are more mobile. Open to different career paths. Hustling." He smiled at me across the table.

Mom raised an eyebrow. "Don't you 'Okay, Boomer' me. I'm Gen X. We scrabbled for everything we had. I had to push and claw past all the established Boomers at my firm. Those white men with wives at home taking care of the house and the kids. Mimi knows it's harder for us. No one's taking care of her, ready to pull her up to the next level. She'll have to grab each rung herself and take it. But"—she smiled at Cooper—"Synergy looks out for its employees. Will this brand-new nonprofit do the same?"

"I'm sure Jackson's taken care of it." Even as he said it, Cooper's jaw tightened, belying his confident words.

"Maybe Mimi isn't as interested in employee benefits as she is in helping people. In doing good in the world," Ben said. "I'm proud of her for wanting to help kids."

"Aw, thanks, Benny." I raised my glass of wine to him. He winked and did the same.

"Still," Cooper said, "I'd be happy to talk to Jackson about the career path and remuneration—"

"No." My heart leaped into my throat. What would Jackson—and Larissa—think of me if Cooper threw his weight around? "Thank you. I'll check it out before I accept an offer. I promise." I nodded at Mom.

"It's kind of you to offer, Cooper. I'm glad Benny found you." Mom beamed at Cooper.

I couldn't keep my eyes off Ben. His soft expression of happiness, of pure freaking bliss, was like nothing I'd ever seen on his face.

He had every right to feel that way. He had the fulfilling job he'd always dreamed of, plus a fiancé he adored and who obviously worshiped the ground he walked on. He had love and financial stability. My little brother was at the flipping peak of Maslow's hierarchy of needs.

And where was I, the older sister who'd always seemed to have my shit together? Still at the bottom, still working on my financial safety. No hope of love.

I'd always made fun of my brother for falling in love so easily. But now, seeing him so transcendently happy, a small part of me wanted what he had.

I poked at my matzah ball with my spoon. I never thought I'd be jealous of my little brother. But I was.

"I hope you find someone like Cooper," my mother said, voicing my own thoughts. "Well, maybe not as good as Cooper." She laughed nervously. "Someday when you've settled into your career."

As little as I remembered from Bree's bachelorette party, I remembered how my Mystery Man made me feel. It was the same way my brother looked: seen and cherished.

"Maybe someday," I said.

15

MATEO

I CLUTCHED the bouquet in the small lobby of Mimi's apartment building. The creamy white plumeria with their shy yellow centers meant I was sorry. Sorry for whatever I'd done on the dance floor to make her run away. And I wasn't ready to give up. Not yet.

Whenever Papá did something to irritate Mom, he'd brought her these flowers. It had always worked. Until one day, it didn't.

Neither of us knew why she left. What I'd done, what we'd done, to make her pack her bag and leave the island in the middle of the night. Papá called her a few times, but after her crushing betrayal, he'd never shown up at her door with flowers.

Maybe his mistake was staying on the island with me. When we heard she'd died, he seemed so broken I never had the courage to ask if he regretted not working harder to get her back.

Mimi, with her beauty, her intelligence, her heart, was worth working for. If only I could get out of my own way and prove to her I was worth it, too.

Before I'd gathered the courage to ring her buzzer, she stepped out, winding a beige knit scarf around her neck. She looked up at me, startled.

"What are you doing here?"

Fuck, I'd forgotten to call or text. Again.

"I came to see you. To apologize. For the mole. For everything." When I waved the bouquet, I practically hit her in the nose. I winced. *Chill out, Mateo.* "How's your foot?"

"It's fine. Are those for me?" She reared back as I shoved the plumeria toward her.

"For you. Sunshine on a gloomy day." A fine mist was suspended between us, not quite falling but not much heavier than the San Francisco fog. It sparkled in her hair and made tiny beads on her wool coat.

She took the bouquet and sniffed it cautiously. "How did you know plumeria is my favorite?"

"It is?"

"Yes, they're straightforward. Unfussy. Simple."

"Like me," I joked.

Her eyes narrowed for just a second. "Mateo, you're anything but straightforward. You're like…like one of those ruffled orchids. Showy. Hard to keep at home."

I mimed shoving a dagger into my heart. "Ouch."

"You know what I mean." Her cheeks pinked. "You're too beautiful for everyday use. Like my mom's hand-painted challah platter."

A compliment? Chalk one up in the win column for Mateo. I didn't feel the drizzle anymore. Everything was tropical sunshine and the scent of plumeria.

"You're going out?" I asked. *Stupid, Mateo.* Of course she was going out. She'd just stepped outside her building.

"I'm volunteering today. For the foundation. There's an event at the library. The kids are reading to animals from the shelter."

"Did you take your allergy medication?"

"I sure—wait. How did you know I was allergic to dogs?"

She'd told me that the night at the bar. She'd told me many

things, and she'd forgotten all about it. The secret weighed in my chest. "Ben told me that's why you don't go to their place that often."

"Oh. Well, yes, I did." She tugged at a lock of hair trapped inside her scarf.

There was another piece stuck, and I wanted to loosen it for her, but I didn't dare touch her. I shoved my hands into my coat pockets.

"I should go," she said.

"Of course." Shit, she'd hate me for making her late. Mimi hated to be late. "Want me to take those to your apartment?" I pointed at the flowers.

"No, I—I'll take them with me. I'm sure I can find a vase or a glass of water to park them in at the library."

I'd definitely scored with the flowers. It gave me the courage to ask, "Can I walk you to the library?"

She tilted her head. "Actually, we could always use more volunteers. Could you stay for an hour or so and hold a shelter pet while a kid reads to you?"

"Absolutely!" Mimi was inviting me along? My grin had to be ridiculously wide. "And I've even been background-checked."

"Your own cousin background-checked you before he hired you for his security team?"

He had, the asshole. Family meant nothing to him. Though since it was me, he had a point. "Yeah, and I'm clear."

"Okay, then. Let's go." She turned and walked briskly down the sidewalk.

I caught her easily with my long stride. "What you do is admirable, Mimi."

"What? You mean, being an accountant?" She eyed me side-long. "Or spending an hour or two on a Saturday helping kids feel more confident about reading?"

"Both. I never went to college." I'd told her that the night at the bar, but she didn't remember. "Your career is impressive. And then to add on what you do for the foundation and other volunteer work besides, it shows your commitment."

"Thank you." She sniffed the flowers cradled in her arm. "Ben's done so much more. He got into nonprofit work first. I'm just following in my little brother's footsteps."

"No, you're not. You're blazing your own trail. Your way." She'd told me all about it that night.

She hummed, neither agreeing nor disagreeing with me.

Why didn't she see it? "You have such drive. You can do anything you set your mind to."

She snorted. "Anyone can do that."

"Not anyone." Not me. We stopped at a street crossing.

Like she'd plucked the thought out of my brain, she asked, "Why didn't you go to college?"

"I wanted to. Had always planned to. I even had a baseball scholarship. But my father got sick my last year in high school. It had always been the two of us, you know? After my mom left." I reached for his ring, but of course it wasn't on my finger. I shoved my hands in my jacket pockets. "I couldn't go to college and leave him, not after all he'd done for me. He needed help at his store. And at home when he got too sick to work. So I stayed."

"What happened?"

The signal changed, and I stepped into the crosswalk. I'd told her all this, too, in the two hours we'd talked. But I didn't mind repeating it. Every time I said it, it was a little easier. "He died a few years later. And his treatments were expensive. I didn't have money for college. I was too old to play baseball by then."

Her shoulder brushed mine. "I'm sorry. About your dad. Ben went to college as a nontraditional student, you know. You could, too."

I shrugged. "I'm happy doing what I'm doing. I'm helping my cousin. Protecting my aunt, who always looked out for me. I don't need college to do that."

She side-eyed me again. But there wasn't any judgment in her tone when she said, "I guess not."

She stopped in front of the library. "Are you sure you want to do this? The literature isn't exactly gripping. It's mostly picture books."

"Of course." *Anything for you.*

Mimi helped me sign in as a volunteer, then the librarian set us up on cushions on the floor. Because Mimi was slightly less allergic to cats, we asked for a pair of them. She had a fat brown tabby named Mrs. Butternut, and they handed me a black kitten named Roger. Roger didn't seem interested in sitting quietly beside me and purring the way Mrs. Butternut was doing with Mimi. He pawed at my hand with his tiny, sharp claws, then he sank them into my T-shirt and climbed toward my neck.

"Oh, no," Mimi said, laughing. "He'll shred your shirt."

"Shred my skin, more like." The little bastard's claws were razors.

"Here, take this toy. I don't think Mrs. Butternut will mind." She handed me a plastic wand with a few feathers attached to it by a string.

As soon as I wiggled the toy, Roger pounced. I yanked it up out of his grasp, and he leaped to catch it. While we waited for a cat-loving kid to show up, I danced the feather for him, and he bounded after it again and again while Mimi uncharacteristically giggled.

Soon, our antics attracted the attention of a little boy with thick glasses. He tucked a picture book under his arm.

"What's your cat's name?" he asked.

"His name is Roger."

"Like a pirate? Jolly Roger?"

I held the kitten up to look into his eyes, then turned him toward the kid. "He looks like a pirate to me."

The kid laughed. Then he held out his hand to Roger, who butted his head into the kid's palm. He stroked the kitten's head. "He's not a very tough pirate."

"I guess when you're as cute as he is, you don't need to be tough to steal someone's booty."

Mimi snorted, but I kept a straight face. "Want to sit with me and read to him?"

"Yeah, okay."

He sat next to me on the cushion and crossed his legs. Gently, I placed Roger in his lap. After his feather chasing, the kitten seemed content to curl up with his head on the kid's thigh.

The kid cracked open the book and paused. "Ah, I have dyslexia. That means I'm not a very fast reader."

"That's okay," I said. "I'm not so fast myself. And I need these." I pulled my glasses out of my pocket. I'd needed them for reading since I turned thirty. I put them on and grinned at the kid. Mine weren't as thick as his, but we had this thing in common. He beamed back at me.

Mimi sucked in a breath beside me. Ugh, I'd forgotten about needing to pull out my reading glasses. My tía called them ugly. I glanced over at Mimi to make sure she hadn't seen me put them on, but she had. In fact, she was staring at me, her mouth open like she'd seen a ghost.

16

MIMI

I CLUTCHED Mrs. Butternut until she mewled and wriggled. I loosened my grip, but I needed something to hold onto because

my

world

had

turned

upside down.

As soon as Mateo slid on those tortoiseshell glasses, the memories flooded back.

Leaning toward him, our elbows touching on the bar. Our shoulders bumping as we laughed until finally I slumped against him, and he held me up.

That night, I told him things. All about Bree and why I wanted a full-time job at the foundation. About how much I admired Larissa but could never seem to impress her. About my mother and wanting to make her proud.

He told me things, too. About his mother leaving them when he was young—so young! About Mateo and his father propping each other up after. About how he cared for his father. How much he loved him. And he'd pulled the ring off his finger…

The ring. Sure enough, his right ring finger was pale at the base, where a ring would have belonged. I stroked the outline of it on the chain around my neck under my sweater. He'd given it to me for safekeeping. So I'd remember that night.

So I'd remember him.

I swore I'd remember, despite the tequila.

Yet I'd broken that promise.

I'd forgotten him. I'd forgotten it all. Except for the fuzzy memory of a man in glasses who'd made me laugh. One who, at least my tequila-dulled brain had thought, might be worthy of a disruption in my driven life.

Mateo bent over the book to listen as the kid haltingly read to him. He stroked Roger's fur slowly, absently, hypnotically.

He didn't even notice that my blindfold had fallen off. That I saw him now. That when I wasn't snarling at him, he was sweet and steady and kind.

Mateo was my Mystery Man.

And I was the woman who'd snubbed him. Who'd looked for something different, someone better, when a good man had stood right in front of me, offering friendship. And possibly more.

Mrs. Butternut curled up and nipped my knuckle. Not hard, but hard enough to pull my attention to the little girl waiting patiently for me. She wore bright purple leggings and a *Where the Wild Things Are* sweatshirt.

"Can I read your cat a book?" she asked.

I blinked. I was here to read to kids, not ogle Mateo. My private earthquake had shifted the ground only for me. "Of course. This is Mrs. Butternut, and I'm Mimi. What's your name?"

"Tara. I like books about animals." She held up her book, which had a dog on the cover.

"Me, too." I'd always wished for a golden retriever, but we'd never had one because of my allergies.

As Tara snuggled next to me, Mrs. Butternut stretched against her thigh. I sneaked a glance at Mateo.

He watched me behind those glasses. If you'd asked me last month if glasses were inherently sexy, I'd have told you no. But on Mateo, they drew my gaze to his magnified ocean-blue irises and the long lashes that wreathed them. Below the simple plastic frames, his jaw was rugged, strong enough to take the blows life had thrown at him. Soft with stubble that I knew the feel of from that night when I'd run my hand over his cheeks, scratched my fingertips through the bristles.

From the abrasion of it on my cheeks when he kissed me.

I lifted my hand to my upper lip as if the beard burn still marked it.

Breaking our stare, I yanked myself back to the here and now. I nodded and exclaimed at all the right parts of the dog story. I praised Tara when she finished.

Just when I thought she'd take her book to the next pet, she asked, "Does Mrs. Butternut live with you?"

"No. I'm allergic. Dogs and cats make me sneeze."

"Who does she live with?"

"She lives at the animal shelter."

Tara's face crumpled.

I rushed to add, "I'm sure it's a very nice shelter. She's not in a cage all the time." I hoped not, anyway.

But that was the wrong thing to say. "She lives in a *cage?* Is she all alone? Does she have parents? Or toys?"

"I—I don't..." I'd never been to the shelter, not once. My eyes would swell shut.

Mateo leaned over. "Mrs. Butternut can come out to the play-room where there are toys. And she's old enough that she doesn't need her parents anymore. She's grown up. She can watch out for the little ones like Roger here." He held up the sleeping black kitten in one huge hand.

Did he know these things? Had he been to the shelter? I hoped so. I hoped the tale he was spinning for Tara was true.

"Roger doesn't live with his parents?"

Uh-oh. Tara's voice had risen to a squeaky register that sounded like the clarinet Ben used to play in middle school.

"No. That's why he's looking for a family to adopt him." Mateo's eyes had gone sad.

Mateo had lost his parents, too. First his mother when he was young. Then his father. Was that why he worked for his cousin? Why he protected his aunt? For the connection to family?

Tara reached out a finger to stroke Roger between his ears. He purred in his sleep.

"I know! I'll ask my mom and dad if we can adopt him!"

Fantastic. The problem that had felt like splinters under my fingernails would go away.

"That would be perfect," I said. "Why don't you go ask your parents right now? Here"—I scooped the kitten out of Mateo's hand and set him into Tara's cupped hands—"hold him carefully while you walk over there. Walk!" I called after her as she skipped away.

"Problem solved." I turned to Mateo. But he frowned. "What?"

"I'm not sure you can solve it that easily. Roger is a living creature who will become a member of someone's family. And families don't always come together as easily as the numbers in your budget. You know what they say about black cats. Unlucky. Unwanted." He stared at a spot on the carpet.

"That's just superstition." Why were we talking about a cat when my memories from that night had come crashing back? "Let me give Mrs. Butternut back to her handler. Then you can walk me home?"

He roused himself to grin, showing his movie-star teeth, straight and white and just a tiny bit imperfect. Though something still shaded the usual brightness in his blue eyes. "It would be my pleasure."

———

ALL THE WAY back to my apartment, I thought of a dozen ways to ask him about that night at the bar. And then discarded every one. Why hadn't he reminded me of our conversation, our connection? Why had he let me treat him like a stranger, and an annoying one at that? Why had he taken everything I'd hurled at him in stride?

I hadn't yet found my courage by the time we reached my building, and I couldn't send him on his way without saying anything. "Come up for a minute?"

Surprise flashed across his face. "Sure," he said. He held the door open, then shut it securely behind us. Silently, he followed me upstairs.

I'd meant to invite him inside, offer him a beer, then find a way to talk to him about what I remembered, but as soon as I fit my key into my door's lock, my mind flooded with memories of that morning after the bachelorette party—his sudden appearance with the bakery sack, hunting for prickly pear, the spilled coffee, and my ruined presentation.

Sure, he'd been clumsy, but he was only trying to be nice. And I'd been a bully. No hangover, not even a ripped pie chart, justified that.

The words burst out of me. "Why? Why did you let me get away with it?"

"With what?" Under the fluorescents in the hallway, the shade was back in his eyes, cautious. Hesitant.

I hated it. Hated that I'd dimmed the brightness by acting like a supreme ass. That he expected me to be rude to him. That he somehow felt he deserved it.

"With putting you down. With being such a jerk." I leaned on the door. "After we—after you—after everything."

His eyes widened. "You remember?"

"Yeah. I don't normally get like that. So drunk I forget things, I mean." Sharp realization sliced through me, and I winced. What had he thought of me? I must have been stumbling, sloppy drunk that night. "I'd taken some allergy medicine that day and... You must have thought I was a fool. You took care of me. Did you do it for Ben? Because Cooper asked you to?"

"They both thought it was a good idea for me to keep an eye on you. But, Mimi, I did it for you. Because I care about you."

"But you didn't then, right?" I had to make it all make sense. To superimpose the stiff, silent Mateo I'd known before, the one who flirted with everyone but me, against the nice man who'd checked on me after my night out, who'd offered to go with me to the gala because I needed a date.

"Of course I did." His blue eyes went soft and round. "You're the smartest person I know. Confident. Beautiful. I like being around you. Even when I can't keep up with you. Even when you're not so happy with me." He ducked his head.

No. The man I'd talked to at the bar was smooth, funny, and kind. And I'd never make him feel less-than again.

"Come here." I grabbed his hand and tugged him through the doorway into my apartment. Standing an arm's length away, I put my hands on my hips to keep from touching him.

"I'm sorry." I stared at a spot in the center of his chest. "I made a mistake. I misjudged you. And I was unkind. Can you forgive me?"

His arms were longer than mine. He reached out, and with one thick finger, he tipped up my chin. "There's nothing to forgive."

His eyes were dappled with gold like a pair of Caribbean tide-pools at midday. Like a shallow pool, Mateo's surface was opaque, reflective, hiding the life, the intelligence, teeming within him. I'd refused to see anything beyond the shiny outside. I hadn't bothered to peer inside, to explore what he concealed.

There was so much more to Mateo Rivera than the easygoing flirt. There was the hurt little boy, abandoned by his mother. The scared young man who'd given up his dreams of college to care for his sick father. The sad, lonely adult who'd dropped every-thing and moved across four time zones because his cousin had asked him.

The kind man who'd saved a drunk acquaintance from potential predators in a bar. Who'd kissed her until she felt less lonely, taken her home, and let her sleep it off.

Who never said a word when she forgot to thank him.

"Thank you," I whispered. My gaze dropped to his lips. They were plush and pink. I remembered their softness when I kissed him that night. I remembered the bite of his stubble against my cheek. I remembered his big hand in my hair, tugging me closer. I remembered the hard press of his chest and the big heart that galloped inside.

All I wanted was to do it again. Sober, this time, so I remembered his taste, his sounds, so I could catalog them all. So I'd never forget.

He shifted closer until his hand cradled my jaw. I stretched up on my tiptoes, but I was still too short to reach him, even in my heeled boots.

"Kiss me? Again?" I asked.

"Yes." He bent until his lips hovered a fraction of an inch away from mine. "Yes," he murmured. Finally, his mouth lit on mine, light as a butterfly. "Yes," he whispered, caressing my lips.

Our first kiss at the bar had been like this. Sweet and tentative. A question and an answer. Hesitant. Restrained.

For my side, I infused the kiss with the many apologies I owed him. For my unkind thoughts and actions. For forgetting what we'd shared and wishing for something more than the man who stood up for me, who helped me impress Larissa, who let himself get roped into planning a fancy-dress party. Who'd done it all for me.

I stretched my arms up around his neck and tugged him closer, my fingers teasing the curls at the back of his neck. I slid my tongue against the seam of his lips and pushed through, tasting him. Sharp, peppery mint. And something spicy. Clove, perhaps, or that spice my dad used to make his special apple cake for Rosh Hashana.

He purred like Roger the kitten and let me invade, easing his tongue against mine, bending me back slightly over his arm. I hung on, meeting him again and again, intoxicated by his kisses, lost in his taste. My knees trembled and my calves shook with the stretch up from my toes. If only I were taller, I could push back against him, rub my tingling nipples against his chest, straddle his thigh and ride it to soothe the pulse between my legs. But with our height difference, all I could do was tug him tighter, closer, and show him with my tongue what I wanted to do when our clothes came off.

Finally, breathless, I pulled back and sucked in a breath. "Wow."

He kissed the corner of my mouth. My jaw. My earlobe. He breathed into my ear, "¡Caray!"

"What—what now?"

"You're asking me? You always know what to do, Mimi. What do you want now?"

My body needed him, naked and in my bed.

But my brain knew better. I'd taken my allergy medicine, and that clouded my judgment. Like when I'd accidentally roofied myself the day of the two parties. I needed to take this slowly.

Mateo couldn't be one of my one-night stands.

He was part of Ben's family. Part of his life. I couldn't take him to my bed—or my couch—for only a night, no matter how much my pulse throbbed for him. That would only end badly, with awkward avoidance at family events, with Cooper's concerned expression, with Ben trying to smooth everything over and trying too hard to make everyone happy.

I needed to be sure this was what I wanted. And to take it slowly.

Did I want a relationship with Mateo?

If we were careful, he didn't have to be a distraction from my goals. I was wiser now than I'd been with Byron. I wouldn't let anyone pull me off course again.

Already, Mateo had helped me with my goals. He was my date to the gala. And he'd helped with the planning, finding us a caterer and a band. I might even enjoy myself at the gala, thanks to Mateo.

He deserved more than a one-night stand. And I deserved something more, too. A chance at happiness. At…partnership?

"Let's go out. Tonight." I'd change into clothes that weren't covered in cat hair, and my mind would clear. Then I could make a rational decision about sleeping with him. About all the complications it would bring.

"Ah." He winced. "I'm working tonight. How about tomorrow night?"

"Sunday night? I have work the next day…"

"We'll start early. I'll have you home by ten. Promise."

"Okay." Twenty-four hours to cool off was smart. I stretched up onto my toes and pressed a kiss onto his lips. "It's a date."

17

MATEO

"¡NO TOQUES LA ESCENA DEL PESEBRE!" My tía shouted at me across her lawn.

"I wouldn't dream of touching el pesebre," I called, carefully skirting the nativity scene as I lugged the giant snowman toward the shed. "Not before Candlemas. Go back into the house, tía. Please."

"You'll put everything in the shed?"

"Yes. Organized alphabetically. Now go into the house and lock the door. Or Miguelito will kill me."

"You know I wouldn't let him harm a hair on your head. Be careful with Frosty. I got so many compliments on him."

"I'm sure you did." I glanced at her neighbor's house just as their landscape lights flicked on and washed the mansion in anti-septic not-too-yellow, not-too-blue light. Their Christmas lights and their giant fake wreath had come down on January 2. No way in hell had any compliments come from them, especially not in the latter half of January. I waited until she closed the front door, then I trudged around the back of the house to the shed, where I wedged the snowman next to Santa's sleigh.

When I returned to the front of the house for the reindeer, tía opened the door again. I rolled my eyes to the cloudy sky and begged Santa María to keep my cousin away from his mother's house.

"Hijo, come inside. I made chocolate con churros."

My aunt's hot chocolate and churros were worth any trouble from Miguelito.

When I sat across from her at her kitchen table, dipping a greasy, almost-too-hot-to-touch churro into a warm mug of dark cocoa, she lifted her mug to her lips but didn't drink. "How are things going with Miriam?"

It was the moment I'd looked forward to—and dreaded—all afternoon. Warmth flooded my face, including my lips, where I still felt the imprint of hers, like a brand.

When I bit into the churro, cinnamon and chocolate burst onto my taste buds. I savored the sugary morsel in my mouth. I hadn't often indulged in them on my tropical island home, but in frigid San Francisco, the sweet treat was a comfort. Swallowing it down, I chased it with a sip of thick chocolate.

"It's going well," I said. "We have a date tomorrow night."

Her eyebrows rose. "A date?"

"She remembered. About the night at the bar. That we... talked." We'd made out right there at the bar, but I wasn't about to tell my tía that. For all she knew, I was a good Catholic boy.

"You sleep with her yet?"

"What?"

"Mateo. Stories of your sexual adventures reached me even here in the U.S. You're not one to wait for a date. Much less a priest's blessing."

The tips of my ears flamed. "Tía."

"So, how was it?"

"We haven't—I wouldn't—not with Miriam."

"Oh?" Her eyebrows flew back up. "What's different about her?"

"She's..." I leaned back against the cushion. "Special."

"Besides being resistant to your charms and rude and dismissive, what makes her special?"

"She's not rude! She's smart. And funny when she wants to be. And she cares about kids. Yesterday, we volunteered at the library and listened to little kids reading. To cats. Even though Mimi is allergic to them."

She sipped her drink. "But does she care about you?"

"I...I think so?" At her apartment, she'd kissed me like she meant it. And before that, at the library with that kid sitting next to her and the cat in her lap, her eyes had gone all soft and warm. Like tía's chocolate. I'd hoped she'd been imagining a future where it was our own kid sitting between us, our own cat in her lap.

Too much? Too fast? When I'd seen that flash of recognition, of memory, on her face, I'd greedily imagined it all. An engagement ring. A white dress. Her belly round with our baby.

I'd never wanted any of that. Casual flirtations and casual hookups had been enough for me.

Until Mimi.

She frowned. "You are a wonderful man, Mateo. Everyone likes you. But—"

"But?" I braced myself.

"But you don't know your own worth. You let people take advantage of you. My son, for instance."

"Miguelito is family. He watches out for me. He'd never take advantage of me." Even as I said it, I knew it wasn't true. Lito cared about me, sure. But to him, I was second-string. His mother and Ben, even his friend Jackson, were at the top level of his affections. They could do no wrong, and he'd move heaven and earth to protect them. Me? Not so much. Still, wasn't it a reflection on me that I let him walk all over me? "He pays me well. And he lets me live in his guesthouse."

Pity softened Rosa's stare. "Niño. You're worth so much more than that. Don't let anyone, not Miriam, and not my son, convince you otherwise. You're so much like your father. My brother had a big heart. He gave it away too easily."

"You're talking about my mother, you know." My tone was light, but heat flashed across my cheeks.

She crossed herself. "I don't want to speak ill of the dead— God rest her soul—but she didn't deserve either of you."

Maybe we didn't deserve her. In my memory, she was an angel with long, blond hair, twinkling blue eyes, and bubbly laughter. How could someone like that not deserve me?

"Think about it. And think about whether Miriam is worth risking your big, caring heart. Hear me?"

"Sí, señora."

She sipped her hot chocolate, then stared into its brown depths. "How long are you staying?"

"My shift ends at six tomorrow morning."

"No. I mean in the U.S. When are you going home?"

I shrugged. "Hadn't thought about it. I'm fine working for Lito."

"You know I don't need protecting."

"You do. Miguelito said Mick—"

"I lived with that man for almost twenty years. You don't think I can protect myself from him?"

"Well, I..." I scratched the back of my neck. One time she and Miguelito had come to the island for a visit when I was a teenager, he had a black eye, and I could've sworn my tía had a bruise on her jaw. She'd worn long sleeves, even in the tropical heat. And now Miguelito had money. Sometimes money caused as many problems as it solved.

"You had a life on the island," she said. "Friends. What do you have here?"

Mimi. I had Mimi here. But did I really have her?

"I have you, tía. And my primo. And maybe, after our date tomorrow, I'll have Mimi, too."

All I wanted out of life was family. Love.

And that day, it felt close enough to touch.

18

MIMI

TEN MINUTES into my first date with Mateo, I was starting to question my decision to date men.

So far, he'd tangled his finger in my hoop earring and nearly pulled it out of my piercing while helping me take my coat off; pushed in my chair at the table so forcefully I'd collided with the edge of the table and rattled the plates, drawing the eye of every diner in the fancy restaurant; and knocked over my first glass of wine—thank God I'd ordered white—trying to signal the waiter to ask if they could adjust the temperature because I was too warm.

Though he'd managed to flirt with the waiter, who'd winked at Mateo when he set a pair of bacon-wrapped figs in front of him. *On the house,* he'd said like I wasn't even there.

The restaurant made my palms itch. It was full of tech bros and their manicured, spandex dress–wearing dates. The bros, awkward and mannerless, used money-backed sharp commands to cover up their discomfort. Their dates simpered and tittered, trying to seal the deal so they could eat meals prepared by a personal chef at home next year.

Maybe the whole thing was a mistake.

I'd taken our date seriously. I'd worn one of the few skirts in my closet, a flared black one that hit right above my knees, with a white blouse. Sure, I'd bought it for my bubbe's funeral, so the blouse didn't show any cleavage, unlike the tech bros' dates. But I'd worn heels, for God's sake. Heels that pinched my toes and made me cranky. Fine, more cranky. When he uncrossed his legs, Mateo accidentally kicked one of them under the table.

I sipped my second glass of wine and tried to interpret the menu for a first date–appropriate choice. Fish or chicken? Everything had a reduction or a foam or a mousse and sounded more complicated than one of my spreadsheet formulas.

I cleared my throat. "Do you, ah, come here often?"

Mateo gave me a tight smile over his menu. He wore his glasses, and my insides warmed a little. "It's my first time here. Cooper recommended it when I told him I needed a place to take a special date."

I fanned myself with the menu. "Did he say what was good here?"

"The filet."

Filet sounded expensive. And it came with mushrooms, which made me shudder. I scanned the menu again and sipped my wine, then I looked up at my date. He clenched the thick leather menu folio so hard it shook. He had passed on a drink since he was driving. Mateo stared longingly out the front window, where a pair of men stood, smoking cigarettes.

My crankiness melted away. We were in this together. And we were both miserable.

"Hey." I reached across the table and set my hand on the soft wool sleeve of his sweater. "Want to get out of here? I don't need a meal this elegant. I could, um...cook?" The extent of my cooking was to boil pasta and cover it with a jar of sauce, but that had to be better than sitting stiffly at this table for two hours. "Or we could pick up a pizza."

"You don't like it here?" Behind his glasses, his blue eyes went round.

"I—I didn't mean—" *Shit.* "No. Restaurants that don't have prices on the menu give me hives."

His shoulders eased down. "It's awful, isn't it? I'll make dinner if you don't mind simple food."

"Simple food sounds great."

After a brief tussle with the check, he paid for my wine and we got back into his Jeep. He drove carefully, no rapid accelerations or hard braking, his head swiveling right and left. So it surprised me when he said, "I'm sorry."

"Sorry? For what?"

"For the restaurant. I wanted to please you. To impress you. Instead, I made you uncomfortable. I can't seem to do anything right around you." His fingers tightened on the steering wheel.

And in that moment, I imagined him not as the suave, flirtatious guy he was with everyone else, or as the clumsy, bumbling lunkhead he was around me. With my mental eraser, I lifted all those layers to get to the scared, lonely man under it all. The one whose mother had left him and whose father had died too soon. Who used a honeyed façade to surround himself with people so he wouldn't be alone.

Even though my family got up in my business too often, it was a comfort to know they were there whenever I needed them. I was glad Ben had adopted Mateo as part of his family.

I waited until he stopped at a red light, then I put a hand on his shoulder. "You don't need to try so hard. I'm already impressed, or I wouldn't be here."

He turned toward me. "You are?"

I nodded.

Leaning across the console, he reached for the back of my neck and pulled me in for a brief, fierce kiss. When we broke apart, his eyes blazed like blue lightning. "Thank you. For saying that. I won't disappoint you."

He tangled his fingers in mine, and when the car behind us honked, he pulled forward, still holding my hand.

A few minutes later, he turned up the hill onto the driveway of Cooper's opulent mansion on the edge of Pacific Heights where the houses had a little more room to breathe. In the daytime, we'd have been able to see the ocean.

"Don't get excited." His lips twisted. "I live in the guesthouse."

"You live with Cooper?"

"Yes. We decided it would offer an extra level of protection for your brother."

"Ben?" My insides went cold. "Why do you think someone would want to hurt Ben?"

He shrugged, steering the Jeep down a narrow lane past the main house. "I don't. I think what happened on the island was a mistake. A one-off. But my cousin protects those he loves."

"Wait, what happened on the island?"

"Ben didn't tell you?"

"Obviously not." He'd come back from his getaway with Cooper broken-hearted because his boyfriend hadn't stood up for him when he should have. But physically, he was fine.

"A man attacked him. We think he was only supposed to be following Mi—Cooper. Something about his company. But then the guy started freestyling. That little dog, Coco, saved your brother."

"He said that. That Coco rescued him. But I thought he was talking about something emotional."

"Coco bit the guy hard enough that he limped for weeks. The attacker followed them to the U.S., according to my cousin. But then we lost him here in San Francisco. So Lito likes having me close. Just in case."

"I do, too, then." I squeezed his hand, glad my brother had someone looking out for him. "Thanks for protecting him."

"It's my pleasure. I care about him. Your brother is a good man."

Mateo parked the car on the concrete pavers that separated the main house from the modest guesthouse. The smaller building matched the mansion with its light-colored stucco and those rectangular-block moldings sticking out under the roof. The exterior lights on the main house shone onto a row of tall bushes that shielded the guesthouse from its large windows.

I leaned across the console to kiss his cheek. "Thank you for watching out for us both. But that's not why I'm here. Understand? I'm here because I like you."

He turned his head and cradled my jaw, holding me in place. He brushed his lips across mine. "I like you, too."

Sunshine bloomed in my chest. But just as I pressed forward to deepen the kiss, my stomach growled.

He chuckled. "No more kissing until after I feed you."

He opened my door and helped me descend from the Jeep. Then he used a keypad to unlock the front door and let me enter first. The house was compact, though it was larger than my one-bedroom apartment. To the right was a modern kitchen and dining area. Straight ahead was a cozy living room with a desk in the corner. And to the left was a hall that, I assumed, led to a bedroom or two.

The furnishings were modern, done in simple shades of gray better suited to someone cool and professional like Cooper Fallon than to sunny, colorful Mateo. And it was immaculate. Not a pair of shoes or stray T-shirt was in sight, and the glass table in the dining area was shiny and smudge-free.

The exception was a long stretch of what looked like toilet paper that ran from the hallway across the living room, over the sofa, and disappeared into the kitchen.

"Did you get TP'd?" I asked.

He clucked his tongue. "Roger."

Something jingled in the hall, and then a flash of black streaked in and twined around Mateo's leg.

"Is that—?"

He scooped up the tiny kitten. "I checked this morning after I came off my shift, and the little girl—"

"Tara."

"Tara's family took home a different cat. That big tabby you had yesterday."

"Mrs. Butternut?" She'd been sweet and calm; I could see why they'd chosen her over a rambunctious kitten.

"The shelter said black cats don't always get adopted. So I did."

"Oh." Of course he had. Mateo's protection extended to orphaned animals, too.

"Your allergies!" Mateo's eyes went wide. "I didn't even think —I'll run to the drugstore for your medicine. Or I can put him in the garage?"

"No." I sucked in an experimental breath and let it out. "I'm okay so far. I have some pills in my purse. We'll see how it goes, okay?"

"Okay. But if you start to feel sick—"

"I'll let you know. I promise." I stroked one of Roger's big bat ears, and he closed his eyes and purred.

Mateo lifted Roger until he looked the kitten in the eye. "Listen, I know you missed me, but there's no reason to behave like that." He turned so they faced the toilet paper disaster. "I'll always come back for you. Understand?"

Roger lolled his head toward Mateo's hand. Mateo scratched him under the chin. "Okay."

Meanwhile, I was about to melt into a puddle right here on the gray rug in the entryway. "Want me to clean that up while you feed him or whatever?"

"No. You sit." He led me to an armless gray chair that faced the kitchen island. "I have wine—red and white—rum, and whiskey. What would you like?"

"White wine, please." The last thing I needed to do was spill red wine on Cooper Fallon's furniture.

Mateo set Roger on the rug, then balled up the toilet paper. He poured me a generous glass of white wine from a small wine refrigerator set into the island before he poured himself a glass of rum with a couple of ice cubes. He checked the refrigerator.

"Chicken and rice okay?"

"Sure."

When he tugged off his sweater, his white T-shirt rode up, giving me a flash of the defined muscles at his waist before he smoothed down his shirt. The plain crew-neck hugged his body, displaying biceps, triceps, and the muscles on his back I didn't know the name of but that shaped him like a funnel right down to his narrow waist.

I took a cooling gulp of wine and fanned myself.

He hefted an instant pressure cooker out of a lower cabinet onto the counter. He winked at me. "My tía would have a heart attack if she saw this monstrosity, but I love it."

"What's so special about it?" Bree raved about the air fryer she'd gotten as an engagement gift, but because I had to google *how to boil an egg* every time, I didn't deserve specialized appliances.

He plugged in the cooker, added a splash of oil, and started chopping some onions and peppers on the counter. His forearms took center stage, and I ogled them, fascinated by the taut muscles and tendons.

Without looking up, he said, "Why is the instant cooker special? It's efficient. Fast."

"That's the way you like it? Fast?" I snapped my jaw shut. Where had those words come from?

He paused his knife and grinned at me over his shoulder. "Sometimes. Though I like to savor my meals." His gaze raked over me. "Linger at the table."

"Linger." He watched as I crossed my legs the other way and pressed them together to ease the tingling at my core.

"A feast can take hours." His voice was a low purr.

"Hours," I sighed.

"Would you like a taste? An amuse-bouche?"

"A—a what?" A drop of sweat started between my breasts and trailed down my stomach.

"One...bite. A promise of what's to come?"

Come sounded pretty good. Was it possible to climax from verbal foreplay? If anyone could manage it, Mateo could. "I do enjoy a well-placed bite."

He set down the knife and picked up a dish towel to wipe his hands. Those massive hands I wanted on me.

The appliance beeped, startling me.

"Or," he said with a wicked smirk, "we can let the anticipation build."

"What? Why?"

"What I want to do to you will take stamina. And stamina requires fuel."

"But—" I rocked on the seat, chasing the throb between my legs. "Do we have to wait?"

He scraped the chopped onions and peppers into the pot, then turned to face me. "You remember what I told you that night?"

The memory came into focus like turning the dial on the AM/FM radio in my dad's ancient Volvo. It brought with it a stab of remembered disappointment.

"That night, I wanted you to stay at my apartment. With me. I propositioned you, and you said no." Humiliation had sliced through me. I'd thought we'd had a connection, and then he turned me down. Did he not find me attractive? He probably hadn't, when I had tequila breath and—

"Mimi. Do you remember what I said?"

"You mean when you refused to fuck me?"

He grabbed a silicone spatula out of a canister on the counter and stirred the sizzling vegetables. "I think I said it more politely than that."

I excavated my memory. Below the hurt feelings, the crushing rejection. He'd smiled with half his mouth and brushed a curl out of my eye. *Mimi, when we sleep together, I want you to remember every moment. Every orgasm. I never want you to forget what I feel like inside you.*

I shivered. "Um, remind me?"

He quirked those lips again. He saw through my ruse. But, like always, he did what I asked. "I said I'd remember my first time with you for the rest of my life, and I wanted you to remember it, too."

The pulse between my legs sent up a chant: Ma-teo, Ma-teo, Ma-teo. We didn't even have to go all the way into the bedroom. We could bang it out on the couch.

"Still, I wasn't too happy with you. To be completely honest, I was hurt."

"I'm sorry about that. But I couldn't. Not when you were so…"

"Wasted?" My cheeks heated. I'd forgotten it all. His kindness. Our connection. And I'd been a bitch to him the next day when he showed up to check on me.

"That's why you gave me this." I tugged the ring out of the neckline of my blouse and held it out flat on my palm. "To remember. I could've lost it."

He smiled. "But you didn't. You don't lose things, Mimi. Besides, I needed an excuse to come see you the next day." His smile dimmed. "Though you'd forgotten."

"I remembered. I remembered a handsome guy whose kindness swept me off my feet. I just didn't remember he was you."

I turned the ring in my fingers, caressing the scratches that dulled its shine. Then I reached behind my neck and released the clasp. I unthreaded the ring from the chain and set it on the island between us.

He stirred the pot. "You don't want to keep it a little longer?"

"Keep it? Isn't it your father's?"

"It was."

I didn't like the way he frowned at the pot, so I asked, "Was your father a Casanova, too?"

That earned me a smile as he slipped the ring on his finger.

"Shameless. But it meant nothing. He wore the ring long after my mother stopped loving him. We Rivera men are like that. Loyal."

"And flirty."

"With everyone but you. It didn't work on you."

"You didn't have trouble flirting with me at the bar that night."

"That"—he finally looked up—"that was different. It was more than flirting. We had a connection. And you started it."

"I did? That doesn't sound like me."

"There was a guy hitting on you. I came over to check that you were okay with it."

"Was I?"

His jaw tensed. "You weren't in any shape to be hit on by anyone."

"Oh." I looked down at my glass of wine.

"But you were relaxed in a way I'd never seen you. So we started talking and…"

"And?"

He shrugged. "The rest is history."

A history I'd remembered at last.

He scraped the chicken into the cooker, twisted on the lid, and set it. He went to the sink to wash his hands. "We have twenty minutes. And I propose we use that time dancing."

"Dancing? You promised me a taste. An amuse-something."

Slowly, he dried his hands, consuming me with his gaze. "Don't you know? Dancing is foreplay."

19

MIMI

HE PICKED up his phone and soon, music with a seductive, syncopated beat played from hidden speakers. He reached for my hand and pulled me into the open center of the room.

"You remember how I suck at this, right?" The shame of his remedial lessons at the club flooded into my cheeks. Natalie hadn't needed one-on-one coaching.

He held my hands the way he had the other night. "Remember the steps. Side to side. Easy. Start with your left foot."

It was a little easier with only Roger for an audience. I stepped to the left and mirrored his steps. Left, right, left, tap. Right, left, right, tap. After a minute, I let the music infuse my hips in a stiff imitation of the way the women moved at the club.

"You've got it. Now, a turn."

"A turn?"

"Keep moving your feet. Now. When I lift your hand, you twirl left."

"Twirl?"

"You can do it, querida." He raised my right hand, released his grip on my fingers, and then pressed his palm to mine. "Turn."

I turned to face the front door.

"¡Ay, ay! Turn back."

"Sorry!" My face burned as I spun to face him.

"Don't apologize. You're learning. You're doing great."

"I'm going to look like an idiot at the gala. Larissa is going to—"

"Don't worry about Larissa. Watch me. I'll signal you. I promise I won't lead you wrong."

I trusted him. He'd taken care of my brother. He'd taken care of me at the bar. And he'd gone along with the whole farce of fake dating, just to help me. So I lifted my gaze from our feet, from our hands, and watched his face. His strong, square jaw and those beautiful eyes that were more like a sun-warmed pool than the stormy gray ocean.

"Now," he said. He lifted our hands and flattened them against each other. I turned away in two steps and back in the next two. His arm went around my back, and suddenly we were dancing close. "Perfect."

And it was. My hips swayed, and when I looked up at him, his breath ghosted on my cheek. His feet stilled, and he leaned closer.

"What does that signal mean? What should I do?"

His hands dropped to my waist. "Kiss me."

He bent, and his lips landed on mine. It wasn't a fierce kiss like in the car. It was as languid and sensual as the music playing. I smoothed my hands up his chest to his shoulders to pull him closer. Although our feet didn't move, it was part of the dance. Our lips, our tongues continued where our bodies had left off. I pressed myself against him, carrying forward the seduction of the dance.

Suddenly, I envied that flexible woman on the stage at the club who'd lifted her leg and twined it around her partner's thigh. I could have soothed the ache at my core. But I had a better than fifty percent chance of toppling over and taking him to the floor with me, so I poured all my need into our kiss.

He pulled away too soon.

"More dance lessons?" I stuck out my puffy lower lip.

"No." He jerked his head toward the kitchen. "Dinner's ready."

Although the cooker was beeping, I hardly heard it over the music and the whooshing of my pulse in my ears.

"Fuel?"

"Fuel." He winked.

I washed my hands in the powder room while he finished up the food.

When he made to carry the two fragrant plates to the dining area, I stopped him.

"Can we eat here at the island?"

"Really?" He frowned. "But I didn't clean up—"

"I'd rather not mess up your fancy table." I glanced at the spotless glass. "And this is cozier."

"All right, then." He set down the plates and scooped the flatware off the table. He set a fork and knife precisely where they belonged. After I sat on the high stool, he fluttered out a cloth napkin across my lap. "Do you have everything you need?"

I smiled at my blond, blue-eyed chef and dance partner. "Everything."

He clutched a fist over his heart, rolled his eyes up to the ceiling, and bit his lip.

"See?" I pointed an outraged finger at him. "You *can* flirt with me."

He settled a hip onto his stool. "Flirt? Wait until I show you my smolder." He raised his sandy eyebrows at me and then lowered his eyelids halfway. A teasing smile lifted one corner of his mouth.

"Oh my God." I laid a hand over the center of my chest, where my heart fluttered like hummingbird wings. "The smolder."

He threw back his head and laughed. "See? You broke me. That smolder would have worked on anyone else. Not my Mimi."

He froze like he wanted to hit delete over those last two words. Never breaking our stare, I picked up my glass of wine and drained it. Then I licked the wine from the corner of my mouth. He followed my tongue's movement.

"Mateo." When I said his name, his eyes snapped to mine. "I think you're the one who's mine."

"We'll see about that." His voice dropped into a lower register. "After dinner, when I show you what I've got planned for dessert."

My mouth went dry when I imagined him laid out on the couch, his plush lips and all those muscles mine to explore. I opened my mouth, but no words came out.

"More wine?" he asked, tipping the bottle toward my glass.

"Please." I splayed my fingers across the base of the glass, grounding myself. Dinner first, then dessert.

As we ate, he told me stories from his father's tobacco shop. About the regulars there and the varieties they preferred. The sweet, summery Virginia blends. The light, berry scents of Cavendish. The spicy Latakia. I could almost smell it wafting on a warm Caribbean breeze.

For the first time, I understood why he smoked. It connected him with his father and brought back memories of their brief years together.

The food, too. It tasted of spices and wholesome love. The kind of love that cared for people, that nourished them. That became a memento of good times past.

I'd never forget the simple meal Mateo had prepared for me. Nothing fancy, no expectations or demands, only nourishment when I was hungry. If I wasn't careful, I was going to fall for this man's cooking and never want to eat anything else.

After I'd consumed the last juicy morsel of chicken, I set my fork on my plate and extended my hand toward his empty dish. "You cooked. I'll clean up."

"No, no, no." He stood and snatched up his plate. "You're my guest."

"Then we'll do it together. I may not have much in the way of cooking skills, but I wield a mean dish brush."

"Ah." He swept up my dish. "The magic of the instant cooker. It's all dishwasher-safe."

Still, I rinsed the dishes, and he loaded them into the dishwasher. The bachata music still played, softer now, bouncy and sensual. I wished I'd taken Spanish in high school like Ben instead of Latin. I wished I understood the words that went with the rhythm coursing through my veins.

While I rinsed out the sink, Mateo's hands landed on my hips. "You're a natural," he whispered in my ear.

"A natural? At dishwashing?"

"No. At dancing."

It was only then I realized I'd been swinging my hips as I worked. His hands encouraged the movement, then he pressed his pelvis against my behind until we swayed together. Continuing to guide me with his body, he lifted his hands from my hips, grabbed the towel, and patted my hands dry with it. Then he reached to the shelf over the sink, pumped a bottle of lotion, and smoothed it over my skin, massaging it into my wrists and fingers.

"Feels nice," I murmured.

"We're only getting started," he purred in my ear, his stubble tickling my earlobe.

He kissed the side of my neck. I leaned my head to my other shoulder to give him more skin to caress with his lips. His hands swept up from my hips over my ribs to cradle the undersides of my breasts.

"Okay?" he asked, his voice a low rumble against my pulse point.

"More," I groaned.

He smoothed his hands over me. Although his hands were big, my breasts overflowed them. His thumbs rubbed across my nipples, encouraging them into needy peaks.

"I've wanted to touch you for so long," he murmured into my neck.

"Touch me."

His hands left my breasts for one disappointing second until he tugged the tail of my blouse out of my skirt and rolled it up my torso, over my head, and off. He set it carefully on the counter before he gazed down over my shoulder. His breath hitched. "Beautiful."

I checked out what he saw. I wished I could wear lacy, sexy bras. I was sure Larissa and Natalie had drawers overflowing with them. Mine was made of sturdy, white polyester-cotton with thick, supportive straps. There was nothing beautiful about it.

But Mateo treated the contraption with reverence, running his fingers over the fabric, even the straps, cupping, squeezing, exploring until, needy, I leaned back against him, unsure how I was still standing.

He followed the band to my back. "May I?"

"Please." It came out as a throaty whisper.

He released the tension and peeled the bra from my chest. My breasts sagged, heavy, and not for the first time, I cursed their weight and the pull of gravity.

But Mateo rubbed his hands across my skin where the band had dug in and lifted my breasts, running his fingertips to my nipples and tweaking them. "I want to worship these. Always."

I stretched up my arms until my hands clasped behind his neck. "Worship away."

Without warning, he spun me in his arms until my ass rested against the edge of the sink. I caught his hungry expression just before his mouth descended on my right nipple, licking, sucking, nibbling. Tension stretched from my breasts to the tingling nexus between my legs until I forgot where we were, until I forgot my own name.

He lifted his head and looked into my face, still idly plucking at my other nipple. "Can you come from this?"

"I—I don't know. I never have, but…"

He didn't wait for me to finish but turned his attention to my other breast, driving me higher. I rubbed my thighs together to get at the pressure building low in my belly, so close. At last, as he clamped his teeth down and sucked, long and hard, I found my release. I stopped breathing as I shuddered, pinned between him and the counter. He eased my nipple from between his lips and lapped at it until the aftershocks eased.

"Never?" he murmured at last.

Cool air caressed my heated chest. "Not like—not like that. It must have been the dancing."

He hummed, and a smug smile lifted his wet lips. He smoothed his hands down my sides. "I like this skirt. I think we'll leave it on."

Then his hands were under my skirt, caressing my panties. He groaned as he traced the high leg openings and the lacy dip at the waist with his finger. "I'm glad I didn't know about these before. I'd have come in my pants. But now they come off."

The words had barely left his lips when he squatted, taking my panties down my legs. One hand behind my calf encouraged me to step out of one leg, then the other, until I was naked except for my flared skirt.

He looked up at me from his knees. "Still okay? Think you can come again?"

"Maybe?"

That smug smile appeared again right before he ran his big hands up the insides of my thighs until they met at my core. All I could do was hold on to the counter behind me while he ran a finger through my wetness and then popped his finger into his mouth. He rolled his eyes and shook his head. "You're going to kill me, Mimi."

He ducked his head under my skirt. His shoulders nudged my legs wider as he gripped my ass cheeks with his massive hands. Then he touched me. I couldn't see anything but the shape of his head moving under my skirt, and somehow that made it more erotic, not knowing what he was using to touch me—his fingers, his tongue, his nose. Or how. A kiss, a caress, a slow slide in.

My body, warm with pleasure, made it so easy for him. My second orgasm barreled through me as soon as his fingers delved inside me while he sucked my clit. One strong hand held me up when all I wanted to do was collapse like a marionette with cut strings.

It was too much, and I pressed his shoulder. He ducked out from under my skirt, the lower half of his face glistening. He licked his lips. "Mimi, when I get you into my bed—" He shook his head.

I couldn't resist the half-made promise or the bulge against his leg. "Let's go now."

He rested his chin against my belly. "I promised I'd get you home by ten. You have work tomorrow."

"No." The word came out as an embarrassing whine. All I wanted was more time, more closeness with this sex god. And to wreck him as thoroughly as he'd wrecked me. "I'll set my alarm. You can drive me back to my place early."

"No, Mimi, I shouldn't."

"Please?" I set my hands on his cheeks.

He turned his face to kiss the inside of my wrist. "Anything for you."

He led me down the hall to his bedroom.

20

MATEO

I STARED AT MY BED, where I'd fantasized so many times about
Mimi. Touching her, cuddling her, fucking her. Was it true, or was
I dreaming again? Had I just made Mimi Levy-Walters come twice
in the kitchen, and was she now actually in my bedroom? Slowly,
I turned.

She stood, dwarfed by the tall doorway, wearing nothing but
her skirt. I knew that because her panties were currently shoved
into my pocket and might conveniently go missing later.

She crossed her arms across her chest, but they didn't hide the
bounty I'd familiarized myself with earlier. "Mateo?"

"Yes?" I blinked up from the rounded curve of her breast into
her troubled brown eyes.

"You're not...having second thoughts?"

I was a fool for standing here, gloating at my windfall, when I
should have been showing her exactly how grateful I was that she
was in my home, in my bedroom. I strode to her side and gently
untangled her arms. "No, no, mi tesoro. I was...savoring my
meal." I bent and kissed her soft lips.

When I lifted my head, those lips had curled up into a soft smile. "Mind if I use your bathroom?"

"Right through here." I beckoned toward the en suite and found a new toothbrush and toothpaste in the cabinet. Then I closed the door and returned to the bedroom.

I tugged at the tail of my T-shirt. Should I be naked when she came out? Or clothed? I glanced at the clock. Nine-thirty. I should really let her sleep. Though she hadn't looked like she'd wanted sleep. Not right away. My dick throbbed against my zipper.

She was so perfect. So responsive. Despite all the humiliating fumbling I'd done around her, I'd finally done something right. Something that pleased her.

Something that pleased us both. I could still taste her. I licked my lips. Perhaps I'd feast on her again before she left. Not perhaps; I would. Something magical was happening tonight. How long would the magic last? Another few minutes? Hours? It was too much to hope for it to continue after I took her home.

I never wanted it to end.

The warm haze of sex cleared from my mind like the morning sun burning away the mist.

I never wanted this new closeness with Mimi to end.

She was in my life. In my home. And I wanted her to be there. Always.

None of my friends from the island would believe it. I'd fucked my way through our town, through the neighboring towns, through the big city. Locals and tourists. As a going-away gift, my friends had given me a giant box of condoms for my bedroom tour of San Francisco. I'd figured the box would last a month.

I hadn't opened it.

And now, the reason for my self-imposed celibacy wanted me, too. She'd said *please*.

My shirt stuck to the cold sweat on my chest. I dragged it over my head, folded it, and set it on the dresser.

From my first time with Anna Perez in her bedroom under a

poster of One Direction—and my second with her cousin Yefri's dick in my mouth in the high school locker room a week later—I'd always figured more was better. More sex, more partners, more pleasure.

No pining after one person like my father.

I looked up toward heaven. God, fate, whatever higher power felt the need to fuck with my life, had shown me.

I'd found my one person. Just like Papá.

Would she stay?

At the sound of the bathroom door opening, I whirled to face her.

My jaw dropped. Mimi's bare skin gleamed in the lamplight, her curves lit up in places and shadowed in others. Her curls floated loose over her shoulders. Her eyes had blue shadows underneath that she must have concealed with her makeup, which she'd scrubbed off. Her lashes were still dark, and her lips were a dusky rose.

She was beautiful and naked and mine. At least for the night.

Her arms twitched like she wanted to cover part of herself, but I strode to her and clasped her hands. Raising them to my lips, I murmured, "Mi tesoro." She was my treasure, my life, my heaven.

Her skin pinked all the way from her cheeks to her chest. "Do you have condoms?" she asked. "If not, I have one in my purse." She tilted her head toward the bedroom door.

"I do." Where had I stashed the box my friends had sent? I'd joked with them that I'd fuck my way through not only San Francisco but the entire state of California. And then I'd met Mimi, and I hadn't wanted to touch anyone but her.

"One second," I said.

I tried the bathroom first, avoiding my reflection in the mirror and the jutting evidence of my arousal in my pants. I opened and closed every cabinet, but the box wasn't there. Fuck! I ran my hands through my hair.

Back in the bedroom, I kissed Mimi, letting my hands wander over her ass as I tugged her toward me. Her hand landed on my hip and then trailed lower, too close to my straining erection.

"One moment." I backed away and dropped to my knees beside the bed. I tugged out my suitcase and zipped it open.

Gracias a Dios.

I lifted the box high like it was the World Cup and then, my cheeks heating, set it on the bed. I shoved the suitcase back underneath.

I was on my knees facing the bed, and I could think of a good use for that position. I beckoned to Mimi. "Come sit."

She followed my order, though she needed a boost to climb onto the tall bed. I placed my hands on her knees. "May I?"

She planted her hands behind her and then, nodding, spread her legs. The lamplight illuminated what I'd learned by feel earlier under the darkness of her skirt.

"Ah, Mimi," I said, irrepressible pride making me smile, "you're wet for me again."

I slicked my thumbs from her inner thighs to her lips and her clit. Then I lapped up her essence like honey from her skin. Mimi moaned and lowered herself to her elbows to watch me work.

I spread her open and delved inside with my tongue, mimicking the throbbing pulse in my dick as I showed her what I'd do later. And, God, what if I showed her my stash of toys? Which would she let me use on her? Would I ever be bold enough to ask her to use one on me?

Focus, Mateo. I had her spread out before me now, and I had all the tools I needed to bring her pleasure.

"Mateo, I—"

I lifted from her center and replaced my tongue with a lazily thrusting finger. "What is it, cariño?"

"I need you. Inside me. I don't think I can…"

I licked her clit as I continued to work my finger inside her. "You don't think you can do what, gorgeous?"

She rolled her eyes up and let out a whimper. "I don't know

how many more times I can come, and I want to come with you inside me."

"Ah." I kissed her swollen nub. "I think you can come as many times as we both want." This—sex—was my safe space. I knew well how to please a partner, especially one as responsive as Mimi. "One more time with my fingers and mouth, and then you can have my cock."

"But I don't…"

She didn't have to finish her sentence because I'd found the spot that made her speechless. She keened something that sounded almost like my name combined with a she-ocelot's cry.

She pushed away my face, my hand. "Enough," she sobbed. "Too much."

"Ah, cariño." I surged up onto the bed and folded her into my arms. "You're so beautiful when you come. I've got you. You're okay."

She was boneless in my arms. I kissed her forehead and found it damp with sweat. I loosened my hold on her. "Are you too warm? Need some space?"

"No." She snuggled closer. "I'm exactly where I want to be."

This time, it wasn't my dick but my heart that gave a giant throb, beating against my ribs. "Me, too."

I scooped her up in my arms and scrabbled with my fingertips to pull down the covers. I laid her back on the bed, shucked off my pants, and scooted in behind her, willing my erection to settle so I could go to sleep. Mimi had to go to work early, and I had an overnight shift at my aunt's place the next day. We both needed rest.

But Mimi had other thoughts. She tangled her fingers with mine and then brought them up to cup her breasts. Then she pressed her ass against my dick. "I was promised another orgasm with you inside me," she murmured. "But I'm too blissed-out to move."

"It's all right. We don't have to." Though my dick had other ideas. It was steel in my shorts.

"No, Mateo." She ground against me, and spots danced in front of my eyes. "I want it."

Kissing up her neck from her shoulder to her earlobe, I ended with a tweak to her nipple. "Then you will have it."

I shoved down my shorts and kicked them off. I grabbed the box of condoms from the foot of the bed, ripped it open, and drew one out. I rolled it on gently, willing myself not to go off too soon.

I caressed the mouthwatering curve of her ass and then wedged one hand under her, gripping her torso against me. With my other hand, I lifted her leg and hooked it around mine. I slicked my fingers through her wetness—God, her arousal was amazingly endless—then carefully guided myself home.

We both gasped when I ended the thrust. In this position, I couldn't get all of me inside, but it was enough to hit the spot I'd found earlier with my fingers. One hand resting on her clit, I pumped my hips. She hummed with pleasure.

Each slide inside her made tingles erupt along my spine. Mimi's breath quickened as I squeezed her nipple and brushed her clit. But I needed more. I needed the heady rush of skin slapping against skin. I needed to be balls-deep inside her.

Slowly, I dragged myself out.

I nudged her forward until she was face-down on the bed. Tugging up her hips, I kneeled behind her. She tucked her arms under the pillow, a half-smile of anticipation on her face. For a moment, I admired the way the lamplight gilded the curve of her ass and the plump lips that beckoned to me. And then, grasping her hips, I slid inside.

Hips to ass, I found heaven. I ground against her, not wanting to leave the comfort I'd found. Slowly, I slid out and then thrust back in. Mimi let out a long groan.

"Is this all right, mi tesoro?"

"Fuck. Yes." She put a hand between us where we joined, and a spark raced straight to my balls. Her hand left my body to touch herself. She moaned. "More, Mateo."

I gripped her hips and did as she asked. I thrust once, twice, three times. God, I was close. But I wouldn't come until she did. I focused on the long line of her spine and the way the lamplight split her back into a light half and a dark one. I lifted a hand and traced the line of shadow.

"Harder," she grunted, pushing back against me.

I was done for. I was going to die right here in this bed, over this woman who'd turned me inside out. I obliged her, gripping her hips and lifting them to meet my thrusts. Our skin slapped, a counterpoint to her moans. My balls tightened.

"Mimi, I—"

She stiffened and interrupted me with a wailing groan. I stilled, letting her climax wring out of her, savoring the squeeze that grayed my vision. Then I thrust again, and once more, and blessed, blissful release emptied me out. I let out a long, appreciative curse.

Mimi's legs were trembling, and I eased her to the bed as I pulled out. I caressed her ass once before I covered her up and went to the bathroom to dispose of the condom.

She was already asleep when I gathered her into my arms and tucked myself behind her.

Over the course of an evening, she'd become my entire world.

I never wanted to let her go.

21

MIMI

I WOKE IN A STRANGE BED, but it was warm and soft and safe. Mateo's big body curled around me, one muscled arm slung around my waist. I traced a vein down his forearm, trailing my fingertip through the coarse hair gilded by sunlight.

Sunlight?

Oh, shit.

I flung off his arm and the covers and sprang out of bed. Why wasn't there a clock in his bedroom, and why hadn't my alarm gone off?

Snatching my skirt off the floor, I ignored his sleepy "Mimi?" and raced stark-naked into the living room. My bra and blouse were on the kitchen floor, and I grabbed them on the way to the front door, where I found my shoes and my purse with my phone inside, still feebly sounding my alarm.

Roger leaped noiselessly to the kitchen counter and watched me with his yellow eyes.

Seven-thirty. Shit. I was supposed to meet Larissa and Natalie at Synergy half an hour ago. If I hurried, I could get there before they left. With one hand, I pulled up a ride-share app, and with the other, I tugged on my skirt.

"Ready for me to drive you home?" Mateo's voice startled me, and I dropped my phone. He'd pulled on jeans and a thermal Henley. He looked absolutely delicious, but I'd already lingered too long.

"No time. I'm late." I wrestled into my bra and fastened it in the back. Where were my underwear?

He rubbed his eyes. "Jesus, I'm sorry. I didn't know you had an early meeting. I'll drive you to work."

"It's a foundation thing. With Larissa." Slithering into my blouse, I raced into the bathroom. No underwear in here, either. At least I'd washed my face before bed. While I peed, I scrubbed my fingertips under my eyes to remove the last traces of mascara. I washed my hands and pushed the toothbrush through my mouth.

Mateo already had his shoes on and his keys in his hand when I sprinted back into the living room. While I toed on my shoes, he leaned over. "You look beautif—"

"No time!" I held up a hand. First my presentation, now this. Why did I always screw up when Mateo was involved?

He pulled open the door, and we raced to his Jeep. He tried to open my door, but I said, "I've got it. Go!"

Dutifully, he slid into the driver's seat. Only after I'd tucked my skirt under my naked ass and buckled my seat belt did he steer the Jeep down the narrow drive past Cooper's house to the street. "To the office?"

"Yes, we're meeting in the first-floor conference room." I checked my phone and winced as I tapped the button to listen to Larissa's voice mail.

Hi Miriam, we were supposed to meet at seven. Are you still coming? We need to approve the budget today.

"The budget! Shit!"

"What is it?" Mateo glanced at me.

"I don't have my laptop with me. I can't make any updates to the budget in the meeting. Do you have any paper? A pencil?"

"Check the glove box. You can't do it on your phone?"

"Oh. Possibly? My spreadsheet would be awfully small. I guess I could try it." I fished in the compartment and came up with a stub of a pencil and a spiral-top notepad.

"Make do with the spreadsheet on your phone. Meanwhile, I'll run to your apartment and fetch your laptop."

"Really? You'd do that for me?"

"Of course, cariño."

"Thank you." I wanted to kiss his stubbly cheek, linger there at the crook of his neck where he smelled divine, but he was driving. I settled back into my seat and dug my keys out of my purse. I set them in the cup holder. "You're a lifesaver."

Mateo knew the shortcuts and ways to avoid San Francisco rush-hour traffic and, sooner than I'd hoped, we were at the office. Grabbing my phone and my purse, I pecked his cheek and pushed out of the Jeep.

I heard a strangled gasp and turned to look over my shoulder. Mateo stared at my ass.

"Your skirt." He passed a hand over his mouth. "Tug it down a bit?"

Shit, I must have flashed him during my descent. I smoothed it, back and front. "Better?"

He shook his head but said, "Yes. I'll see you soon."

Carefully holding down my skirt and praying the wind wouldn't cause me to flash my early-arriving coworkers, I scurried to the conference room.

Larissa and Natalie faced the screen at the back of the room, where Natalie projected a floor plan from her laptop. When I clattered to the door, they swiveled to look at me.

Natalie suppressed a grin, but Larissa raised an unamused eyebrow. "So glad you could join us. Natalie was just walking me through the venue arrangements, but we'll cover the budget next.

You do have the figures?" She stared pointedly at my clutch, obviously too small to contain anything useful.

"I do. I'm ready." It was a lie, but I pulled up the spreadsheet on my tiny phone screen while Natalie finished talking about coat check and the green room for the speakers.

Mateo wasn't back by the time Larissa asked for the budget presentation, and she frowned as I started to talk them through the numbers.

"Wait," she interrupted me. "Don't you have printouts or anything to show us on the screen?"

"Not—not right now." My voice quivered. Why had I let Mateo sex me into forgetting my responsibilities, my goals? Last night, I hadn't remembered my own name, much less that I had to deliver a presentation at seven the next morning.

Larissa thumped her hands on the conference table. "Then why are you even here? If I can't rely on you, this isn't going to work, Miriam."

"She's got the figures." Natalie nodded at the phone in my hand. "Mimi, why don't you write them on the whiteboard?"

"Great idea." But as it turned out, it was a terrible idea. My bare thighs made a sucking sound on the conference-room chair as I stood.

"Oops." My cheeks flamed. Quickly, I smoothed down my skirt and turned to the whiteboard.

"I expect foundation members to present a professional appearance, Miriam. That skirt is much too short."

The marker squeaked on the board. "Yes, of course, Larissa," I mumbled.

"Ah, good morning to my favorite power trio." Mateo's tone was jovial, but I heard the strain in it.

"Mateo!" Larissa's voice took on a flirtatious lilt. "What are you doing here? You said you had to work."

Slowly, I turned to the door. Mateo had a tote bag slung over one shoulder and my laptop bag over the other. In one hand he held a cardboard carrier with four cups, and in the other, a sack from the bakery down the street.

"I thought you'd like breakfast at your breakfast meeting." He set down the coffees and the sack and then gave Larissa air kisses on each cheek. Natalie had stood to investigate the offerings, but she held out a hand for him to shake.

He approached me at the whiteboard and murmured, "I brought a change of clothes. And panties." Then he placed a smacking kiss on my cheek.

Louder, he said, "I apologize. I made Mimi late this morning. I couldn't let my angel go. If you had this face on the pillow next to you, could you?"

Heat blasted to my cheeks. "Mateo," I growled.

He caught the hand that had been about to slap his biceps and brought it to his lips. "Mi tesoro."

"Swoon," Natalie said.

Larissa said, "You can make up for it by joining us."

"Join you?" A frown passed over his face so quickly she might have missed it. But after last night, I had a new sensor for Mateo's expressions, and he didn't look pleased.

"We need a consult on the menu. I haven't been able to choose which dessert to serve."

That was a lie. We'd chosen the flan last week, but if it distracted her, I was thrilled to let it ride. Mateo handed me my laptop bag, and I powered up my computer and connected it to the projector while they discussed the merits of flan versus tres leches.

When they'd decided—again—on the flan, I cleared my throat. "I'm ready to walk you through the budget figures now."

"Oh, good." Larissa laughed, high and false. "If only Mateo had a head for numbers, we wouldn't need you at all."

I froze, my voice gone. If she didn't need me, that had to mean I was off the list for the assistant director spot, too. Why the hell was I even here, trying so hard?

For the kids, I reminded myself grimly. For girls like Bree. For them, I'd keep trying, keep falling short, and do it all for free.

"Larissa." Natalie's voice was quiet but firm.

"She was late and unprepared until Mateo got here." Larissa gave me a steely stare. "I could hire any accountant to do what she does."

"Ah," Mateo said, his voice like gravel. "But you didn't hire an accountant. Mimi does this work pro bono, from the kindness of her heart. She does it for the children. In her spare time. I think you'd have a hard time finding someone as talented as Mimi willing to do that."

I was glad I'd washed off my mascara because it would have run down my face. I swiped under my eyes and flashed Mateo a watery smile to express my gratitude. He understood. He saw me.

Larissa glanced up at the screen, her jaw set. "Fine. You can have another chance. Give us the numbers."

My body went cold. Like a puddle slowly freezing from the top down, my skin tightened, and the grateful tears pooling in my eyes dried up. I became a pillar of cold, hard ice. Despite Natalie's and Mateo's defense, I was on shaky ground. All because I'd let myself get distracted from my goal. Not only was my chance at the assistant director position slipping out of my grasp, but I was letting down the kids.

My one-night stands didn't stay long enough that I almost missed important meetings and showed up unprepared. None of them had made me look unnecessary in front of the person I wanted to hire me. They stayed safely in the non-work side of my life.

Crossing the work boundary was one thing Mateo had in common with Byron. He was all over my life—involved in my work, part of my family, and now setting my love life on fire.

He'd brought me flipping panties. To the office. That was a line I'd never crossed. Not even with Byron.

My mother's voice whispered in my ear. I couldn't show

weakness like this again. Not if I wanted the job at the foundation. Not if I wanted to keep helping the kids like Tara at the library.

And I wanted all that. I'd prove it to Larissa.

Though—I glanced at Mateo, sipping his coffee and looking expectantly at the screen like he actually cared about the gala budget—now I wanted him, too.

22

MATEO

ALTHOUGH ALL I wanted was Mimi back in my bed, on my kitchen counter, hell, wherever I could get her, I worked the night shift that week. I didn't even have to lie to Larissa to miss the foundation meetings where I took too much of the spotlight from Mimi.

I tried to text Mimi, but she was gruff and uncommunicative, responding in single words. With the gala three weeks away, she was busy, and I understood that. I'd thought she had a good time, but I worried. Maybe she hadn't enjoyed our night together as much as I had?

Or maybe she was pissed at me again. It was the second time I'd caused her to be less than prepared at one of her committee meetings. Larissa had sniped at her, criticizing the smallest mistake like she was looking for an excuse not to hire her. Why? Mimi clearly deserved the job. Why did Mimi put up with her bullshit?

On Friday morning, when I pulled into Miguelito's driveway, my headlights illuminated Ben walking his dog Coco across the motorcourt. Her brother might clue me in to what was going on in her head.

"Ben!" I leaned my head out my Jeep's window. "Can I walk with you?"

"Sure. Now?"

"My cousin's at the gym?" The last thing I wanted was for Miguelito to find me alone with Ben and get jealous. I'd never try anything with his fiancé, but he hadn't yet forgiven me for the bad behavior of my youth. Plus, my cousin wouldn't understand my love troubles. He would never pine for anyone the way I had for Mimi.

"Yeah." Ben yawned. "He's one of those irritating morning people."

I parked the car and, after greeting Coco, fell into step beside Ben. We walked out the driveway and down the hill toward the bay. The sun had started to spread its rays at our backs, but I zipped my jacket up to my chin. San Francisco in January was cold for someone who'd grown up in the tropics.

I glanced at Ben. He was taller and thinner than his sister, but they had the same dark, curly hair. Same strong noses and deter-mined chins. Though his smiles came easily and Mimi's were rare as a hundred-degree day in San Francisco. Except post-orgasm, I'd discovered.

I blinked. Better not think about Mimi's pussy while I was with her brother.

I cleared my throat. "You doing all right? How's work?"

"So far, so good. It's nice to get paid again. I mean, it was amazing of Cooper to finance my school that last semester, but we Levy-Walters kids are independent, you know."

"I know." It was exactly the segue I needed. "Why do you think that is?"

He pushed out his lower lip. "I guess because of my mom. She worked hard for what we had. She overcame a lot to get to where she is. I mean, women lawyers drop out of the profession like flies as they get older. She fought her way through a lot of patriarchy and sexism to stay in. She always told Mimi and me you had to prove you were the best if you wanted to get anywhere."

He scuffed his toes on the gravel path. "For me, it was a lot of pressure, and I kind of cracked. Not Mimi. She took it to heart. She's following in Mom's footsteps, sort of. Not into law, but in her own field."

I nudged his shoulder with mine. "You turned out fine. You got exactly what you wanted."

He glanced back at the mansion. "More, actually. I never thought someone as amazing as Cooper would fall for me."

"You're pretty amazing yourself." If my cousin hadn't already marked Ben as his when I met him, I might have tried to snag him. But as beautiful and kind as Ben was, Mimi had a special spark to her, a sharp shininess like a cut gemstone, that I couldn't resist. Not even family bonds or my powerful cousin would have kept me from her.

"Thanks." He paused while Coco sniffed a spindly tree. "How are things going with Mimi?"

"She didn't say anything?"

"Ooh!" His eyes went wide. "Cagey, answering a question with a question. No, she didn't even tell me you guys were dating. Not until Cooper outed her. Why? Did something happen?"

My cheeks burned. This was not how I'd envisioned this conversation going. "She really didn't say anything?"

"You know Mimi. She's not into talking about her feelings and shit. Besides, she's been holed up in her apartment every night for the past week, working on stuff for the gala."

I mumbled, "Not every night."

He pulled Coco to a stop on the sidewalk. "Spill it."

"I took her out for a special date Sunday night. Well, I tried to. The place Miguelito recommended wasn't really...us."

"That jerk!" His nostrils flared. "He didn't tell me you two had a *special date.*"

"I asked him to keep it on the down-low. I didn't want expectations, you know?"

"Well? Were expectations met?"

I couldn't hide my grin. "Surpassed, actually."

"Stop it!" He slapped my arm playfully. "Really?"

"Really. She's amazing. I think I—" No. Ben couldn't be the first to know I was falling for his sister. I'd tell Mimi herself when I was ready. When she was ready. When she wasn't sending me one-word texts.

"So, what's the problem? Why are you out here in the freezing cold dawn talking to me and not snuggled up warm next to my sister in bed?"

"I just got back from work. Besides, she, um, she's not responding to my texts." Now I sounded like a teenager.

"Did you call her? Or drop by her place?"

"No, I worked nights this week. And she's not a big fan of my dropping by. She wants to be texted first."

Ben chewed his lip. "Sometimes Mimi—both of us, really—can get stuck in her routine. In her work. That was me before Cooper and I got together. I hardly ever went out with friends. I got scared after I got laid off, you know? So I just focused on school and my job. I guess my mom's mindset kicks in during times of stress. And Mimi's *stressed* right now. She wants this job at the foundation so bad. And she's still doing her other job. She probably feels like she can't take her eye off the ball. She's panicking."

"She's afraid of me?" Nothing scared Mimi. Even after I'd ruined her presentation, she showed up to her meeting with Jackson Jones. And she'd gone commando to Monday's meeting. She was fierce and unstoppable as a hurricane.

"Afraid of what it might mean if she let herself go. If she let herself fall for you." He watched Coco for a second. "There was this guy."

"A guy?"

"Byron. She dated him at the first company she worked for. Before Synergy. Their manager left, and the controller needed to fill the job. Fast. Mimi and Byron both had interviews. She deserved it more because she'd been there longer, worked harder than he did. Still, she helped him prep for it. He interviewed first, and they offered him the job right there. Without even talking to Mimi. Turned out, he told them she wasn't ready."

"That cabrón!"

"Yeah. She quit after that. Dumped his ass, went to work at Synergy. Hasn't dated anyone since. Won't let anyone close, especially at work. And with guys she meets, it's one night only. I mean, except for you."

Though we'd had only one night. Were Mimi's one-word texts her way of letting me down easy? Goosebumps rose on my arms under my sleeves. "I'd never do that to her," I said. "I'm not like him."

I looked down at myself, at the jacket Cooper had given me when I'd shown up in San Francisco without one. At the jeans and sneakers I wore to work.

I twisted the ring on my finger. I didn't work in an office like Mimi. Unlike Byron, I had no college degree. No real savings to speak of. I slumped, the exhaustion of my night shift washing over me. "I'm not worthy of her."

"No!" He clutched my arm. "No, Mateo. You're amazing. Look at me."

Reluctantly, I lifted my eyes to his.

"I don't say this about everyone. Believe me, Mimi has dated some real assholes. Like Byron. As driven as she is, she thinks she's attracted to guys who are like her. But that's not what she needs. She needs someone like you." He squeezed my arm. "Someone to care for her. To help her. To—to love her. You are absolutely worthy of her and never, *never* think otherwise. Do you hear me?"

His ferocious tone reminded me of Mimi. I thought back to all the times she forgot to eat. Monday, when I brought her clothes and her laptop to her meeting. She needed someone like me to support her, especially working what amounted to two jobs plus volunteer work on the weekends. I could be what she needed.

"I hear you."

"Now." He chewed the inside of his lip. "What are you going to do?"

Grow up. "I'm going to help her. I don't know what yet, but I'll figure it out."

"Maybe"—he tilted his head—"you don't need to *do* anything to help her. Just be there for her. And don't let her push you away."

I grunted, my mind already whirling to what Mimi needed. She'd mentioned she was worried about what to wear to the gala. I'd help her with that. After a power nap. Because right then, I would've face-planted into the steering wheel before I made it to the dress shop.

Ben rubbed my arm. "You've got this. Just remember, you're exactly what she needs. Okay?"

"Okay." But was I?

"Now, go sleep," he said, pushing me toward the guesthouse. I hadn't noticed that he'd led me back to it.

"Thanks." I pulled him into a hug, and Coco, as usual, danced at our feet.

"Anytime. You're a good guy, Mateo."

Inside my house, I fed Roger then collapsed onto my bed for a few hours' sleep. When I woke, I still had dark circles under my eyes, but I had enough energy to optimistically pack an overnight bag, ensure Roger had enough food for the next twenty-four hours and no access to toilet paper, and get back in my car. I headed toward the Excelsior.

———

A LITTLE AFTER six that night, I pressed the buzzer at Mimi's building, a sack of takeout in one hand and a garment bag in the other.

A wave of gratitude washed through me when she answered. I couldn't tell through the tinny speaker if her monotone meant she was reluctant to let me up or perhaps only tired, but she buzzed me in, and that was what mattered.

When I walked into her apartment, she leaned against the counter in her neat kitchen. All I wanted to do was lift her up onto it the way I had on Sunday night and taste her again, but that would have to wait. She needed other types of care first.

"Hey," I said, kissing her cheek before I set the food on the counter. "I brought you dinner."

"And a change of clothes?" She lifted one dark eyebrow at my garment bag. "That's bold."

"This?" I grinned. "This is for you."

"For me?"

"Did you have lunch today?"

"I did." Her stomach growled. "Well, if you count a fun-size pack of M&Ms and a hundred-calorie bag of almonds from the vending machine as lunch."

I shook my head. If she'd let me, I'd get up early and pack her a nutritious lunch every day. "We'll look at what I brought later. First, we eat. Do you like Thai food?"

Her stomach rumbled again. "Yes, please."

I laid the garment bag across her sofa, then we washed our hands and set the food on her kitchen table.

She was quiet while we ate. I watched her, trying to figure out if she focused on the food because she was starving or tired or because she was planning how to snip me out of her life like a wasteful expense.

A dozen times during dinner, I opened my mouth to ask her what she was feeling, what she'd been thinking, to try to crack her open and see the emotions she kept hidden so well. But each time, I chickened out. I wasn't ready to hear it if she'd decided we were done. Not yet. Not until I'd shown her what else I'd brought her.

After we filled our bellies, I set the leftovers in her fridge for her lunch tomorrow.

"Are you ready to see what's in the garment bag?" I asked, leading her into the living room.

"Okay." Her cheeks were pink, her eyes bright from the meal we'd eaten. Still, she eyed the bag with trepidation.

One summer, I'd worked in my tío José María's tailor shop. I remembered how dress sizing worked, and I'd reproduced Mimi's measurements from the memories of how my hands splayed across her body on Sunday night. Still, my fingers trembled as I unzipped the bag. She wore mostly black and gray, and her clothes tended to conceal rather than accentuate her curvy figure. What I'd brought was well outside her usual wardrobe. If she gave it a chance, if she gave me a chance, I was certain she'd look stunning.

I pulled out the first dress, an iridescent blue-violet tulle confection.

"What's this?" She curled her lip.

"For the gala. You have to try it on."

"Have to?" She raised an eyebrow. "It's not my style."

"Try it." I held it out to her. "For me."

She hesitated for a few seconds. At last, she rolled her eyes. "Fine."

Grabbing the hanger, she flounced to her bedroom and shut the door.

I waited five minutes before I went to her door. "Do you need help with the zipper?"

"No. I'm fine. I just—" She opened the door and squinted one eye. "Does this look good on me?"

The tulle gathered at one shoulder, floating over her breasts, toga-style, before cinching at her waist. Then it flowed out again over her hips and puddled on the floor.

"We'll have to get it taken up at the hem." I cast a critical eye over the rest of it. "You look amazing in it."

"I do, don't I?" she murmured, twisting in front of the cheap mirror on her wall so the skirt swirled. "I never would've tried on something like this. But it…it's gorgeous."

I leaned over her bare shoulder to whisper in her ear, "You're gorgeous. The dress is only a vehicle for your beauty."

"Oh my God, stop." Her cheeks went red.

"Where's your phone? I'll take a picture."

"In my purse. You can take a picture with your phone and send it to me."

"Really?" I slid my phone out of my back pocket.

"It's fine." She turned to the side and popped a knee.

I snapped the photo and texted it to Mimi. Sliding my phone back into my pocket, I said, "Turn. I'll get the zipper and bring you the next one."

When she turned her back to me, I lowered the zipper all the way to her black panties. I wanted to trace a finger over the waistband, but if I started that, she'd never see the other dresses. So with one last, longing glance, I turned away to fetch the second gown.

I passed it to her through the cracked door.

"Ooh, a black one," she said.

"I knew that would appeal to you."

Two minutes later, she opened the door and beckoned me in. This one was a heavy black brocade fabric with a V-neck bodice and an A-line skirt that flared out over her legs.

"It has pockets!" she squealed, tucking her hands into them.

"Thought you'd like that."

She twirled again in front of the mirror. "This one is really more my style. I mean, the other one made me look like a...a fairy princess, but this dress means business."

I held up my phone. "Give me that *get out of my way, you're blocking my spotlight, Jay-Z,* look."

She gave the camera a fierce stare, and I snapped the picture. "Turn."

After she turned her back, I lowered the zipper. This time, I ghosted my fingers over the silky skin of her lower back, and she shivered.

"One more," I murmured.

"But this one is perfect."

"One more."

"Fine."

I returned with the final dress, weighty with rose-gold sequins.

"Pink?" Her lip curled.

"Try it."

She shook her head. "No way. There's not enough fabric here. And all that sparkly shit? It'll make me look like a disco ball."

"Try it." I held it out to her. "Indulge me."

She didn't answer, only shut the door in my face.

I wiped down the counters in her kitchen and started the dishwasher. After ten minutes, she hadn't emerged, so I tapped on the door. "Everything okay?"

"I can't get the zipper up. But I don't think I like this one. It's too…"

When she didn't finish, I asked, "Can I come in?"

"Yeah. Since you've already seen me naked and…"

The dress had stolen the ends of her sentences, and when I stepped into the room, she stole my breath.

In the lamplight, the sequins shimmered like sunset over the water. The bodice gaped over her chest. I aligned it with her shoulders and slowly zipped it from below the swell of her ass all the way to her nape. As I went, the stretchy dress snugged against her like a second skin.

Fluffing her curls around her shoulders, I peered at her reflection in the mirror. The dress was a long-sleeved faux-wrap style with a slight flare to the skirt that puddled at her feet.

"I—I don't think—" She turned, and her upper thigh poked out of the long slit.

When I spoke, my voice was hoarse. "What don't you think, Mimi?"

"It's not very…professional, is it?"

I swallowed. "You're stunning. And the dress is appropriate for a gala like this."

"I don't know." She bit her lip.

I stepped out of the frame and snapped her picture. With her teeth capturing her plump lower lip, she was a man-eater in that gown.

Sidling closer to admire her in the mirror, I ran my hand over her ribs, all the way down to her hip. The sequins were bumpy and rough against my palm, but the curve of her body was irresistible. I stroked the long line of her back, following the zipper down her spine and over the arc of her ass.

When she hummed in pleasure, I molded my body to her back and tugged her curls to one side. I kissed her neck, and she sagged back against me. On a whim, I raised my phone and snapped a mirror selfie of us, not bothering to look at the screen to see if I'd captured us both. I curled my other arm around her waist and slid it up to cup her breast, weighing it in my palm. I snapped another photo.

"I guess…I guess this dress is the winner for you?"

I kissed up to her earlobe. "You're exquisite, no matter what you wear."

"I could wear my college sweatshirt and leggings, and I'd be exquisite?"

"Resplendent." I nipped her earlobe, and she gasped.

"One of your henleys and my fat jeans?"

"Your fat jeans?" I pulled off her earlobe, momentarily distracted.

"The baggy jeans I wear when I have my period and I'm bloated."

I caressed the curve of her belly and teased at the opening of the slit just below her hip. "Now you're just trying to turn me on."

"You can't be serious."

I captured her gaze in the mirror as I inched my fingers inside the slit to stroke her upper thigh. "You're beautiful to me all the time, Mimi. And baggy jeans give my hands more room."

I brushed the front of her panties with my thumb, and she shuddered.

"Unzip me. I want your hands on me. Now."

"Sí, mi tesoro."

I took my time sliding the zipper down her back, kissing every inch of skin as I revealed it. When the zipper reached the bottom of its track and the fabric shushed to the floor, I held Mimi's hand as she stepped out of it.

She must have put on the strapless bra to try on the off-the-shoulder dress. It cinched around her ribs, the underwire contouring around the lower curves of her breasts. On top, the upper swells spilled out of the cups, showing off the deep valley in between.

I couldn't resist. I stuck my nose into that valley and explored the silken hills with my tongue. Only when I'd mapped them did I reach behind her to unfasten the four hooks that secured it. I took my time, easing the hooks one by one. When I peeled the garment from her skin, there were red furrows where it had poked into her. I kissed them, laved them with my tongue, hoping to take away the ache.

She moaned my name.

I worked my way up to her nipples the way I'd driven her wild Sunday night, wetting one to stroke and pinch it with my fingers while I licked and nibbled the other. Groaning, she let her head fall back. Her responsiveness made my dick stiffen against my leg.

Supporting her back, I worshiped at the altar of her bosom, tracing her curves, lapping at her pebbled skin. Tonight, this fantasy of a woman was mine. Mine to please, mine to adore.

Her breath hitched. "I'm—I'm—"

I sucked her nipple into my mouth, biting down firmly. Her legs shook, making her body tremble in my arms. I held her through it, easing up on the pressure but not pausing the work of my mouth and fingers.

"Who's making you come, Mimi?" I growled. Jesus, I was a greedy bastard. But I needed to hear my name on her lips.

"You are. You are, Mateo," she murmured.

"I need you, mi vida."

"Yes." The word ended with a sigh and a greedy whimper.

I guided her to the bed, pushed the dresses to the floor, and laid her down. Slowly, I drew her panties down her legs, lingering at the juncture of her legs to inhale the scent of her arousal into my lungs.

Locking my gaze with hers, I tugged off my long-sleeved T-shirt. Then I flicked the button of my jeans and dropped them to the floor.

Her eyes widened. "You're not wearing underwear?"

"Are you scandalized?"

"Yes." But she rubbed her legs together.

"Ah-ah," I teased, gripping her knees and tugging them apart until she was spread before me, glistening and swollen. "I'm taking care of you tonight."

"Then take care of me. I need—"

I cut her off with a swipe of my tongue through her slit. Her knees quaked in my grip.

"Condom." She tipped her chin toward the bedside table, where a shallow glass bowl held a handful of colorful condom packets.

"I like it." I snatched one up. "No fumbling in drawers."

One corner of her mouth tipped up. "You can fumble in my drawers anytime."

I fake-gasped. "That's my line, cariño."

"No." She smirked. "Your line is, 'How deep, baby?'"

I grunted as I rolled on the latex and then grasped myself at the base. If she kept going with that kind of talk, I was going to come before I was even inside her. Sex was my domain, and I needed to wrench back control. Leaning both knees on the bed between her spread thighs, I purred, "I'm not asking. I'm going deep, baby."

Lifting her hips off the bed to position her where I needed her, I shoved inside in a single thrust. I held my breath until the fire-works in front of my vision cleared. When I looked at her face, her mouth gaped in bliss.

"Legs around my back."

She dug her heels into the lower part of my back, and I tightened my grip. I rocked my hips against her. "This okay?"

She opened her mouth, but no words came out. A first with Mimi. She licked her lips and breathed, "Uh-huh."

I reversed and plunged back in, deep as I could go, grinding my stomach against her clit. Her eyes fluttered closed, and she squeezed around me. My eyes rolled back in pleasure, the delightful compression around my dick creating an echoing tightness in my balls. Pleasure swept up my spine and coiled in my center. Fuck! One day I was going to take my time with Mimi.

Today was not that day.

I thrust in twice more until I teetered on the edge. I eased my thumb onto her clit and thrummed it fast. "Come with me, Mimi."

She let out a sound somewhere between a cry and a sob before her muscles squeezed me. I saw stars when my release rocketed through me. Mimi's legs shook. Or maybe the shaking was me.

Still inside her, I nudged her up farther onto the bed until there was room for my knees. Then I bent over her, careful not to squash her, and kissed her lips, her cheeks, her forehead. "Mi vida," I murmured.

"I took Latin in high school, but I know that word from the Ricky Martin song. *Vida* means life. Are you saying I've taken your life? Killed you? La petite mort?"

An embarrassed chuckle escaped me, blowing the damp curls off her temple. "It's an endearment. It means—" No, I'd gone too far for retreat. "It means you're my life."

She scrambled up onto her elbows, almost knocking into my nose. "What, like, 'til death do us part?" Her expression of horror would've made me laugh if it hadn't sliced into my chest and robbed me of my breath.

I gathered enough air to say, "It's just a saying, you know? Like, when I called you *baby*, I didn't mean you were an actual infant." Nervous, I watched her. Would she buy it? Or would she see right through my thin excuse and chase me out like she'd done with every other guy since that asshole, Byron?

She narrowed her eyes. "Let's save it for in front of Larissa."

"Wait a minute." Grasping the base of the condom around my suddenly shriveling cock, I pulled out of her and strode to the bathroom, my heart pounding in my chest. After I'd tossed the condom and washed my trembling hands, I tugged on my jeans and my shirt. Mimi watched me, still naked and sweaty on the bed.

Finally, I sat on the edge and clasped my hands together so she wouldn't see how they shook. My lungs, my throat, were almost too tight to speak. Controlling my voice as best I could, I said, "This is part of the ruse for Larissa? Sleeping together is part of our date to the gala? *That's* what this is?"

"No." She sat up and put a hand on my arm. "All I meant was that—that…" She rested her head on my shoulder, and it took all my strength not to touch her. "That it scared me a little. I've spent a long time focused on my job and on my goals. Getting close to someone"—she swallowed—"wanting you, having feelings for you, it scares me."

My heart thumped once, paused, and then set off racing. "You have feelings for me?"

She lifted her head and met my gaze. "I do. I care about you."

My heart burst like a balloon, raining confetti over my insides. I clutched her shoulders and kissed every part of her beautiful face. "Mimi, I—I…"

I couldn't say it, not with the warning in her cooling brown eyes. But I felt it deep inside.

I loved her.

23

MIMI

I WAS ALREADY HALF-AWAKE when the ding of the intercom sounded from the other room. It was the first Saturday in a while I didn't have an early meeting for the gala committee or, God forbid, a wedding, and I was too cozy in my bed to get up, the covers snugged under my chin.

And a warm man at my back.

The bed shifted, and I blinked my eyes open. Mateo sat up and tucked the covers more securely around me.

"What are you doing?" I asked.

"Answering the door." He stood, but instead of picking up his jeans from the floor, he walked naked to the bedroom door, his hair not a flattened tangle like mine but sexy and rumpled like a GQ model's. His morning erection bobbed in front of him.

"Wait, why?"

"I ordered coffee and breakfast. I'll just buzz them up."

I sat up. "Delivery is expensive. I have coffee—I think—and there's a bakery not six blocks away. Why—"

"Because"—he returned to my side of the bed and kissed me,

soft and lingering—"this way, we can eat breakfast in bed. Naked."

I grasped his hand. "Eat breakfast...or something else?" I rubbed my thighs together to contain the slickness that gathered there.

"Aha. Now you see the wisdom of my plan. A bite of pastry, a bite of Mimi." He nipped my earlobe.

The door dinged again. "You know," he whispered, "if you lived in a newer building, you'd have an app to open the door, and I could snack on you right now."

"New buildings are expensive, too. Hurry back?" I bit my lip. I could get used to this. Breakfast in bed with a guy who loved giving oral as much as I loved receiving it? Cancel my weekend plans.

"Two seconds." His voice was a low rumble.

I watched his round, naked ass work as he disappeared through the bedroom door.

I lifted my hand to smooth my hair and found the silk elastic I used at night to gather up my curls snarled in my hair. Shit. I had to look like Medusa while Mateo looked like a guy in a glossy cologne ad.

Tugging it free, I combed my fingers through my curls to introduce some order to the chaos. I breathed into my cupped palm. Should I brush my teeth? The thought of leaving the warm, comfortable nest of my bed made me shiver. Though if I went down on Mateo, the last thing he'd care about was my morning breath.

Plan made, I was fluffing the pillows when Mateo appeared in the doorway, his face pale. He clutched one of my gray throw pillows at his groin and another behind his naked ass.

"Ah, you have a visitor."

"A visitor?"

"Your mother is here."

"What?" My cheeks prickled as the blood drained from my face. "Now?"

He closed the door behind him. "Yes. Sorry, I…" He gestured at his pillow-covered middle, and I winced as I imagined the scene. My mother giving up on my buzzing her in, then breezing through the door with the key it was clearly a mistake to have given her and finding a naked stranger.

"Did she say anything?"

"She asked to speak to you."

"Shit." I hauled my ass out of bed and took half a minute to find some underwear, leggings, and a sweatshirt.

More slowly, Mateo gathered his clothes from the floor. "I'll just…"

"Stay here. For now. Please." I dropped a reassuring kiss on his lips.

Who knew what my mother would say? I'd never been unlucky enough for her to walk in on one of my one-night stands. Usually, I sent them home well before dawn.

I walked out the door and gently closed it behind me. My mother sat on the couch, legs crossed, wearing winter-white slacks and a navy and white striped sweater. She'd draped her coat over the arm of the sofa like she was staying for a while.

"Morning, Mom. What are you doing here?"

She stood and kissed my cheek. "What kind of greeting is that for your mother when you haven't answered my texts or calls for a week?"

"Sorry. I meant to. But I've been so busy with work and the foundation—"

"And the sexy naked man?"

"Yes. Him, too. Why are you here so early?"

"I told you. I wanted to make sure you weren't dead on the floor, your body being eaten by rats. But I see someone much more pleasant has been eat—"

"Mom!"

"Your sex glow is absolutely obscene." Her smile widened. "I'm so happy for you."

"Mom!"

"What? I hate thinking of you all alone in this apartment. I'm glad you're enjoying your sexual freedom." She gasped. "Is this your *new, casual* man?"

My stomach flipped, and not in the joyful way it did when Mateo kissed me. "If you don't mind, I'd rather not discuss my sexual freedom with you."

She shrugged. "Suit yourself. I was a little distracted by his big schlong, but I think I remember you said he's a relative of Cooper's?"

I covered my hot cheeks. "Why don't I introduce you?"

"That would be lovely. Tell him he doesn't have to put on clothes on my account."

"Gross, Mom."

I returned to the bedroom, where Mateo perched, fully clothed, on the comforter. He'd made the bed and picked up the clothes I'd tossed on the floor. He fidgeted with the ring on his finger.

He reached for my hand. "I'm sorry, mi tesoro."

I squeezed his hand. "It's okay. Come meet my mother."

He nodded like I'd asked him to stand in front of a firing squad.

He followed me from the bedroom to the couch. Mom stayed seated, scanning him from head to toe.

"Mom, this is Mateo Rivera. You remember I mentioned we're seeing each other? He's Cooper's cousin."

She held out her hand, and I thought for a second he might bow over it and kiss it like a prince in a movie, but he only shook it.

"Mateo, this is my mother, Jeannie Levy."

"Sorry about earlier," he said, releasing her hand. "Usually, I try to make a better first impression on my girlfriend's mother."

Both of them stared at me when I gasped. *Girlfriend?* No. We were *so* not there yet. Sure, I'd broken my no-repeat rule for him, and I'd even admitted I had feelings for him, but *girlfriend?* I wasn't ready for that. Not with him. Not with anyone.

"We don't have to pretend for my mother." I'd make her swear never to reveal the truth in front of Ben or Cooper. And my lawyer mother might not understand boundaries, but she knew something about confidentiality.

"Pretend?" His eyebrows scrunched down.

The intercom dinged, and Mom stood. "I'll just go see who's downstairs. Give you two kids a minute."

She shut the apartment door behind her.

"Mimi, I—what's wrong?" He clasped both of my hands gently, like he did when we danced. He rubbed circles on the backs with his thumbs.

"Nothing's wrong. I just...I didn't expect you to meet my parents. I wasn't prepared to give a narrative."

"A narrative?" He grinned, showing one dimple. "That sounds more complicated than this is. We're dating. We're sleeping together. I'm not seeing anyone else. So you're my girlfriend."

"That *sounds* simple. But—"

"No but. Turn off that big brain of yours for a minute and go with it. This feels good, yes?" He tugged me closer and put our joined hands behind his back so I embraced him. No, it was more like I draped over him. Like butter on hot corn.

"Y-yes."

"We're simple, you and I. I like you. A lot." He kissed my lips, light and sweet. "And you like me." He raised his eyebrows.

I hesitated for only a moment. I'd already admitted it. To him and to myself. I nodded.

His shoulders lowered. "Good. Then no more fake. You're my girlfriend. And I'm your man."

Before I could answer, Mom opened the door and walked in with a pair of coffees and a pastry sack. "Breakfast is here."

"Ah." He kissed my cheek before releasing my hands. He took the food and drinks from my mother. "I'll turn breakfast for two into breakfast for three while you ladies relax."

Mom arched her eyebrows and settled back onto my couch.

She watched Mateo walk into my kitchen, then patted the cushion beside her.

I sank onto it.

"So?" she asked.

"So?"

"Tell me about your *boyfriend.*"

"Let's not use that term. Like I told you, it's new." Measured-in-minutes new.

"And?"

"It's good? I guess? We're going to the gala together. He's teaching me to dance."

"That's what they're calling it now?"

"Mom!" I glanced at the kitchen. My coffee maker hissed. Was he hearing this humiliating conversation?

"I like him. And not only because he's got an enormous, baby-making schlong. I guess it's too much to hope that he's Jewish?"

"Mom! No! It's not like that. We're not going to be making any babies together. Besides, you're always telling me to focus on my career. Not men."

"Where are my grandchildren going to come from? Ben gave me a grand-dog. I can't take a grand-dog to the zoo. There will be no bris, no bar mitzvah for Coco. I'm counting on you, Mimi."

"But what about my career? What about proving myself? What about smarts, drive, and confidence?" When had my mother come down with grandchild fever?

"With the right partner, you can do all that. Take your father and me, for example. I have the career I do because he helped me. He spent time with you kids while I put in the hours at the office. Maybe I was slow to realize it, but seeing Ben be Cooper's support reminded me. I think Mateo could be like that for you."

As if to prove her point, he emerged from the kitchen with a plate and a mug of coffee. He set the plate on my coffee table.

He handed the mug to Mom. "Do you take milk? Splenda? Mimi is out of sugar and cream."

If he'd sniffed the milk, he'd probably have reported I was out of that, too.

"No, black is fine. Thank you."

"I make it strong, so let me know if you change your mind." He returned to the kitchen.

Did Mateo want to be a supporting actor to my starring role? No, that wasn't how things worked. Ben had his own life, separate from Cooper's. He had his own career with his new foundation. Even my dad had his tutoring business.

Mateo wanted something. Maybe all the help he'd given me meant it was something to do with the gala or the foundation. Maybe he wanted a position there, and he was counting on me to give it to him once I became the assistant director. And I was fine with that, as long as it wasn't my position he wanted.

That made sense. That was how the world worked. Being Mateo's girlfriend wasn't too different from my one-night stands. We gave each other pleasure and enjoyed each other's company. It was simple, transactional, reciprocal. Sure, I cared about him, but I didn't need to get my feelings any more involved, not—not *love* like I'd thought I had with Byron.

Love made me vulnerable, clouded my vision. Love had already lost me one promotion. I couldn't let that happen again. Not when there was still a chance my goals were within my reach.

My economics professor in college said there was no such thing as a low-risk, high-reward investment. Had I just found it in Mateo?

He walked in from the kitchen with two more mugs and three small plates and forks. He set them on the coffee table and sat in the chair closest to me. "Now we feast."

He'd cut each pastry into three pieces, and he'd made an omelet, also cut into three pieces.

"Thank you, Mateo," Mom said. "You didn't have to do this."

"It's my pleasure." And he hit us both with the double-barreled blush and dimple combination.

Mom didn't say another word. I hoped she wasn't swooning the same way I was.

Eating the breakfast he'd conjured from my barren kitchen in less than ten minutes, I was sixty-six percent sure she was right. That Mateo was just the man I needed.

———

EARLY MONDAY MORNING, Mateo used one hand to pull his Jeep into the no-parking zone in front of the Synergy building. His other hand gripped mine.

He'd had his hands all over me, had hardly stopped touching me, all weekend. Well, since I'd pushed Mom out the door late Saturday morning. We'd gone to his place, and I'd stayed with him Saturday night. Although his bed was so much more spacious than mine, which didn't seem large enough for his giant frame, he slept snugged up behind me, his big hand wedged between my breasts like he owned them. Sunday night back at my place, I wasn't sure we'd slept much at all. I could see the bottom of my bowl of condoms.

If letting Mateo call me his girlfriend meant fabulous sex multiple times a day, I definitely saw the benefits of it. His growly *You're my girlfriend and I'm your man* would have made even Gloria Steinem's toes curl. I was one hundred percent on board the sex-with-Mateo train.

Even the annoying little voice—an echo of my mother's—had gone quiet. The voice that told me I had to earn affection and respect. That what Mateo offered me wasn't real, he couldn't really care about me, and I was a fool for letting him distract me from my goals. I'd packed that annoying voice into a box deep inside me.

The sex wasn't the only fantastic part of my weekend with Mateo. Saturday afternoon, when I told him I needed to go down to the building's basement to do laundry, he'd brought me to his place to do it using the machines in the guesthouse. He said he wanted to check in on Roger, but Ben would've done that. When the allergy meds I'd taken as a precaution made me so drowsy I'd fallen asleep on his couch, Mateo had folded my laundry much more carefully than I'd have done.

His voice broke me out of my rhapsody about crisply folded T-shirts. "Why do you always meet so early?"

"It's my fault, mostly. I work during the day, so we have to meet outside of work hours. Natalie sometimes has commitments in the evening, so we meet before work."

He nodded. "And why do you meet at Synergy?"

"A couple of reasons. The foundation doesn't have a physical location yet—"

"You mean Larissa hasn't gotten off her ass to choose one."

"That's not exactly fair. She's saving the foundation money on rent."

"That's my Mimi. Always so frugal."

"Frugal is a nice way of putting it. Ben calls me cheaper than the wine at Walmart."

"There's nothing cheap about you, mi tesoro." He leaned across the console to brush a kiss over my lips.

I shivered and kissed him back. I could really get used to this boyfriend thing.

Like he read the thought on my face, he grinned. But he said, "And the other thing?"

"What other thing?"

"The other reason you meet here, at Synergy."

"Oh. The free bagels."

"Now you've sold me. I'll walk you in like a good boyfriend and snag a bagel."

"Actually...would you mind not coming in?" I winced even as I said it, anticipating the hurt look on his face. I rushed on. "You've helped a lot with the gala, and I really appreciate it. We all appreciate it. And if you want a position at the foundation, I'll be happy to help once I get this job. But I need Larissa to see my work now. And you're kind of...distracting."

"Ah." He sat back, and his expression cleared. "Larissa is like a crow, attracted to new, shiny things. She doesn't appreciate the treasure already in her nest."

I wanted to tell him to stop referring to me as a treasure. Grown-ass women didn't get chills when men referred to them as something to be hoarded.

But I loved it.

"Thank you for understanding."

"Of course. Stay there, cariño. I'll get your bag and open the door."

He slipped out of the driver's seat, and I actually did it. I waited for him to open my door. Like some kind of princess or a red-carpet celebrity. Who was I, and where had independent, fuck-the-patriarchy Mimi gone?

Maybe she was in the box with that annoying voice.

He swung open my door, my laptop bag slung over his shoulder. He gripped my hand while I found the running board with my toes and hopped down to the pavement.

Mateo didn't just hand me my bag. No, he steadied me as I stepped onto the sidewalk. He tugged the sides of my coat together and leaned in to kiss my cheek.

"Can I see you tonight?" he whispered in my ear.

"I… Okay. You're not working?"

"I'm on the day shift this week. I'm off by seven. I can bring you dinner?"

"Or I could meet you at your place?" Mateo's giant bed was much more comfortable for the two of us.

He pulled his phone out of his pocket and tapped at the screen. A second later, my phone buzzed in my purse. "Why don't you go there right after work?"

I checked my phone. "Is that your door code?"

"I've seen you making eyes at the tub. Take a soak in it while you wait for me."

I may have fantasized about the giant tub, especially with the new ache between my legs. I'd pick up some bath salts on the way there. Stretching up on my tiptoes, I kissed him. "I'd like that."

"First the golf course and now in front of your place of work? Really, Miriam." A chilly voice froze the blood in my veins.

I plastered a bland smile on my lips and turned. "Good morning, Larissa."

"Morning, Miriam. Mateo."

I didn't miss how her voice turned silky-smooth when she said his name.

Mateo must not have missed it, either. His arms came around me, hauling me tight against his body. "Good morning, Larissa. How was your weekend?"

"Fine. Busy. You know, with all the gala planning."

My throat tightened. "Wait. I thought we arranged everything. You didn't need me to help?"

"No, no." She waved me off with her leather-gloved hand. "I took care of it. I only need you to make the reimbursements."

"But I would've been happy to help," I said.

"I did try to call you Saturday afternoon, but you didn't answer your phone."

Goddamned nap. I'd taken my eye off the ball for a second, and suddenly, Larissa didn't need me. My face burned, but I tried to keep my voice light. "Okay, I'll get the receipts from you inside."

"Mateo," Larissa's voice was saccharine-sweet. "Do you have time to join us? I could use your input on the decorations."

He squeezed my shoulders. "Sorry, I'm on my way to work."

"Too bad. We could really use your perspective."

"Mimi has a good perspective. I'm sure she can help."

Larissa's lip curled. "Miriam's good with numbers. Not aesthetics. How about I email her the choices, and she can show you later?"

"I guess we can look at them together?" He searched my face for the answer.

I stepped out of Mateo's grip. It was one thing for him to help me. It was something else for Larissa to rely on him instead of me. Yet another clue I wasn't her top candidate for the assistant director job.

Larissa confirmed it with her next words. "If only you had accounting experience, you'd be the complete package, Mateo. How about I text you the options? Then I'll call you tonight and we can discuss it?"

She had his number? I sucked in cold air through my nostrils. What. The. Hell. She needed his help and not mine, *and* he'd been talking to her behind my back? This was Byron all over again. The sharp pain in my chest was a signal I'd made the same mistake I'd made with him. Mateo was a distraction, and my dream of a paid position at the foundation was imploding right here on the sidewalk in front of my place of work. Despite what I'd promised myself, I'd caught some feelings along with the great sex.

That voice burst out of its box. *What have feelings ever done for you? Trust your smarts, drive, and confidence.*

I brushed my chilled hands together like I could dust the feelings off them. I focused on them and not Mateo's face. "You know what? I don't think I can make it tonight. I've got a lot to catch up on from the weekend."

"But—"

"I'll meet you inside, Larissa." I held out my hand for my bag, and after a brief hesitation, he handed it to me.

"Bye, Mateo."

"Mimi, wait."

I flung my hand into the air in a backwards wave and marched toward the building's entrance. I had work to do. Goals to achieve. And I wouldn't let Mateo or his endearments, his muscles, his superior lovemaking, or his five-star cooking get in my way.

Byron had made a fool of me once. I wasn't about to let it happen again.

24

MIMI

I WAS ALONE in my apartment that night finishing up the final budget for the gala when my laptop screen blinked to black. My hand automatically went to wiggle the cord, but it wasn't there. And in a flash of frustration, I realized where I'd left it.

Mateo's place.

I'd been working on my spreadsheets for the foundation on his couch late Saturday afternoon after my nap when he'd kissed the back of my neck. An innocent kiss at first, but then he'd trailed down my shoulder, and work was done for the day.

He only checked that I'd saved my work before he closed the screen, unplugged the cord that stretched across the couch, and then laid me down and given me the best oral of my life.

Second-best oral? Also Mateo. And third. He stood in triplicate on the Olympic podium of cunnilingus.

I had to memorialize him like that. Like Han Solo in carbonite, flash-frozen with his head between my thighs.

We couldn't keep going. Not when Larissa thought we were a couple and she could conscript Mateo into free labor whenever she wanted. When she actually wanted him instead of me.

I'd been ridiculous this morning when I'd thought Mateo was going behind my back to steal the assistant director position. He wasn't like Byron. He didn't want the position, and no matter how much Larissa liked him, he wasn't qualified. Jackson would never approve it.

But would I still be in the running for the job without Mateo's help?

Probably not. And that made my skin tingle in a way very unlike the way Mateo's oral did.

In a way that reminded me how I'd felt when the big bosses told me they'd given the promotion to Byron.

I stared at my reflection in my laptop's dead screen. I wanted the foundation job more than anything. But I wasn't acting like it. I'd let my performance lapse. Now, at least in Larissa's view, the best part of me was that I came as a package deal with Mateo. In a way, my mom was right about the benefits of having a helper.

But I didn't want that. I wanted to shine on my own. Not with Mateo's reflected light.

And there was only one way to do that, to prove that I deserved the job on my own merits.

I had to end it. The real relationship and the fake one.

A weight sank into my chest. He'd be hurt. Hell, I would, too. Those fledgling feelings of mine already cried out at the thought of what I was about to do.

Maybe we could still be friends. Though, after what we'd done together, how would that work?

In my reflection on the dark screen, the stubborn twist to my lips told me it wouldn't. Every time I saw him, I'd remember how kind, how gentle he'd been. How beautiful he'd made me feel.

I thumbed my phone awake and pulled up the photo. The one he'd taken of me in the pink-sequin dress. One of his enormous hands held my phone to capture us in the mirror, and the other splayed reverently across my ribs.

I hovered my thumb over the delete icon. I should really get rid of it. Toss it out along with these irritating feelings.

Instead, I swiped away the photo app. Someday I'd be strong enough to use it as a reminder of how I'd let my emotions lead me astray.

Someday in the far distant future. Like, when I was old and gray and driving a flying car.

For now, Mateo and I would go back to being acquaintances, stuck in Ben and Cooper's social circle, always a little too careful around each other.

I slammed my laptop shut so I didn't have to look at my lips curling down at that idea.

I picked up my phone. I could call Ben and ask him to bring me my charger. But that was the coward's way, and I was no coward. I'd suck it up, get back my cord, and break things off.

Levering off the couch, I changed my lounge pants for a pair of jeans and reluctantly strapped back into my bra. I wiggled into a black turtleneck. No more distracting neck-kisses.

The pink sequins winked at me from my closet. I had to pay Mateo back for the dress, too. He'd refused to take my money over the weekend, but since we wouldn't be dating anymore, I couldn't let that stand. I'd use a cash app to pay him. Then he couldn't refuse.

I tapped under my eyes with my cold fingertips to stop their prickling. It wouldn't do to show up with red eyes and a runny nose. He'd comfort me, and there would go my resolve. Sniffing, I focused on what I had to do. Get my charging cord from Mateo. Pay him back for the dress. Break up with him. If I looked at it as three items on a checklist, it wasn't so bad.

I pulled on a jacket and grabbed my purse and bus pass. I considered taking a car, but I needed the process of walking to the stop, flashing my pass. I needed the hard plastic seat, the bright interior lights, the suspicious stares of the other riders to keep me from dissolving into a puddle of emotions.

I brisk-walked to my stop, my shoulders hunched against the cold. Emotions. They were the last things I needed. Focus. Drive.

Cold-hearted purpose would get me what I wanted more than anything.

Which was the assistant director job.

And to get that, I needed my charger and an empty social schedule.

By the time I trudged up the hill to Cooper's mansion, I'd managed to box up my pesky emotions and shove them into a deep, dark corner of my heart. The chilly air froze the tears inside their ducts where they belonged.

I marched down the brightly lit drive and across the pavers to the guesthouse. I knocked on his door. It was well after seven, so he ought to be home. I spared not a thought for his proposal that I be waiting for him in his fancy jetted tub.

Okay, I spared one longing thought as the cold prickled on my cheeks.

When Mateo opened the door, a mouthwatering scent of meat and potatoes and spices wafted out. It curled into my nostrils and beckoned me inside.

Breathing through my mouth to resist the delicious aroma, I said to his chest, "Hi. Can I come in? I left my charger here this weekend."

Only then did I run my gaze from the center of his T-shirt up to his face, which welcomed me with a grin.

"Please," he said. "And stay for dinner. I made enough for two."

"No, thanks." I swallowed the saliva that had pooled when he'd said "dinner." I'd been too caught up in my spreadsheets after work to remember to eat. "Just the charger."

When he stepped aside, I slipped past him, trying not to breathe in his scent, to brush up against his warm, hard chest.

I looked for my charger but didn't see it plugged into the outlet where I remembered leaving it.

"I, ah, had to pick it up. Roger found it." He went to the built-in bookcase and plucked the coiled-up cord off a high shelf. He held it out to me, and sure enough, there were tiny kitten tooth-prints on the plastic cord.

I ran my fingers over the indentations. "Looks like he didn't manage to chew through it."

"No." He chuckled as he ran his hand through his hair, and I tried not to gape at his triceps. "I was glad not to come home to a fried kitty. He must have found something else to play with. He's figured out how to open drawers, you know."

"What has he gotten into?" I shoved the charger into my bag.

"Sock drawer. I fold them into balls, and, well, my bedroom looked like the outfield after batting practice."

I couldn't help it. I laughed. "Roger," I called. "Come here, you bad kitty."

His bell jingled, and he raced from the hall with the bedrooms. Standing on his hind legs, he sank his front claws into my jeans. I tucked my bag under my arm, scooped him up, and cradled him in my arms. I rubbed a finger against his cheek, and he purred. But when I remembered I needed to tell him good-bye, the warmth in my chest cooled.

"Your allergies," Mateo said. "Did you take your medicine?"

"No." Reluctantly, I set Roger on the floor. "I'm not staying long."

His plush lips turned down. "You're not?"

"No. This—this—" I squeezed my bag against my side. I'd checked off one item on my list; now it was time for another. "This isn't going to work out. You and me."

His chest lifted and then caved in, rounding his shoulders. "I know."

"You do?" Maybe this wasn't going to be as hard as I'd thought. Maybe he thought we were a mismatch, too. I ignored the sharp pang behind my breastbone.

"I always knew." But he didn't meet my gaze as he bent to pick up Roger and cuddled him against his chest.

His back to me, he curled his shoulders around the kitten and bent his head. And suddenly, he was a little boy, abandoned by his mother. A young man, standing alone beside his father's hospital bed. And now I was the one abandoning him.

"Mateo, I—" I touched his back, and when he flinched, I snatched my hand away.

Cold-hearted purpose. That's what I'd come here with. But the curve of his back melted it away.

Something stuck out from under his T-shirt sleeve. A bandage? Had he hurt himself? Without touching him, I plucked up his sleeve. A square patch stuck to the skin of his inner arm, lighter than his tan.

"A nicotine patch? You're quitting?"

His shoulders inched down. "Trying. For real this time."

I swallowed. "For me?"

"No." He turned to face me. "For me. For my health. But also...also for you." One side of his mouth tipped up into a sad half-smile.

He was quitting smoking, something he'd been doing for years, something that connected him with his father, just because I hated it. No one had ever made a life change like that for me. The words dried up in my throat. I patted down his sleeve and let my fingertips linger for a moment on the smooth patch.

He'd done nothing but try to help me. From the night at the bar, when he'd saved my drunk ass from potential sexual predators, to the foundation meeting, when he'd buttered up Larissa, to the meals he was always trying to get me to eat, he'd always worked for me. Never against me. Not like Byron. It wasn't his fault Larissa tried to take advantage of the obvious way he cared for me.

I trailed my hand over his hard pec and rested it on his breastbone where his kind heart beat. Roger nestled his tiny head against the side of my hand, fighting to be closer to that pulsing symbol of Mateo's gentle goodness.

"I'm sorry," I said. "Forgive me?"

"Of course. Though there's nothing to forgive. I under—"

"No." I stepped closer until we were toe to toe. "For what I said. I didn't mean it. Not really."

"You"—his eyebrows crashed together—"you don't want to break up?"

"No." Shit, I'd smashed his brittle heart. I didn't deserve his forgiveness. "Not unless you want to."

He stopped my words with a kiss, hard and demanding. I opened and let him in. Let him do what he wanted. I could give him that after my cruel words this morning and just now.

Roger gathered himself and leaped to the floor with an annoyed mewl. His hands free, Mateo banded his arms around me and pressed me to his chest. His heart thrummed frantically, unlike the slow, easy beat I'd fallen asleep to last night.

"I thought I'd lost you."

"I'm sorry," I mumbled into the soft cotton that stretched over his tripping heart. "I'm sorry."

"Food first, or…?"

"Or." I raked my fingernails down his back the way he liked. "Definitely or."

"Bedroom." He clasped my hand and led me there. On the way, I tossed my purse onto the couch.

Inside the bedroom, something hummed like he'd left the bathroom fan running. Mateo didn't so much as glance in that direction, all his focus on me. He walked backward until the backs of his knees hit the bed, then he tugged me to him. "Miriam," he breathed into my ear as he tugged my turtleneck up over my head.

After a brief, breathless struggle, I was free of it. He tossed it to the floor, where it landed next to something bright blue that rattled against the floor.

Before he descended onto my neck, I narrowed my eyes. "What's that?"

He palmed my breasts over my bra. "What?"

"That. On the floor." It was made of plastic or silicone, less than a foot long and a couple inches in diameter. One end of it tapered and the other flared out wide. It looked almost like a—

He gasped and leaped for it. "Nothing." He shoved it into the open drawer of the nightstand and slammed it shut.

"Are you sure?" Laughter bubbled up into my chest. "Because it sure looked like a—"

"Roger must have thought it was a toy. I mean, one of his toys. And—and—turned it on." He reached back into the drawer, and the humming ceased.

He didn't touch me. He'd gone cold and stiff.

"You know my brother is gay, right? Not that your sexuality needs my stamp of approval. But why didn't you tell me about your toys? I could have..." Even though it had stopped announcing itself, the dildo in the drawer pulled my focus to it.

"No, no, I wouldn't."

"Wouldn't what?" I propped my hands on my hips. "You wouldn't want to ask for what you want?"

"No, I..."

"Mateo." I reached past him and drew out the dildo. It was heavy in my hand, but I liked the way the curved base nestled into my palm. "Take off your clothes."

His eyes widened, and he licked his lips. Then, slowly, he reached behind his neck and pulled off his shirt. He dropped it on the floor next to mine. Then he paused.

I took a moment to admire his chest, muscled and lean. I ran one finger through the springy hair between his pecs. Goose-bumps rose on his skin. His fingers flexed at his sides, but he didn't move to touch me.

"Good boy." I leaned over and licked his nipple, then I sucked it into my mouth and gently bit down. Releasing it, I looked into his half-closed eyes from under my lashes. "I'm going to make you feel so good. Now, take off your pants."

While he wrestled off his jeans, I peered into the drawer and found a bottle of lube. I uncapped it and poured some into my palm to warm it. Butt stuff wasn't really my thing, or at least I'd never found a partner who'd given it to me in a way that rocked my world, but I'd had plenty of talks with Ben and knew the basics.

When Mateo was naked and standing beside the bed, I slicked the lube onto his erection, which went even harder as I caressed it. Slowly massaging him root to tip with one hand, I reached behind and slathered up his balls, too.

He groaned. "Feels good." His hands landed on my breasts, and they followed the fabric of my bra to the back clasps.

"Ah-ah," I said, squeezing the base of his dick. "Hands at your sides. I'm getting you off first."

His eyes widened. "But I—"

"Shh." I kissed him quiet as I continued the slow slide of my hands over his length. He'd always been so selfless in bed. I was so far in the red on orgasm count he should have repossessed my pussy. "Tonight is about you. Lie back."

He tugged down the covers then lay on the sheet, his erection curving up over his belly. I poured more lube into my hand. "Tell me if anything doesn't feel good, okay?"

He knew better than to protest again, especially while I fondled his balls. "Okay."

I kneeled between his legs, and he bent his knees. I trailed my finger down his taint to his hole and pressed it with the flat part of my thumb. He groaned. Okay, that sounded like a good sign.

Encouraged, I lubed up my thumb and eased it inside the tight ring. He gasped.

I stilled. "Did I hurt you?"

"No, mi vida. Feels fucking fantastic."

He loosened around my thumb, and I backed it out to slide two fingers inside. It felt different from my vagina, of course, but I tried a similar technique to what I liked, scissoring my fingers and feeling around for the bump of his prostate like Ben had described.

He stiffened, and I looked up to find the tendons in his neck corded. "Keep—keep going," he gasped before he let out a string of curses.

I did as he asked, adding my thumb next to my fingers' slow push and retreat. He squirmed, pushing back against my hand, trying to take more, but I had no more length to give.

"The—the toy. Please."

I reached for it on the nightstand and lubed it up. I flicked it on and held it against his hole.

He moaned. "Yesssss."

Gently, I inched it inside him while he gasped and trembled. "Still good?"

"So good."

My skin tingled with a flush of warmth. I was almost as turned on as he was. My pulse throbbed between my legs, aching for the hard cock in my hand. Later. I'd have him later. Now, I needed to show him that he deserved my attention, my desire. How I cared for him.

I nudged the tip of the dildo toward the spot I remembered from before. When his chest stopped heaving and his balls tightened, I knew I'd found it. I buzzed the spot for a few seconds, then eased off. I returned to it again and again until he gasped, "Mimi, I—"

His dick hardened under my other hand. Knowing I'd pleased him, aroused him, made him lose control, I hummed, and my heart kicked into a faster rhythm. My skin buzzed with the power to make this man, the one I cared about, happy.

Keeping the buzz going inside him, I jacked him slowly, echoing the pulsing in my pussy. I tucked my heel against the seam of my jeans, trying to relieve my own building pleasure.

Finally, he shouted, and his release splattered across his chest. I kept the tip of the toy where it was, and his come—well, it kept coming. Longer than I thought possible. His knees trembled beside me.

I'd done that for him. My cheeks stretched with my grin. I was a sex goddess. Admiring his body, wracked with pleasure, was almost as good as preening over one of my perfect spreadsheet formulas.

Finally, his hoarse shout downshifted to a long groan, and I clicked off the vibe. His cock gave one last twitch, and his legs flopped out to either side. Slowly, I eased the dildo out of him.

"Don't move. I'll be right back." I gave him a soft, lingering kiss and then went to the bathroom where I washed my hands and the toy. I returned with the damp hand towel and wiped off his chest.

"C'mere," he murmured, sounding sex-drunk.

I tossed the towel onto the floor and snuggled in next to him, still in my jeans and bra. I kissed his neck, then his stubbled chin. "Good?"

His arms banded around me, tugging me right up against his warm chest. "Perfect. Just let me rest a minute and then—"

"Then we'll eat. And then I'll take a turn with the toy. You rest."

It was the least I could do. To return a bit of the care he'd given me.

25

MATEO

I'D PLANNED to wake her up before I left for my seven o'clock shift at tía's, but when my alarm went off, Mimi froze, Scooby Doo–style, in mid-tiptoe toward her jeans on the floor.

"Morning," I mumbled, rolling over to turn on the lamp. We both blinked in the sudden light. "Do you have an early meeting today?"

"No, we're meeting tonight." She tugged on her jeans. "Now that the gala is two weeks away, we're meeting every day. I need to finish up the foundation statements I was working on last night before I go to work."

"And you do all this for free." I'd meant it to come out light and joking, but my words were flat. Mimi deserved so much more than to run from her full-time job to a second part-time job. She deserved more than Larissa's mean-girl veneer of sweetness that hid the foul scorn beneath. She deserved to be loved and appreciated. And paid for her work.

"I do it for the kids. And for the assistant director position."

I couldn't help it. The words exploded out of me. "Why would you want to be Larissa's assistant?"

She didn't say anything for a minute, reaching for her turtle-neck and tugging it over her head. "I want to be paid for what I love to do."

"Do you love to work for Larissa? Honestly?"

Her lower lip poked out, sexy and stubborn. "Larissa is driven, like me. I wish I had a career like hers. But what's more important, I love to help kids, especially those with Tourette's and other neurological differences. I support the foundation's mission."

"There are tons of foundations that help kids. Cooper contributes to several. He could get you a job, a paid one, at any of them."

"You mean you could." She put her hands on her hips.

I wished I wasn't naked so I could— Fuck it. I leaped out of bed and marched around it until I faced her. I didn't go toe-to-toe with her—I didn't want to intimidate her—but I propped my hands on my hips to show her I was serious. "I could."

Her gaze dropped from my face to my groin. Quickly, she ripped her eyes away and stormed out of the bedroom, a Valkyrie no less fearsome for her small size.

I followed. "Mimi, wait."

She snatched her purse off the couch. "Mateo, I want to do this myself. I got this volunteer position, and I want to earn the assistant director role. I don't want anything handed to me."

"Ah." Pride warmed my chest. My Mimi could do anything she set her mind to, and she wanted to prove that to the world. Who wouldn't admire this amazing woman?

Larissa. That's who.

"Mimi, you are a treasure. Everyone sees that. But Larissa wants to take your golden shine and tarnish it. She'll never give you that job. Don't you see that?"

She paused, her purse slung over her shoulder. "Larissa's achieved what I could only wish to do. She might be cold, but she's fair. She's difficult to please, but she'll consider me along with the other candidates, and if I'm the strongest, she'll hire me."

"Even if she does, she'll keep you down. Take credit for your work. You can't want that, can you?"

"Oh, that's funny." Her bark of a laugh had no humor in it. "Coming from you, always in your cousin's shadow. Living in his guesthouse. Working security." Her lips twisted like she wanted to take it back.

It was too late. She'd spoken her truth. Run me through with it, like my father's razor-sharp plug cutter.

She didn't respect me. She was no different from the people back on the island who liked me for my pretty face and the way I gave head. And I was no different from the randos she kept that bowlful of condoms for.

My words came out quiet through the needle-sized opening in my throat. "That's what you think of me."

She winced. "Not—Mateo, I…"

"So going to the gala with me, all this"—I gestured at my naked body—"was for show. To get you the assistant director job. What was going to happen after the gala?"

Her lips tightened, and I knew.

"You were going to dump me. After you pranced me out like a pony in a tux for Larissa, you were going to ghost me."

She said nothing.

I stalked around her to the front door and flung it open, not caring that my father's gold ring was the only thing I wore. She'd ripped my heart out of my chest, shredded it, and then stomped on the pieces. If I were smart like Cooper, I'd have seen it coming. Mimi was shiny, precious, vivacious. Too fine for someone like me to keep.

I held the door open, my anger burning so hot I didn't feel the winter chill. "I'll consider myself already dumped. Tell Larissa whatever you want, but I can't"—my voice cracked, and I had to clear my throat—"I can't do this anymore. You want to do this on your own. You don't need me. You don't want me."

She peered up at me through her lashes, standing close enough that I could have twisted one of her rogue curls around my finger, that I could have leaned down and kissed those stubborn, pouting lips.

"I'm sorry," she whispered.

I could have taken it back then, said I'd go with her to the gala. But I loved this woman, and now I had to stop. Seeing her looking gorgeous in that rose-gold gown when I knew she'd never be mine would torch the ruined sludge she'd left of my heart.

I should have learned weeks ago, when the alcohol and her hangover had scrubbed away her memory of me and our connection at the bar that night. I was forgettable, and I'd never be good enough for her.

"Go," I said.

She went.

Fool that I was, I watched her walk across the motorcourt toward the street.

Fuck.

"Mimi!" I called.

She turned.

"You didn't drive here, did you?"

"No, I took the bus. I'll catch it back home."

The bus? This proud woman would be the death of me. Already had been. "No, you won't. Give me one minute to put on some clothes, and I'll drive you."

"No, I—"

"Thirty seconds." If she stubbornly kept walking, I'd catch up to her before she made it to the bus stop. Where the fuck was there a bus stop in Pacific Heights? How long had she walked to get here last night in the dark?

I sprinted to my bedroom and threw on jeans and a shirt. Not sparing time to brush my teeth, I grabbed my toothbrush so I could take care of it at my tía's and jogged out to my Jeep. Mimi had the sense to be standing beside it.

Silently, I unlocked it, and just as silently, she got in.

I might be frosted over with anger, but I was no monster. Even the woman who'd used me to advance herself at work and then broken my heart deserved a safe, warm ride home.

Who was I kidding? She deserved so much more than a safe ride home. More than the fucking assistant job under Larissa.

She deserved plenty more than me.

26

MIMI

Me: U up for drinks tonight?

I WINCED as I hit send, then I shoved my phone face-down on my desk like that could erase my pathetic cry for help.

Bree was probably busy doing couple things with Josh tonight. And I shouldn't need her support. I'd ended a fake relationship. There were no actual feelings in a fake relationship. I was fine.

That was a lie. Actually, two lies.

Guilt squeezed my heart. I'd never meant for Mateo to develop real feelings. But the pain in his eyes, the way his voice broke when he'd told me he couldn't keep pretending, had cracked through me like lightning and split open my shriveled, black heart.

Though guilt had never felt like this, so crushing, like Thanos's fist.

Was it only guilt? I mean, sure, I cared about Mateo, but I hadn't actually loved him.

Had I?

My monitor blinked to black, and I hurried to move the mouse to wake it up again. I was supposed to be working. There was no space for emotions at work.

Hands-down, that was the best part of work. Being busy. Checking things off my list. Focusing on the black digits on my white spreadsheet.

I stared blearily at my screen. What had I been doing, again?

Relief tingled through me when my phone buzzed.

Bree: YES! Raisa's at 6?

                                           Me: C U then

"Mimi." Monique's voice behind me made me drop my phone. I whirled in my chair to face my boss. "Hey. What's up?"

"Have you finished those journal entries?"

My cheeks flamed. I'd been staring into space for at least ten minutes before I'd texted Bree. I couldn't afford to do that so close to month-end.

"Sorry. Just another twenty minutes or so. I'll send you a message when they're done."

Her forehead creased. "Are you all right, Mimi? You seem…off."

"I'm fine." I tried to give her a reassuring smile, but my face didn't seem to be working.

"I talked to Jackson. He said you've been burning the candle at both ends helping him with his foundation."

She'd talked to Jackson Jones about me? Shit, did that mean she was disappointed with my performance? Was I about to lose my boring-but-stable job?

"It's fine. I'm handling it."

"Mimi." She stepped further into my cube and lowered her voice. "I know you're handling it. You're a superstar in this department. But I worry that you're trying to do too much between Synergy and the foundation. You'll burn out."

My heart tripped in my chest. "No. I'm good. Synergy is my

top priority, and month-end is on track. The gala is in two weeks, and after that, I promise I'll have more time to spend at work."

"That's not what I'm saying, Mimi. I'm saying you need to take care of yourself. Or find someone to do it for you. Like that handsome security guard you were talking to the other day." She winked.

I knew she meant to be friendly, but her words stabbed like a sharpened pencil into the raw, cut-open part of me that had opened up when Mateo had shivered, naked in the doorway of his guesthouse, and told me to go.

"I can take care of myself. And I'll get those journal entries done and over to you in fifteen. Okay?"

She pressed her lips together. Her lipstick was blue today. Like Mateo's eyes.

Crap. I needed to scour those silly details about Mateo out of my brain. Tequila would help.

"Okay. But I don't want to see you here after five o'clock tonight. You hear me?"

"I understand. Thanks, boss."

She nodded and left my cube.

———

"WANT ANOTHER?" Bree drained the last dregs of her margarita and looked over her shoulder for our server.

Did I ever. After unloading the whole humiliating story of my fake relationship and very real breakup onto my best friend, all I wanted to do was drink tequila until I couldn't feel the emptiness.

But tomorrow was a workday, and I didn't have Mateo sitting across the bar from me, ready to swoop in and rescue me when I needed it.

"No. Thanks." My eyes prickled, and I rolled them up to the ceiling. A string of crimson paper hearts stretched from the pendant light above us to the one at the next booth.

Bree turned around just in time to see me swipe under my eye.

"Oh, no, babe. Don't let him make you cry."

"I'm not crying." Shit, now I was lying to Bree. And crying. I didn't cry. Not even when Byron broke my heart and destroyed my career in a single dick move. What the hell was wrong with me?

She patted my hand. "There are plenty of guys out there, and one of them is going to be the kind you need."

"That's the thing." I pointed at her. Shit, was I already drunk? I only pointed at people when I was buzzed. I slapped my hand on the table. "I don't need a guy at all. All I need is myself and my work."

"Sure, sure." She licked a few grains of salt off the rim of her glass. "You're, like, a superhero. An Amazon. Like Wonder Woman. Though, wait. Wonder Woman pined over Steve Trevor. Don't do that. Be like…like Valkyrie. All she needed was some ale. Am I right?"

The server set down another margarita for her and a glass of water for me. I smiled at her and then lifted the water in the air. "To independence."

Bree clinked it with her margarita glass. "Though didn't Valkyrie get a love interest in one of those movies?"

"Yeah. Somehow, Hollywood doesn't find women who aren't into love sexy."

"But you"—she waved her glass, and margarita splashed onto the table—"you're sexy. And it's okay not to be into relationships. Hookups are sexy."

"Hookups are great. All the pleasure, none of the baggage." Though none of my hookups had given me as much pleasure as Mateo had. I'd just have to try harder next time. Which wouldn't be for a long time. A long, long, long time. My eyes prickled again.

"Hey, hey." Bree clasped my hand across the sticky table. "It's okay. Come over this weekend and hang with Josh and me. We'll do an Avengers movie marathon and drink every time something explodes. Okay?"

"How about Saturday night? I have to do gala stuff most of the weekend, but I should have a break then."

"Yay! It'll be just like when we were in college. We'll get shit-faced and fall asleep on the couch."

Huh. That didn't sound nearly as fun as it used to. I guessed a lot of things were different now that we were thirty. Being a responsible adult sucked.

"Come on. Let's call Josh to pick you up."

"What about you?"

"I'll get a rideshare." Back to my lonely apartment.

If I weren't so allergic, I'd get a cat.

Maybe I'd get a cat anyway. The allergy meds would make me sleepy, and when I was asleep, I didn't feel the ache in my chest.

————

THE TEXT CAME as I waited for Natalie after work at the country club where we were supposed to walk through the space with the decorator, a week before the gala.

Ben: When can I see you?

I pulled up the calendar on my phone. There were no blank spaces between now and the gala.

Me: After the gala?

Ben: That's a week away. I need to see you before then.

Me: Why? Is something wrong?

While I waited for him to type his response, my mind raced. Had something happened to him or Cooper? Or Mom and Dad? After that miserable night at the bar with Bree, I'd kept myself so busy—it was my first Mateo-free week since December—that I hadn't called or texted any of them.

Ben: I don't know. You tell me.

I gritted my teeth. That was my little brother, always sticking his nose into my business. I looked up and saw Natalie approaching from the parking lot. Quickly, I ended the text.

Me: I'm good.

And why wouldn't I be? The gala was almost here, and I'd know soon after that if I was going to get the assistant director job. Everything I wanted was within reach. All I had to do was work my ass off to ensure the gala went off without a hitch.

Last week's wallowing at Raisa's with Bree was a one-off. PMS. Mercury in retrograde.

"Hey, friend!" Natalie bustled in, looking perfect as always in a spotless oyster-pink wool coat, a charcoal gray sheath dress, and knee-high boots that made her tower over me as she bent down to hug me.

"Hey." I hugged her back. Before the gala planning, I'd never have thought someone as elegant and well-connected as Natalie would call me a friend.

Her brother Andrew sauntered up behind her, a golf bag over his shoulder. "Hey, Mimi. Good to see you again."

"Hi, Andrew." I shook his hand. Natalie seemed to drag him everywhere with her. Was it a rich-people thing? I mean, yes, Ben had lived with me for a while, and we did things together, but he'd never come with me to a foundation planning activity.

"Is Mateo here?" he asked.

Pain sliced through my chest. "No, not today."

"Too bad. I liked hanging out with him the night we went dancing."

I gave him a weak smile. So had I.

"I'll let you ladies get to it. Nat, come find me out on the range when you're done." Andrew jerked his thumb behind him at the corridor I remembered from the night I'd come here with Mateo.

He'd told that ridiculous story about me being his kryptonite. He'd put his hands on me, adjusting my grip on the club, and I'd practically swooned.

"Go play," Natalie said. When he'd walked off, she turned to me. "Gail's right behind me. She just needed to get some things out of her car. Larissa's running late and says to start without her. Where's Mateo?"

"Not coming. But I'm ready to start." I turned toward the ballroom.

Natalie held my arm. "Oh, no. You guys are fighting?"

"Something like that." Over the course of the gala planning, we'd gotten closer. I wouldn't have minded telling her, but my throat tightened up, and if his name crossed my lips, tears would flow.

There were no tears when a job was on the line. Mom had taught me that.

"Let's get down to business." I pivoted toward the ballroom and took a deep breath.

"Mimi, wait."

I paused and turned back.

Natalie's eyes creased with concern. "Are you okay?"

"Of course. I'm fine." My voice only cracked a little.

"You know you can talk to me, right? We're friends."

When I curled my lips up into a smile, my face felt rusty like the Tin Man's in *The Wizard of Oz*. How long had it been since I'd smiled?

I'd guess about a week.

But I had business to attend to. Foundation work, like my real job, was safely unemotional. "Hey, actually, I do have a question for you. I emailed our original venue to see if we could get the deposit back—I figured it wouldn't hurt to ask—and they said they never received our deposit. I checked the receipt book, and I found a copy of the cash receipt I wrote out to Larissa for it. Did she say anything to you about it?"

Natalie's eyes narrowed. "No. That sounds suspicious."

"Wait, no, I wasn't saying I suspected Larissa of any wrongdoing. She's notorious for losing receipts. But I've never known her to misplace cash. Maybe she gave it to the caterer instead? Or the florist?"

"Not that I know of. Didn't you give them checks?"

"I did. But I was hoping…" I was hoping I wouldn't have to ask Larissa about it. She'd take it as an accusation for sure, and then I'd never get that job. I bit my lip and glanced away from Natalie. A familiar tall, blond figure sauntering through the lobby caught my gaze.

"Flavio?"

He turned and cocked his head like he was searching through his mental files for my name.

"Miriam Levy-Walters," I said. "I work with Larissa at the foundation. We met a few weeks ago on the driving range."

"Ah, good to see you again." His lazy gaze trailed off me and sharpened when it snagged on Natalie's pearl necklace and earrings and trailed all the way down to her designer shoes. "Do you also work at the foundation?"

"Natalie Jones." She stuck out her hand. "And no, I'm just helping with the gala."

"Natalie Jones of the Jasper Jones family?"

I remembered that her father died years ago. She had to have been young when she lost him.

Her smile tightened. "That's the one."

He didn't release her hand. "I'd love to talk with you later. I think our families can help each other out. Come to the bistro when you're done? My treat."

Natalie peeled her hand out of his grasp. "Sorry, I have an engagement. Another time, perhaps."

He slipped a card out of his pocket. It looked like a personal one, just his name and phone number. He handed it to her. "Call me. Or come find me here. Anytime."

She took the card and gave him a strained smile. "Nice meeting you, Flavio. We've got to get to work."

"Sure, sure." He glanced at Gail, the decorator, who hurried toward us with her giant tote bags. "If you need anything at all, let me know." He nodded at the card.

When he'd swaggered off toward the hall that led to the driving range, I said, "That's weird, right? That he'd want us to call him if we need anything?"

Natalie tossed the card into the umbrella stand. Her face was stiffer than I'd ever seen it. "It's the Jones name. It happens all the time."

It still seemed odd to me. After all, what could a golfer like Flavio do if we ran into issues? Maybe he was richer and more powerful than I thought, and the staff would jump to do his bidding. Did he come from a family like Natalie's?

I had no more time to wonder because Gail herded us into the ballroom to talk about roses and potted palms and twinkle lights.

As she pointed out where she planned to place the decorations —the ones Mateo had suggested to go with our theme—as Natalie and Gail looked at me like I could speak for Mateo and give them his opinion, the crack I'd put in my own heart when I'd pushed him away that morning at his place widened into a ravine.

Over the past week, I'd kept myself busy with work and the gala so I wouldn't have to think about him. So I'd have no time for regret.

Regret was a distraction, just like Mateo. I couldn't afford that nonsense. Not only did I have work to do for Synergy, for Monique, who'd noticed me slipping, but I had a gala to put on. And a full-time, paid job to earn. I needed to focus on what mattered.

Helping neurodivergent kids mattered. My career mattered.

My feelings were irrelevant.

I just needed to convince my cracked-open heart.

27

MATEO

"OH." I stopped at the door to Miguelito's normally empty workout room. It wasn't unoccupied today.

My cousin grunted at me from the leg press. Sweat darkened the neckline and underarms of his gray tank and dripped down his square jaw. His arm and leg muscles weren't as big or defined as mine, but I put in double the time in the gym since my job was to look intimidating. At his job, he intimidated his opponents through his superior smarts.

Early mornings, he always worked out at the gym at the office. Even though he had a better gym in his house.

I knew why he liked to work out at the office. Boy-scout Cooper Fallon wanted to set a positive example of fitness for his employees. He wouldn't require them to exercise; no, he just went in every weekday, did his workout, complimented them on their form, and then carried on with his day on the sixth floor.

I didn't need that role-model shit. Not from him. Not today.

Today was day ten of my post-Mimi life, and I was still enjoying being pissed-off and grouchy and alone.

I dropped my bag on the floor, then stripped off my hoodie

and flung it on top. I stalked to the mat and started a set of burpees.

While I warmed up, I didn't think about the appreciative way Mimi used to trace the outlines of my muscles. I didn't think about how I'd used my upper body strength to support my weight while I'd surged over her, driving into her the way she liked. And I definitely didn't think about how she'd appreciated my body right up to the point she decided she wanted someone with a brain, someone who could figure out her complicated rules about achieving her goals on her own when all I wanted to do was help her.

That someone definitely wasn't me.

When I finished the set, I walked in a circle to slow my heart rate. I wiped sweat from my forehead.

Exercise was easier since I'd stopped smoking. My heart rate was lower. I breathed deeper. It all irritated me. Not quite enough to take up smoking again, but I wished Mimi hadn't changed my life. I already spent too much time agonizing over the photo of us on my phone, the one where she wore the sequined dress and I kissed her neck, a look of blissed-out contentment on her face. I didn't need another reminder blinking on my fitness watch.

"Something you want to talk about?"

I hadn't realized Miguelito's machine had stilled until he spoke. He leaned forward, elbows on his thighs.

"Nah, I'm good." My muscles were warm and ready, and I glanced at the weight rack.

"Go ahead. Load it up. I'll spot you."

"But you—you've got to go to work. I'll just use the machine." I waved at his fancy chest press.

"I'm going in a little later today. It's fine." He stood and walked to the weight rack.

I hated wasting his valuable workout time arguing, so I did as he asked. I loaded the weights onto the bar, then I faced it, curled my hands over the bar, and lifted it from the rack while my cousin stood beside me, arms crossed.

Starting my reps, I bent my knees then pressed the weight up until my arms were straight. I lowered it until it hovered above my aching heart.

"Primo"—I almost dropped the weight; he hadn't called me that since we were kids—"are you, ah, happy?"

"What the fuck, Lito? We don't talk about that shit." I pressed up again.

"We used to. We used to talk about a lot of shit back when we were teenagers and Mamá and I visited the island. Guys. Girls. Hopes and dreams."

I snorted. "Yeah. You actually achieved your hopes and dreams. And here I am, working as—" I froze, my arms extended, until they trembled. I lowered the bar onto the rack and blinked at his stony face. "I mean, I like working for you. I didn't mean—"

"Do you really? Like working for me?"

"I do." I shook out my trembling arms. "I love watching out for tía. Making sure she's safe. I feel...useful."

"You don't want more?" He cocked his head. "A more impressive title? Or more education so you can get an office job?"

"An office job?" I shuddered. School had been hard enough. I couldn't imagine sitting at a desk hunched over a computer keyboard every day. "Why would I want that?"

"To"—his eyes darted to the open door of the workout room—"to impress Mimi?"

"Oh. Is that what Ben says she wants? Some guy who'll make bank and look good in a suit? Someone who's not an idiot?" I knew it was true, but it rubbed me raw that she'd talked with her brother about it. And that her brother had told my cousin.

Miguelito rolled his eyes. "I'm paying you pretty well, and you know you look amazing in a suit. Plus, you're smart."

"Fuck you and your charity. You know you only hired me because your mother made you." So I wouldn't have to look into his mocking face, I walked to my bag and plucked out my water bottle. I took a long swig.

He shoved my shoulder, and my water went everywhere. Into

my eyes, down my shirt, onto the spotless floor. Fucking ninja had snuck up on me. I wiped the water from my face. "What the hell, Lito?"

"What the fuck are you talking about? If you weren't smart, do you think I'd have put you in charge of my security? Of my own mother?"

"Well, I—"

"No, Mateo, I wouldn't. I didn't hire you because Mamá told me to. She didn't. She'd prefer it if she didn't have a security detail at all. I didn't hire you because you're my cousin. I hired you because you're competent and because I—because I trust you."

I gaped at my cousin. "You trust me? But you background-checked me!"

"You have to admit you weren't the most trustworthy person when we were kids. You used to steal my dates. And at first, I didn't trust you not to make a move on Ben. But now I do. You've developed some integrity since then."

"Developed integrity?" I yelped. "I always had fucking integrity. It was your dates who didn't. None of them were good enough for you. If they were, they would've shut me down when I flirted with them. None of them did. Not until Ben."

He propped his hands on his hips. "Be that as it may, you've proved again and again that you deserve my respect. And that's why I hired you. But if you'd rather have a different job, we can work that out. I want you to be happy, primo."

And we were back where we started. At least I knew what he was talking about now. "I'm happy working for you. Protecting your mom. I'll let you know if that changes, okay?"

"Okay."

He just stood there with his hands on his hips, like we hadn't had a major breakthrough. My cousin had a brilliant brain, but his heart was sometimes slow on the uptake.

"Bring it in, primo."

He wrinkled his nose. "We're both sweaty, and you're soaked."

"Exactly." So I wrapped my arms around him in a bear hug, which was exactly what we both needed after a moment like that.

"Enough!" But when he stepped back, a smile teased at the corners of his mouth. His gaze flicked to the open door behind me, and he lowered his voice. "So what are you going to do about Mimi?"

The sunshine I'd swallowed when Lito told me he respected me faded to dense black like the fog rolling in at night.

"Nothing. I'm not doing a thing about Mimi. She's made her choice clear. She wants that job at the foundation, and dating me was only a show. She doesn't want me to be part of her life."

"But—"

"No, Lito. This isn't something you can fix with a kind word or even a bucket of cash. Mimi and I split up, and it's what's best for her."

"What about what's best for you?"

"What's best for Mimi is best for me, too. I love her, and knowing she's happier without me…" It would have to keep my stupid-healthy heart beating for the rest of my life. "It's for the best."

"Okay." He frowned. "But you deserve love and happiness, too. Maybe Mimi isn't your person. But that doesn't mean the right person isn't out there for you."

He cleared his throat. "I thought someone I loved was it for me. And if I couldn't have him, I didn't want anyone. I'm glad Ben was able to push past all that. Because I'm happier now with Ben than I've ever been. Than I'd have been even if…even if that other person could have loved me back."

I couldn't imagine him loving anyone other than Ben. Though when he'd come to the island, before Ben had chased him there, he'd been a disaster. Had that other person broken his heart? The fucker.

"Someone is going to love you like that one day." He put his hand on my arm. "I know they will."

I mumbled down at my sneakers, "Maybe it's not worth it."

"Of course it's worth it. That's what I'm telling you."

"I get"—I swallowed to lubricate my dry throat—"I get that the love part is great. I loved Mimi, and I thought she cared about me. And it was perfect. But then she left me. People are always leaving me." I stopped when my voice broke.

"Ah, fuck, Mateo." And this time, he reeled me in for a tight hug. "Not everyone's like your mom. And your papi would've stayed if he could. I'm not saying you can have your person forever. But isn't love—even briefly—worth it?"

I nodded. Short as our time together had been, Mimi was the best thing that had ever happened to me. The memories of our weeks together would forever light up my memory in rose gold like the sunset over the beach.

Gently, I disentangled from his embrace. "Thanks, man."

"Anytime. Though, ah, if you want actual good advice about love, Ben's probably the better man for it."

I smiled to hide the pain that pricked from my battered heart. I couldn't talk to Ben. Not about his sister. Probably not about anything at all since he reminded me too much of her.

"I think I need some time before I think about falling for anyone else."

"Got it. You'll be okay, though?"

My smile was more stable this time. "Yeah. I think so."

"Good. I've got to go shower. I'm running late." He was out the door in a flash.

Running late? He'd said he wasn't in a hurry to get to the office.

Goddammit. I wiped the wetness that wasn't sweat from my cheeks. My fucking primo had ambushed me with his encouragement and made himself late for work.

I glanced at my watch. If I didn't hurry, I'd be late to my shift. And he hadn't said a word.

I loved that fucking asshole.

28

MIMI

BEING at the country club without Mateo last week was nothing compared to walking into the gala alone on Valentine's Day.

I had no gentle giant to hide behind as I stepped into the country club's ballroom on the too-high heels Ben had helped me pick out, in the way-too-sparkly rose-gold sequins, with my too-generous boobs too close to popping out of the wrap-style gown.

And I could have used his sturdy support tonight, especially with the printouts in my clutch. I gripped the papers, wishing I didn't have to ask Larissa about the foundation's rainy-day account that had been emptied last night.

Most people wouldn't have even known about the rainy-day account. I checked the balance once a month when I updated the balance sheet. But after a few weird transactions I'd had to ask Larissa to explain, I'd set up an alert on it.

The oddest thing about it was the deposit in my PayMo account that matched it. I'd reversed the deposit, but something funny was going on. I had to find the courage to ask Larissa about it tonight. And tact so it didn't sound like an accusation. Not a good look from someone who wanted her to hire me.

But if I didn't straighten this out, it would look like I'd embez-
zled from the foundation. That would be hard to explain to the
state board when I went to renew my CPA credential.

With all that hanging over me, I'd considered armoring myself
in a pantsuit or even asking Ben to help me find a different dress,
definitely in fade-into-the-background black. But the bright
sequins buoyed me like I still had Mateo's strength beside me.
And, despite what I'd told him, I needed that.

Natalie loved the dress. I'd sent her a photo of it—the G-rated
one, not the one Mateo had taken with his hands splayed across
my breasts and hips and his lips at my neck. She'd been texting
me daily with questions about the gala even though she could've
planned the event in her sleep. I saw through her ruse and loved
her for it. She worried about me, thinking Mateo and I had fought.
Little did she know.

All my attempts to scrub him from my life had failed.
Although I'd washed them four times, my sheets still carried his
scent. Every time I got a whiff of cigarette smoke, I thought of him
and wondered if he'd been able to quit for good.

And here I was, wearing the dress he'd chosen for me. When
I'd tried it on, he couldn't keep his hands off my skin, my hips,
even the curve of my belly.

Despite the gown's long sleeves, I shivered.

Maybe I was coming down with something.

"Mimi!" Natalie strode to me, so sophisticated with her long
legs and elegantly flowing wine-red gown. Even though the cowl
neck swooped practically to her navel, her better-behaved boobs
stayed hidden under the silk. "You look fabulous!" She grasped
my shoulders in a half-hug, careful not to crush the carefully
arranged drape, and air-kissed me so we wouldn't spoil our
lipstick.

"Thanks. You're stunning, as usual."

"Thank you." She flipped her blond hair to the side and
looked over my shoulder. "Where's Mateo?"

I didn't want to give Larissa another strike against me, so I'd been careful not to mention our breakup during our gala meetings. I'd prove to her I could stand on my own, even wearing a boob-revealing gown at a gala where I felt like I'd peeled off my skin to let everyone gawk at the muscles and tendons beneath.

"He couldn't make it." I gave Natalie a tight smile.

Her smile drooped. "Oh, no. I hoped you two would work it out."

There was no point in lying to her anymore. "Honestly? We were never together. It was all fake. Though I'd rather you didn't tell Larissa. She doesn't need another thing to criticize me for."

"Wait, what?" She scrunched her nose. "Fake?"

Revealing the lie felt like I'd taken off a forty-pound backpack. I breathed as deep as my shapewear would allow.

"We were just friends. Well, not even that." Friends would've called each other in the two weeks since our fight at his place. "He was helping me out because Larissa said I needed to bring a date to the gala. And then things got out of control when he became part of the committee."

She winced. "Sorry, that might've been my bad. Though it didn't look fake. Especially that night we went dancing." She gave me a piercing stare that was oddly reminiscent of the look her brother Jackson had given my dead laptop. Like she could fix me, too.

"Well, it was. Fake. At first. Then it was less fake and..." And the ten days it had been real had been the best of my life. I hated to admit it, but I missed what we had. Though I couldn't say that. Tonight, I had to be Wonder Woman, a boss bitch who was killing it at her volunteer job. Not a sad, lovelorn sack like Barbara Minerva before she transformed into Cheetah.

Lovelorn? No, I wasn't lovelorn.

Was I?

I squared my shoulders. After a quick glance to ensure the girls were behaving, I said, "We're not together anymore, and I'm not planning to see him again except when I have to for family things."

Her kind brown eyes went so soft my own eyes prickled. "I'm so sorry. Are you all right?"

"I'm fine." That lie dripped easily from my tongue. I'd been lying to myself about it for two weeks.

She squeezed my arm. "Let's go find a drink and relax. You can tell me all about it. Or not, whatever feels better for you."

"I'd rather...not, I think."

"That's fine. Regardless, we've worked our asses off. We deserve a drink."

We turned to face the crowd of early arrivers gathering around the high-top tables in front of the bachata band, who were setting up on stage. Which one of the men was Mateo's coworker? If Mateo were here, he could've pointed him out. Introduced us at a break in the music.

But he wasn't here. Neither to shield me nor to ease the conversation.

I missed him. Not for the hundred little things he'd done for me. For himself. I missed turning to him when I thought something was funny to see if he laughed, too. Touching him and feeling him shiver with pleasure. Swaying to the music together, trusting that he wouldn't let us falter as long as I kept moving my feet.

Shit. Had I fallen for the big lug?

Natalie clutched my hand. "What's the matter? You went pale all of a sudden."

"Nothing, I..." But I had an excuse not to finish. I nodded at the older version of Natalie who sailed toward us. She wore a cranberry-red beaded gown and towed a tuxedoed Black man with close-cropped hair graying at his temples.

"Natalie."

"Mother." Natalie straightened. Her caring, concerned expression blanked, and a sardonic smile lifted one corner of her mouth. She turned and air-kissed her mother.

"Introduce us to your friend," the woman commanded.

"Mother, Charles, this is Miriam Levy-Walters, the volunteer treasurer for the foundation. Her brother is Ben Levy-Walters, whom you would have met at Ben and Cooper's engagement party in December. Mimi, this is my mother, Audrey Jones Hayes, and my stepfather, Charles Hayes."

"Nice to meet you," I said. Everything about Mrs. Hayes said *expensive*. Her royal confidence made me wonder if I should curtsy. Or bow? I stuck out my hand.

Mrs. Hayes took it, her skin incredibly soft. Mr. Hayes shook my hand next. "Natalie has told us so much about you."

"She has?" I glanced at Natalie, whose cheeks pinked right at the tops.

"I've never seen her as happy as she's been working on this gala," he said. His brown eyes sparkled, and I couldn't help but smile.

"Which is ridiculous, really," her mother said. "She's managed dozens of them with me. Where's your date, Natalie? I haven't seen Daniel in ages."

She waved a hand carelessly. "He's here somewhere. Probably making a deal in line for drinks."

"He never stops working." Mrs. Hayes nodded in approval, reminding me of my own mom. Suddenly, endless work sounded exhausting. I needed a drink. And a chair.

"Never stops working? That doesn't sound like any fun." Jackson Jones strolled up to us, two glasses of champagne in his hand. He handed one to me. "Mimi, you've worked your ass off on this gala, and it's time to sit back and enjoy it."

"Thank you." My face and neck heated, all the way down to where my boobs disappeared into the low neckline.

"I hear you worked hard, too, Nat." An Amazon of a woman, dark-skinned, thin, and breathtakingly beautiful, stepped up beside Jackson and handed her second glass to Natalie.

"Jamila!" Mrs. Hayes said. "Such a pleasure to see you. Natalie, say thank you."

"Thank you," Natalie rasped. She swallowed. Her eyes had

gone huge and round. I'd never seen her shaken like that. What was happening?

"Nice dress," Jamila said, her gaze trailing down the low neckline. "I can't believe you went and grew up on us. I remember when you used to come visit Jackson at college. You always wore the cutest ruffled dresses, and your hair was in pigtails."

Natalie twisted one long curl around her finger. "That was a long time ago."

Jamila barked out a laugh. "Don't I know it. Remember that time when…"

I didn't realize I'd stopped listening to gaze out over the gathering crowd, hunting for a pair of strong shoulders and careless blond waves, until Mr. Hayes' voice landed low in my ear.

"Miriam, if I may, I think this gala isn't your scene any more than it is mine. The secret to success at these events is to get yourself a partner who'll smooth the way like Audrey does for me." He reached out a hand, and Mrs. Hayes took it.

"Charles." Mrs. Hayes stepped in close, leaning against his shoulder. "If you'd only make an effort—"

"Why should I make an effort?" He grinned. "You do all the work for me. In fact, I'm sure there's someone I should be talking to right now."

"You do need to find Mr. van der Poel to find out what he knows about the new data privacy legislation."

"See what I mean?" His deep brown eyes sparkled. "Jackson, Jamila, come on. We have some networking to do. And these two deserve to drink champagne in peace. If you'll excuse us, ladies. Enjoy the party." He winked at his stepdaughter, nodded at me, and held out his elbow to his wife. She took it, and they disappeared into the crowd, along with Jackson and Jamila.

"Yeah." Natalie's smile was fragile as glass. "That's how you and Mateo would've been."

I tipped the last drops of champagne into my mouth. I needed another if she was going to keep throwing him in my face. "Come on. We need to network, too. Larissa's orders." Plus, I needed to find the director and ask her about the withdrawal and the strange deposit.

"Fuck Larissa. Hanging out with you is way more fun than networking. But if you want to mingle, I can be the Audrey to your Charles." She tossed her long hair over her shoulder. She knew exactly how to work these parties in a way I never could.

"I'll never be like your mother or Charles. I don't belong here at all." I looked down at my sparkly gown like I'd been projecting it with Loki's magic, and at any minute the illusion would crumble, leaving me in my usual saggy, black clothes.

"Sure you do. You just need the right partner." She bent her elbow like some duke in a period film.

"Thanks, Natalie. You're a good friend." I slipped my hand through her arm. "Now, where should we go fir—"

Larissa floated up to us, popping the delicate bubble of normalcy Natalie had blown around me. She wore a strapless black mermaid-style gown covered with intricate beadwork that extended to the swishy tulle at the bottom. Around her neck was a flashy statement necklace of glittery red crystals with a giant fake ruby suspended just above the dress's bodice.

"Larissa, that dress is gorgeous," Natalie said. She peered closer. "Hand beaded?"

"Isn't it?" Larissa smoothed a hand over her side.

"And that necklace." Natalie named some high-end jeweler I'd heard celebrities mention on the red carpet before award shows.

Larissa nodded. "It's the most amazing piece I've ever worn."

It was real? I swallowed, and that tug in the back of my brain, like the answer to a math problem I'd almost solved, was back. I didn't know Larissa's take-home pay since, against my advice, Jackson paid her directly from his personal funds. According to the salary comparison websites I'd checked, it wasn't enough to afford gigantic, genuine rubies. Was it possible to rent jewelry like that? My mind spun, trying to figure out the jeweler's business model and how they'd insure the pieces.

Larissa woke me out of my calculations by saying, "Let me introduce you to Flavio, my date."

He'd been standing behind her, talking to one of the club's black-uniformed staff members, but he stepped up when she plucked his sleeve. He'd been wearing golf clothes both times I'd met him here before, but tonight his tuxedo molded to his physique, from broad shoulders to narrow hips. He didn't stand up straight like Mateo always did but slouched, hands in his pockets, comfortable in his tux and in his own skin like he owned the place.

"Oh, we've already met," Natalie said. "When we came here with the decorator last week."

"Yes." He wagged a finger. "I gave you my card, Miss Jones, but you haven't called me yet."

"Talk to Larissa. She's the one who's been keeping us busy with party planning."

"Ah. But now the party planning is done, and I have a business proposition—"

"Not now, Flavio." Larissa's smile teetered into a grimace. "Where's Mateo? I want to ask him why the band isn't wearing sombreros and those tight mariachi pants."

Natalie rolled her eyes so forcefully I thought her fake eyelashes might fly off.

"He isn't here tonight," I said.

"Trouble in paradise?" Larissa's ash-blond eyebrows sailed up.

I wanted to tell her no, but the lie stuck in my dry throat.

"Oh, no." Her voice dropped an octave. "You broke up?"

Natalie stepped closer and clutched my suddenly cold hand. "Let's not talk about that tonight. Tonight is for celebrating our hard work." But she gave me a look so full of sympathy that my sinuses tingled.

I sniffed. I wasn't sure my own fake eyelashes would stand up to tears. Besides, I'd cried enough of them into my Mateo-scented pillow. I clamped my mouth shut to keep the sob inside.

Natalie must have seen the tremble in my jaw. "Excuse us. We were on our way to get a second round."

"Remember, you're representing the foundation tonight," Larissa hissed. "Only two drinks, Miriam. No mistakes."

I straightened. I had to ask her about the rainy-day account. But not in front of Flavio and Natalie. "Larissa, could I—"

"No time." Natalie clutched my arm and dragged me through the crowd to the closest bar.

"But I needed to ask her something about the foundation—"

"Fuck the foundation," Natalie snapped. "We're on a mission. Breakups call for champagne and chocolate."

With Ben, it was red wine and greasy pizza. But that hadn't lifted the heaviness in my belly. Maybe Natalie's remedy would. I'd find Larissa when my eyes weren't so leaky.

I put on an apologetic smile. "I'm allergic."

"To champagne?"

"No. Chocolate."

Her eyes softened with sympathy. "You poor thing. Chocolate is the best breakup remedy I know. We'll have to drown your sorrow with…carbs. You're not allergic to them, are you?"

"Only the chocolate-flavored ones."

Two glasses of champagne in a corner of the ballroom later, the room had taken on a Crisco-smeared quality.

"I think I need to eat something more than salmon on toast points," I said. I did *not* need a repeat of Bree's bachelorette party —or its aftermath.

"Good idea." Natalie stopped a server with an effortless wave of her hand. "Excuse me, can you ask the kitchen manager if they can start the dinner service?"

"I—I guess? We'll have to ask Mr. Flavio."

I scrunched my nose. The alcohol hadn't lessened the tightness in my chest, but it had loosened my lips. "Why him?"

She tilted her head to the side. "Tonight, everything goes through him."

Everything should have gone through Larissa. Or one of us. "Why?"

The server shrugged. "He says he's in charge tonight. He *is* the owner."

"Flavio *owns* the country club?" That fact pierced through my foggy brain.

"Yeah?"

"That Flavio"—God, I wished I knew his last name—"over there?" I pointed at the center of the dance floor, where Larissa stood beside him.

"Yeah. I'll ask the manager to ask him." She turned on her black shoe and left me there, goggling.

"Flavio owns the country club," I said.

"You didn't know that?" Natalie asked.

"No, did you?"

"No, but why do you look like that?"

"He's Larissa's fiancé. The foundation is paying the country club five figures. Per hour. It's a lot of money, and it's a conflict of interest." I'd written the checks, and Larissa had signed them. I hadn't thought to look into the ownership of the venue, but now that I knew, I'd have to report it. Added to the funny business with the accounts, it was too much to ignore. I scrubbed at my hands. They felt dirty.

I'd sat through Synergy's mandatory compliance training once a year since I'd joined the company, so I could recite the policy on conflicts of interest by heart, but the foundation was too small for a training program like that. Could it have been an honest mistake?

"I knew something wasn't right," Natalie said. "The foundation never seemed to have as much money as it should. That's why I agreed to help with the gala. I, ah"—she gripped her champagne flute—"I thought at first it might be you skimming from the foundation, but after I got to know you, I couldn't square it. I asked Jackson if he thought Larissa might be shady, but she came so highly recommended that I think he's a little afraid of her."

A brick weighed in my belly. I hadn't noticed anything wrong with the accounts until last night's strange withdrawal. Had I been so focused on my career goals that I'd missed something as huge as embezzlement?

"I—I found something. Last night. One of the foundation accounts was emptied. By Larissa." I opened my clutch and handed her the printout. "Today, there was a strange deposit in my PayMo. I reversed it, but the number matched the balance in the rainy-day fund."

"Last week, when we were here with the decorator, you said there was a missing deposit. What did Larissa say about it?"

"She said she gave the cash to the decorator."

Natalie shook her head. "Gail is a friend. She agreed to take her payment after the event. She waived her standard deposit."

My head spun. This was too irregular. We'd never pass an audit. Something was definitely wrong. But Larissa had won that award last year. I couldn't believe she'd intentionally defrauded the foundation. Who could do that to the kids?

"We should tell Jackson," Natalie said. "I know he takes a hands-off approach to the running of the foundation, but he won't be happy to hear this."

"I'd rather talk to Larissa first. See what she has to say for herself."

"Okay, but…" She bit her lip. "There's more. I didn't want to say anything until I was sure, but I think she's been pocketing the money she's supposed to be using for rent. Jackson mentioned he's been paying for office space, but she and I always meet at Starbucks."

My eyes widened. "Jackson's been giving her money for office space? The foundation accounts should pay for that. Besides, she's been working out of her condo."

Natalie shook her head. "We need to tell Jackson. This"—she shook the papers in her hand—"this is proof."

She dismounted from her chair and waited, eyebrows raised.

She was right. It was too much to be a mistake. But there went the assistant director job. Jackson Jones would never forgive me for letting this happen on my watch.

I slid off the tall stool. "Okay. Let's talk to him."

She scanned the dance floor for her brother, and I looked the other direction, toward the entrance.

My gaze snagged on a pair of strong shoulders and a blond head that towered over the crowd. My breath caught in my chest.

Mateo?

Every thought evaporated from my brain. The foundation, Larissa's fraud, even my friend standing beside me. A wave of hope washed through me. Hope that he'd forgiven me. That he'd come here to see me. That—I swallowed—he wanted to be part of my life again.

Because I wanted that.

But when he turned his head, I realized it was only Cooper Fallon, standing next to my brother at the ballroom entrance.

When my stomach plummeted, I stopped denying it.

I'd been in love with Mateo all along.

29

MATEO
ONE HOUR EARLIER

I HAD everything a single guy needed on Valentine's Day: a beer in my hand, a six-pack in the fridge, and a second six-pack behind that. Plus football on a giant TV. No, it wasn't football season, not even American football season, but although Miguelito never watched anything but the financial news, he had an amazing cable television package. The MLS channel was replaying a marathon of last year's World Cup matches.

And I had the best buddy ever, even if he had to hide under a blanket. I ripped a tiny triangle off a strip of beef jerky and fed it to Roger, who purred contentedly under the cashmere throw blanket on the sectional in Miguelito's TV room. Then I tossed a larger piece to Coco, lying on the floor at my feet.

The tapping of dress shoes across the tile gave me plenty of time to cover Roger with the blanket before Ben walked in.

"Hey, Mateo, can you help me with my tie? I still haven't got the knack."

I set down my beer and walked around the sofa to stand in front of him. He had a fresh glow to him even more gorgeous than the satin-trimmed, tailored tuxedo. I wiped my jerky fingers on my sweatpants so I wouldn't spoil the glossy tie.

"Boss?"

"No." He sighed in ecstasy, rolling his eyes up to the ceiling. "Freaking Tom Ford. Look at the cuffs." He held up one forearm to show off the satin cuff and covered buttons.

I whistled. "He must really love you."

"I know, right?"

A smile cracked my face. Was I jealous that my cousin had snagged the love of his life while my heart was shattered? Absolutely. Still, I couldn't be mad in the face of Ben's incandescent happiness.

"Lito couldn't tie this?" I straightened the ends and let muscle memory take over. My father had liked to wear bow ties to Mass on Sundays.

"He tried"—Ben's neck flushed under his collar in a shade that reminded me too much of his sister's skin—"but he kept, um, getting distracted. That's why we're running late. He's taking a shower now."

I forced a chuckle.

Always too perceptive, Ben asked, "Are you going to be okay?"

"What?" I drew the bow tight. "Of course. I've got beer and football. I'll order a pizza later. Life is good."

"Mateo." Ben laid a hand on my T-shirt, right over the gaping hole in my chest. "I'm sorry you and Mimi didn't work out. I was pulling for you."

"Might as well pull for San Marino," I muttered, straightening his tie.

"I'm not into the sportsball. What's San Marino?"

"San Marino?" Miguelito walked in, his own tie dangling around his neck. "Only the worst European football club ever. You don't want to see a game there, do you?"

"Where even is—never mind. Mateo was comparing himself to

them, and I knew I didn't like it." He exchanged a look with his fiancé.

"I meant what I said the other day," he said gruffly. "You're my primo, and I love you. I value you. You're good enough."

I needed those words. I soaked them in through my skin like vitamin D in sunlight. They pooled in my belly, warming me from the inside.

"Oh, Mateo," Ben said. "Of course you're good enough. Mimi might be my sister, but she's a fool if she doesn't see it."

My sinuses prickled. I hooked Ben with my right arm and Lito with my left and hauled them in for a crushing hug. I sniffed back my tears, not wanting to let them land on their tuxedo jackets. "Thank you," I whispered through my constricted throat.

Ben hugged me tight while Lito gave me a few awkward backpats.

"We both love you, Mateo," Ben mumbled against my shoulder.

"But." Miguelito gently disentangled himself from my hug and tugged Ben to his side. "I can't condone this wallowing you're doing." He waved at my faded, frayed T-shirt and droopy sweatpants. "Why aren't you dressed?"

I tugged my shrunken tee down to cover my stomach. "I am dressed. I'm all set for a night with my favorite clubs."

Miguelito flicked a glance at the television. "Leipzig-Chelsea? You hate them both."

Fuck, I'd been too busy wallowing to pay attention to who was playing. "Maybe they can both lose?"

"Fuck that bullshit." My cousin sliced a hand through the air. "You're going with us to the gala. You're going to shoot your shot with Mimi."

"What?" Chills raced down my spine. "No, I'm not. She doesn't want me."

"Of course she wants you." Ben ran a placating hand down my biceps. "She's just forgotten."

I bared my teeth and stepped away from his touch. "Because I'm forgettable."

Ben's mouth dropped open into a horrified O. This time, Miguelito gripped my shoulder, gritting his words out through his teeth. "You. Are not. Forgettable. Everyone who meets you loves you. Your mother? She had her issues, unrelated to you. And Mimi was a fool to let you go. She's probably regretting that decision right now."

I snorted. "Of course she is. She's shown up to that gala alone, and Larissa's—dammit, Larissa's shitting all over her, isn't she?"

"One way to find out. Come with us. Win her back."

I turned to Ben. I mean, I loved my cousin, but his dating record was shit.

"Give her another chance," Ben said. "If she fucks it up again, I don't care if she is my sister. She's going into cold storage."

"I could never come between you and Mimi. You have to take her side. But I'm keeping Lito." I slung an arm around my cousin's shoulders.

He pulled away, brushing invisible wrinkles out of his tux. "Come on. I'll help you pick out a tux upstairs."

"The Versace brocade, babe," Ben said. "You can never quite pull it off, but it'll look amazing on him."

Miguelito's lips curled down, but then he shrugged. "It's a little too flashy for me. But perfect for my primo."

As I turned to follow my cousin upstairs, Ben snagged my wrist. Raising his eyebrows, he said in a voice too quiet for his fiancé to hear, "I'll take your guest home. I wouldn't recommend bringing him here again. Cooper won't be as friendly about it as Coco is, and he might take back those nice things he said about you."

I reached over the back of the sofa, uncovered Roger, and handed him to Ben. "Thanks, man. I owe you one."

"Nah. Make my sister smile again, and all is forgiven." He slapped my shoulder and tapped away, Roger almost invisible against his black tuxedo jacket.

"Coming?" Miguelito called from the landing.

I raced upstairs to join him. Even if I didn't win her back, I'd save Mimi from Larissa's ice-cold jealousy and help keep her in the running for the job she so desperately wanted.

Fifteen minutes later, I followed my cousin downstairs. I was dressed and styled, and he'd spritzed me with some amazing-smelling cologne he said he'd never liked. It reminded me of night-blooming flowers and the warm ocean breezes back home.

Ben got up from the kitchen stool where he'd been waiting. He pretended to shield his eyes. "O-M-G, I can't even with all this hotness. Mateo, if Mimi doesn't take you back, it'll be no problem to find someone to help you forget her. Hell, I'd help."

Miguelito growled deep in his throat.

"Kidding! Totally kidding. But walking in with the both of you, I'll feel like Scarlett O'Hara at the picnic at Twelve Oaks." Ben grasped his fiancé's hand and led him toward the door to the garage. "Let's go, handsome. We're late."

Miguelito brushed something from Ben's shoulder. "Is that cat hair?"

"Couldn't be, babe. Where would I find cat hair in our immaculate home?" He winked at me over his shoulder. "Come on, Mateo. We've done the fairy godmother magic. Now all that's left is to win back your princess."

Silently, I followed them out to the garage. What if Mimi didn't want to be won back?

I squared my shoulders. I'd never know if I didn't try.

30

MIMI

I TURNED AWAY from the entrance. I couldn't watch Ben make heart-eyes at someone who looked so much like the man I'd thrown away and lost.

"Sorry, what were you saying?" I asked Natalie.

But she was distracted, too. Her brother Andrew slouched next to her, his eyes darting around the room. "She didn't come," he mumbled, just loud enough for me to hear.

Natalie hugged him. "It's still early—"

"She's not coming. She's afraid. She doesn't love me enough to…"

I blinked at the pair of them. If I were Ben, I'd get caught up in what sounded like a juicy situation. But Andrew's words were too much like my own thoughts. Someone I loved was missing, too.

"I'm leaving," he said, his voice stronger. "Great party, sis." He shook himself and gave me a tight smile. "Fantastic job, Mimi."

"Stay," Natalie pleaded. "There's time."

"No. She's had enough time. And, fuck, here comes smug Jackson. I can't." Andrew dived into the crowd just as Jackson Jones sauntered up to us. His brown eyes were champagne-bright.

"Where'd Andrew go? He hasn't given me his donation yet. But you're going to love this. I just accepted a ten-thousand-dollar check from that van der Poel asshole. He wanted to give it to you, Nat—isn't he your date?—but I told him it was my fucking foundation, and ten Gs wasn't going to get him into your pants.

"Anyway, I wanted to thank you two again for pulling this together. Whatever I pay you, it's not enough for what you've done here tonight." He waved at the dinner tables sparkling with crystal and silver, at the band and the couples dancing, at the people who'd come in their finery on Valentine's Day to support neurodivergent kids.

Natalie snorted. "You don't pay us anything, Jackson. I helped because you're my brother and I didn't want you to fall on your face with your first big event. Mimi helped out of the kindness of her heart. Because she loves supporting kids."

I did want that assistant director position, though. "Well, that's not entirely—"

"Wait." Jackson frowned. "I'm not paying you?"

"No." I mirrored his frown. "Well, I mean, you are paying me for my work at Synergy, but my work for the foundation is pro bono."

"But I've been transferring money into the payroll account every two weeks. Larissa said she'd distribute it among the staff."

Natalie gasped.

I went cold. The foundation didn't have a payroll account. Larissa said Jackson paid her directly, and I didn't have to worry about it. I'd planned to talk to Jackson about how to better manage the foundation funding and its impact on his personal taxes, but I'd wanted to wait until after Larissa decided about the assistant director position. Bile surged in my belly.

I swallowed. It was a big accusation. But there was no other explanation for everything Natalie and I had seen. "I think Larissa's been enriching herself through the foundation. She kept the entire payroll. And there have been other questionable expenses. Conflicts of interest. I have documentation I gave Larissa cash for a deposit, but she didn't give it to the vendor. It's disappeared. And I have this"—I pulled the folded papers out of my clutch— "proof that Larissa drained the foundation's rainy-day fund last night. I'm sorry I didn't realize it before now."

"Oh, fuck." Jackson scanned the papers. "Fucking amateur move not to even mask her IP address. It'll take me two seconds to confirm it was her."

He ran a hand over his face. "I suck at the business end of things. I should've gotten Cooper to help me with this. But she came so well recommended. And, frankly, she scares me a little." He drew himself up. "I'm going to need copies of the rest of that documentation for my lawyer."

"Of course. I can get it to you tomorrow morning."

"Send it to me Monday. You shouldn't work on the weekend. Let's hope she goes quietly and money can straighten out this mess." He pulled out his phone, dialed, and murmured into it.

"I never thought—" I whispered.

"I did," Natalie said. "That guy Flavio is her partner in crime, not her fiancé."

"He did give off a certain vibe."

Jackson pulled the phone from his ear. "Security's going to locate her and avoid making a scene." He tugged at the roots of his hair. "Now, where am I going to find a new foundation director to straighten out this mess?" He scanned the crowd like they were a line of candidates.

"Jackson, you numbnuts," Natalie said. "Your new director is standing right in front of you." She grabbed my shoulders and pulled me in front of herself.

"Mimi?" His face cleared. "Of course! Mimi, will you step in?" He named a salary in the range I'd researched.

"I—" Oh, shit. I'd been comfortable with the idea of the assistant role, following someone else's lead. But being the leader myself? "Am I qualified?"

Natalie, who still had her hands on my shoulders, leaned in and spoke into my ear. "I'd help, I promise."

"Help." I grabbed the word like a lifeline. "I'd need lots of help."

"Whoever you want," he said. "You can hire a staff. And an auditor."

My cheeks burned. How had I missed Larissa's embezzlement? "Are you sure you want me?"

"I can't think of a better candidate. I've seen your good work. Besides, Nat vouches for you."

"Can I think about it and let you know Monday?"

"Of course." He looked down at his phone. "Looks like they found Larissa. I have to go deal with her."

"What are you going to do?" Natalie rubbed her hands together. "Have the police cuff her?"

"You've watched too many police procedurals, Nat. For now, I'm going to see what she has to say for herself."

"Mimi and I are coming with."

"We are?" I blinked. Did I want to see Larissa taken down? She'd stolen money from the kids we were supposed to be helping. Hell, yes, I did.

Jackson's security team had detained Larissa in a small conference room off the lobby. Jackson spoke to the team lead, a tall, muscular woman with close-cropped hair. "Where's Flavio?"

"Couldn't find him. But he left his date." She nodded at Larissa, who lifted her nose into the air.

"This is ridiculous, Jackson. I don't know what Miriam thinks I've done—"

"She doesn't think you've done anything. I do. I think you've been stealing money that was supposed to help kids."

I ducked behind Natalie, but Larissa's frosty blue gaze found me. "Miriam doesn't know anything about how nonprofits are run. She doesn't get it. I'll show you exactly—"

I stepped out of Natalie's shadow. "Maybe I don't know how to run a nonprofit, but I understand accounting. And taxes. I think you do, too. What you've done isn't right. I've got the receipts—or the lack thereof—to prove it."

"Do you?" She raised her eyebrows, and a smile teased on her lips. "Jackson, I think if you look at Miriam's personal accounts, you'll see that she's the one who took the money out of the emergency fund."

Cold realization washed through my veins. "You were trying to pin this on me? To make me take the blame for your theft? I knew that money wasn't mine. I had PayMo reverse the charges."

"Besides," Jackson said, "I can trace the IP. I'm pretty sure I know where it'll lead."

For the first time, fear crossed her smooth face. "You can't do this to me. I have connections. People who'll see to it you can't prove anything."

Jackson shrugged. "I don't have to prove anything. Your employment is at-will, and I no longer need your services. I trust Mimi. She has evidence of what you've done. We can probably find more from the previous nonprofits you've been associated with. So be smart, Larissa. Get out of town and find honest work in the private sector. If I hear that you're trying to steal from another nonprofit, I'll take you down."

Larissa's chest heaved, but she remained silent. Her expression shuttered. "I don't think I want to stay here, anyway. I'm leaving."

With a cautious look at the security chief, she slipped toward the door but stopped next to me. "Watch out, Miriam. I see how you want to be part of this world." She glanced at the Joneses. "You're like me, ambitious. Putting on a show for them. Wanting the spotlight. Well, that spotlight can burn you."

"We're not alike." She was more right than I cared to admit. I had wanted to be like her, to soar like she'd done. But now I saw she hadn't flown at all. She'd used invisible strings to create the illusion of flight. And I'd rather toil in obscurity forever than do what she'd done. "I'd never steal."

She narrowed her eyes. "Wouldn't you? Women like you and me don't have the safety net *they* do. We have to claw and scratch our way to the top. It costs money to look like we belong. And sometimes you have to fake it until you make it."

On the surface, what she'd said sounded a lot like Mom's mantra of *smarts, drive, and confidence*. But she'd twisted it in a way I never would. "I'd rather be poor and unemployed than take money that was donated to help children."

She arched an eyebrow. "Good luck with that. Only rich people can afford a sense of moral superiority." With a sniff, she sailed through the door. No one stopped her, and her heels clicked away down the hall at speed.

Jackson thanked the security team, and they filed out and closed the door.

"You're letting her get away?" Natalie propped her fists on her hips.

"Nat, I'm giving her a second chance. I've made mistakes, too."

"Mistakes?" Her voice rose in outrage. "Embezzlement is hardly a mistake!"

"Jackson, I have to agree. It's a felony," I said.

"It was wrong, and I'm going to give her an opportunity to make it right. Other people gave me that chance—many chances —when I fucked up." He rubbed a spot between his eyebrows. "But I promise we'll keep an eye on her. If she tries it again some-where else, we'll come after her. I'll cover anything she took from the foundation with my personal funds."

She'd stolen from the organization I'd worked so hard for. From the kids. "But—"

"You'll put measures in place so this never happens again, right?" he asked.

"Of course." It was a promise.

"Now, we still have a gala going on out there and donors to squeeze." He rubbed his hands together. "Larissa was supposed to make a brief speech and then introduce me. Can you do that, Mimi?"

"A speech?" Speeches were not my thing. This was why I'd become an accountant.

"Just welcome everyone, thank them for their contributions, and then say, 'Here's Jackson.' Nothing complicated."

"Do you have a speech prepared?" Natalie asked.

He chuckled. "You know me. I plan to wing it." He strode out the door.

Natalie hugged me. "I'm bummed about Larissa's theft, but I'm so excited for you. You should've been in charge all along."

"But I don't know anything about directing a nonprofit. Maybe you should—"

"I promise I'll help you. You've got the skills you need. You're organized, driven, and above all, you care about the kids the way Larissa never did."

Natalie's confidence propped up my own. "Okay, if you think I can…"

"I know you can." She hugged me again. "Ready to make your way to the stage?"

My smile was unsteady. Sure, I'd achieved—surpassed—my goal. But now I had to step up and do the work. Without the safety net of someone else's leadership. But Natalie believed in me. With her help, I might manage it.

"Okay." We walked out together.

But as soon as I stepped into the ballroom, my gaze landed on the person I'd been looking for all night. Someone tall and blond and wearing a tux. And this time, it wasn't Cooper Fallon.

31

MIMI

"LET'S GO, MIMI," Natalie said. "Oh."

More like *Ohhhh.*

What was Mateo doing at the gala? He stood alone, scanning the crowd. Gone were the jeans and tight T-shirt he usually wore. Tonight, he was gorgeous and elegant in a brocade tuxedo that hugged his shoulders and muscular torso and skimmed his powerful thighs. His bow tie was crisp and snug under his chin.

He looked like he belonged there in the glittering ballroom.

Shit, had he come with a date? He wasn't that cruel. Though I deserved it after what I'd done to him. A fist clamped onto my heart.

"I need a minute."

"A minute?" Natalie hummed in appreciation as she looked him up and down. "I'd need twenty. At least. Go on. I'll get the audio techs ready for you."

Natalie was gone in a click-click-click of her heels. But my gaze stuck to Mateo.

I took a step toward him, and that's when he spotted me. His expression froze, his eyes wide. Then he perused me from my updo to the overspill of my breasts, to where the dress hugged my spandex-wrapped hips, following the long slit in my gown all the way to my toes in my beige heels.

His gaze rocketed to my face, and I wished I could smooth away the uncertainty that settled in the groove between his eyebrows.

I tripped toward him, as fast as I could go in the too-tall heels, until I stood in front of him.

"Mateo, I—"

"Mimi." My name was a sigh, a hope, a reunion. He reached out a hand as if to touch me but yanked it back.

Me? I must have been angling for the night's most-awkward-moment award. Horrified and unable to stop it, I watched my hand extend toward him for a handshake.

He glanced down, and his eyes creased in pain as if I'd kicked him. Still, always the better person, he folded his hand into mine and squeezed it.

"Mimi." This time when he said it, my name came out strangled and stiff.

He released the pressure on my hand, but I hung on like Roger on the sisal-wrapped cat gym.

"Mateo, I'm sorry. I should never have said those things to you. I shouldn't have made you feel like you were a stepping-stone in my career. All you did was help me, and I threw it in your face. I never meant to hurt you."

His mouth tightened until his plush lips went pale. "It's all right."

"No." He had to understand this, that no one should take advantage of him. That no one could insult him and push him aside the way I'd done. "No, it's not. I took everything you gave me. And you gave me so much. Help with the gala. This dress. And so much more. Yet I was ungrateful."

His mouth was a thin line. "It's fine. I'm glad everything turned out for you."

I was doing this all wrong, but I didn't know how to stop. So I dug in deeper. "It did. It really did. Jackson just offered me the director position. Not assistant director. Director. And I think I'm going to do it."

His stiff face cracked, the corners of his mouth turning up. "That's great, Mimi. I'm happy for you."

"But I—" Why was this so hard for me? Why was I stuck on everything that was irrelevant? Why couldn't I tell him how I felt about him?

I looked up into his eyes, kind and soft and warm as a summer sky. And I understood why I couldn't speak. This was all wrong. It wasn't enough for me to tell only him. The world, or at least everyone in this ballroom, had to know how wonderful he was. He deserved not only my appreciation, but a roomful of it.

I levered up on my tiptoes and pecked his lips. "Stay here, okay? Don't move."

Turning toward the stage, I weaved among the people waiting for the band to resume until I reached the steps and ascended them.

"Ready?" I asked, taking the microphone from Natalie.

"I don't see Jackson yet."

"That's okay. I have to say something first."

"You do?"

I flicked on the microphone and turned to face the ballroom. "Good evening, everyone. Good evening."

I waited until the room quieted and I'd caught most of the guests' attention.

"Welcome to the first annual Valentine's Day Celebration of Brain Differences. I'm Miriam Levy-Walters, the financial consultant for the foundation. I want to thank you all for your generosity tonight."

I scanned the crowd. Most of them looked bored. Or cranky because they hadn't eaten anything yet. My knees quaked when I thought about what I wanted to say.

And that's when I did something that I'd cringe about for the rest of my life.

"Do you know the problem with math puns?" I raised my eyebrows and smiled.

Ben knew this one. "No, what's the problem with math puns?" he shouted.

I grinned. "Calculus jokes are all derivative, trigonometry jokes are too graphic, algebra jokes are always formulaic, and arithmetic jokes are pretty basic." I paused. "But I guess the occasional statistics joke is an outlier."

The silence stretched out to two seconds. Three. Then, from the side of the stage, Natalie bellowed, "Ha!"

My cheeks flamed. I guessed rich people didn't appreciate math jokes. I sucked in a deep breath and said, "Before I introduce Jackson, I'd like to recognize a few people who brought tonight's event together.

"First, Natalie Jones. Natalie brought a vision to this gala and executed it flawlessly. Thank you, Natalie, for your contributions and for your friendship."

I smiled at her while the guests clapped. She threw back her shoulders and beamed first at me and then at the people assembled below us on the dance floor.

When the applause subsided, I continued. "I'd also like to recognize Mateo Rivera, who not only helped bring you the food and entertainment tonight but also helped me in so many ways."

I paused, frowned. That wasn't it. Not all of it, anyway. A few people clapped, thinking I was done, but I held up a hand and found Mateo in the crowd. When he gave me a tentative smile, I continued.

"Mateo gave me so much more than help. He gave me loyalty. Encouragement. Support. Unconditionally. No matter what I threw at him, he was always there for me. I wouldn't be standing up here tonight without him.

"I didn't know the first thing about putting together a gala like this. But he gave me the confidence to keep going in the face of adversity. To go for what I wanted to achieve. And even when it was difficult, Mateo made it easier for me. He held me up and sustained me through every challenge."

Closer. I was almost at what I wanted, needed to say.

"He cared for me. And I discovered that I care for him, too. Mateo, I love you. I want to be your partner in this and in everything else."

Natalie squealed and clapped, and a few of the people gathered on the dance floor joined in. They had no idea that this was monumental for me.

But Mateo did. His tentative smile had turned into a full-on grin, and he arrowed toward me through the crowd.

I'd just professed my love for him in front of a thousand people, but I didn't want to be standing on stage with a microphone in my hand when he made it to me. I wanted to drag him off somewhere private to back up my words with kisses.

Into the microphone, I said, "And now, please welcome the person who started the foundation, whose ideas, philanthropy, and commitment to neurodivergent kids are the reason we're here tonight. Jackson Jones."

I shoved the microphone into Natalie's hand, not caring if Jackson was ready or not.

I was ready. I scrambled down the steps to Mateo and threw my arms around his neck. He lifted me off my feet and kissed me once, hard, before he whispered into my ear, "I love you, Miriam Levy-Walters. How long until I can take you somewhere and prove it?"

I whispered back, "I have to stay to the end, but..."

"But?" I felt his smile against my cheek.

"But I know where the green room is. I could, um, show it to you?"

"Lead the way, mi amor."

32

MATEO

I SHOULD HAVE KNOWN BETTER than to hope to get my hands on Mimi in the green room. We were stopped as soon as we stepped off the dance floor.

"Mimi! Mateo!" Marlee, Jackson's assistant, whisper-shouted under Jackson's speech. "That was unbelievably romantic. You two are together now?" She clasped her hands under her chin, grinning widely.

I tugged Mimi's hand and reeled her into my side. "We are."

Mimi gazed up at me, her beautiful brown eyes snapping with her impatience to get me alone. But I could hardly believe that private, army-of-one Mimi had announced her love for me up on the stage. I needed to hear it a dozen more times before I truly believed it.

Marlee squealed. "I'm so happy for you guys!"

"Sweetheart." A tall, rangy guy in glasses slid an arm around her waist. "I, ah, think they might need some alone time."

"Oh." She blinked. "Of course you're right, Tyler. I'll find you later, Mimi. I want to hear all about it!"

As Mimi tugged me away, she muttered, "Marlee loves love. I'll never hear the end of this."

We'd almost made it out of the ballroom when Ben stepped into Mimi's path, Miguelito by his side. Ben held his arms out wide, and we had no choice but to step into his embrace. He crushed us together.

I heard him whisper in Mimi's ear, "I'm so happy for you."

He released her but held onto me. "I adore you, Mateo, but if you ever hurt her, I'll ask Cooper to disappear you."

I yanked out of his grip. His eyes twinkled, but was it with humor or malice?

"I love your sister," I said.

"I know. I love her, too."

Mimi stepped in front of me, bristling. "Stop it, Benny. I'm a big girl, and I know what I want. And it's Mateo."

She wrapped her arm around my waist, and it was only natural for me to sling my arm around hers. For support. Because she'd just cut my knees out from under me.

"Say it again, Mimi," I murmured.

"I love you, Mateo. I want to be with you." She squeezed me tighter.

Her words braced me enough to shoot Ben a triumphant look. He folded his arms and leaned back into Miguelito.

I hardly dared to look at my cousin, but I couldn't help it. I needed his approval. And to check that he wouldn't "disappear" me, whatever Ben meant by that.

Miguelito nodded at the pair of us. "You fit well together. Take care of each other."

It didn't feel like he was giving us an instruction so much as he was stating a fact. I landed a light kiss on Mimi's upturned lips. "We do. We will."

Jackson's speech must have ended because the band started to play. And as much as I wanted a few minutes alone with Mimi, this was the best chance for me to get away from the well-wishers while I got my hands on her.

"Come on, Mimi. Let's show them our dance moves." I grasped her hand and towed her to the center of the dance floor, where I laid my hands lightly under hers.

"You remember?" I asked.

She smiled up at me, and everything about her glittered, from that amazing dress to her smoky-quartz eyes. "I remember it all."

"Good." I counted us off, and we began to move.

We started with our feet, the simple steps bringing back the muscle memories we'd formed at the club and then again at my place. Then I dipped my hips. When Mimi did, too, I almost swallowed my tongue. The slit rose high on her leg, and all I wanted to do was touch the smooth skin of her thigh and watch her shiver.

No, Mateo. Keep it G-rated. Or at least PG.

I switched my grip on her hand to signal a turn, and she moved with me like we'd been dancing together all our lives.

"Beautiful," I said.

Her cheeks pinked. "Only because you're doing all the work."

"No, mi amor. You're doing it, too. And in heels."

"What?" Uncertainty creased her brow.

"Don't look down. You're doing great. Now we twirl."

I shifted my grip and led her into the spin, then I spun. I twirled her back, tucking her back into my front, and groaned into her ear. "Mimi, I'm going to die. Right here on the dance floor."

"Oh, no! Did I step on your foot?" Her steps faltered.

"No." I spun her back around to face me. "Miguelito's ass is smaller than mine. There's hardly room in these pants for me, and no extra room for the hard-on you're giving me."

"I love your ass in those pants." Her grin was wicked. "I'll love it even more out of them."

"Mimi," I groaned. "You're murdering me."

"Really?" She brushed her bare thigh against my pants. "I thought I was your vida. Your life."

"You're all of it. My life, my heart, my love."

She moved closer to me. "I don't think I'll ever get used to that."

"You will." I placed our joined hands behind her neck, and we pressed together. "I'll tell you every day."

"I guess I have a track record of needing to be reminded."

I chucked. "I guess you do."

"Mateo." She planted her feet, stopping our dance. "I will never forget you again. I'll never forget tonight."

I was already warm under my tux from the dance, but her words made happiness bubble hot like tía's chocolate in my chest.

"Let's get out of here." I dropped my hand to her hip and guided her off the dance floor toward the exit.

"Are we finally going to the green room?" Her lips twisted up into a sexy smirk.

I mirrored her expression, already planning the kisses I was going to lay on those lips. Later.

"We're going home so I can show you a truly unforgettable night."

"No." She dug her heels into the carpet. "I have to stay until the end."

"Mimi, you've put your heart and soul into this. Everyone will understand if you take one night off. You deserve it. And I'd like you to spend it with me."

Her lush mouth turned serious. "Not just one night, Mateo. All the nights."

"Absolutely, mi sol. And all the days, too."

"So you understand why I have to stay, right? This gala is a commitment, just like I'm making to you."

I groaned. "Why do you have to be right all the time?"

"I'm not. I was really, really wrong about you." She put a soothing hand over my heart where it was still mending itself back together. "You'll tell me the next time I'm being too stubborn to see what's right in front of me?"

I lifted her hand to my lips. "Of course."

"And challenge my assumptions?"

"If you'd like."

"And wear your glasses to bed one night?"

"What?"

"They're so sexy. Please?"

I smiled at my irresistible girlfriend. "Anything for you, mi vida." I led her back to the dance floor, counted us off, and twirled her again.

Hours later, after Mimi had overseen the silent auction and directed the cleanup crew, after she'd helped the last happily drunk donor slide into the back seat of his car and be driven away, we walked out of the country club together, hand in hand. Lovers. Helpmates. Partners. And all of it real.

EPILOGUE

MIMI
6 MONTHS LATER

I WAS LATE.

Impossibly, inhospitably, terrifyingly late. Dinner-well-after-sunset late. Better-order-pizza late. Might-as-well-give-up-now-and-hide-under-the-covers late.

I ran up the stairs to my apartment, the bag with the challah in it bumping against my leg. Someone on the hall was cooking something delicious. I should ask them if they had enough to spare for seven more guests.

Seven! Why the hell had I thought it was a good idea to host Friday-night dinner in my tiny apartment?

Because it was my turn. Mom and Dad had hosted it forever. Even Ben and Cooper had hosted it once.

Me? I always had an excuse.

Fine, the excuse was always work.

Unraveling the disaster Larissa had left at the foundation was taking more effort than I'd ever dreamed. At least once a week, one of her former associates came by, looking for a kickback or a payment for something—they never told me exactly for what.

I always told them we were running the foundation differently these days. Then I told them about our mission until they got bored and left.

Sometimes they left a little cash for the kids. That made me smile.

Though not as much as today's big donation. I couldn't wait to tell everyone about it. When they got here in—I checked my phone—half an hour. Shit!

I unlocked the door and shoved it open.

That's when I discovered the delicious smell was coming from my apartment.

I rushed into the kitchen, where I found Mateo and his aunt Rosa bent over the oven. The savory, mouthwatering aroma unfurled from my oven. The one that hadn't baked anything except sugar cookies from a tube in weeks.

"Um, hi," I said loudly enough to be heard over the range fan.

Mateo whirled to face me. He and his aunt wore white aprons. Did I own white aprons? Hell, any aprons at all? I didn't think so.

"Mi vida." He held out his arms to me, and I stepped into his embrace. He smelled like roasted meat and potatoes and allspice.

"I—what's going on?"

"We came over early to help, but you weren't here, so we started without you."

"You are the best." I tilted my face up for a kiss. "I love you."

His kiss was closed-mouthed, PG-rated for his aunt, but it carried warmth and care and a promise of *later*. His massive hands rested on my lower back, holding me in place. He needed a moment of reconnection, and I was happy to share it with him.

He nuzzled my cheek. "I love you, too."

His voice, rumbling through his chest, gave me tingles in a place that made me wish his aunt wasn't standing next to us.

I turned in his arms, not quite ready to break our connection. "Thank you, Rosa. It smells delicious."

"You're welcome, cariño." She leaned over and kissed my

right cheek. "Mateo said you planned to make brisket and pota- toes. I hope you don't mind that I gave it a little flavor."

The allspice. And...hot peppers. What would Mom say?

Who cared? "It smells fantastic."

"Thank you. You work so hard. For los niños. I'm happy to help you."

Rosa knew. She worked hard for her own cause of domestic abuse victims. "Thank you."

"Speaking of work..." I should put down the bags of groceries, wash my hands, and help them, but I couldn't make myself move away from Mateo. "I have some good news."

"A big donation?" Mateo tightened his arms around me.

"No fair guessing. But yes. I'm going to wait until everyone else is here to tell you who it's from."

"What do I get if I guess it first?" His hand stroked down under my raincoat to my ass and squeezed it in a bordering-on- R-rated way.

I pushed away, my cheeks flaming. "Nothing. So don't bother. I won't tell."

I turned to the table to set down the grocery bags, but he was there, pressing his hard body to my back and banding his arms around my waist.

"Here's what I want for *not* guessing." And he whispered something so filthy in my ear that I was definitely going to have to change my panties before my other guests got here.

"Fine. Twist my arm." Wow, it had gotten hot in the kitchen.

Rosa cleared her throat. "I'm just going to start the potatoes. Mateo, go help Mimi get ready for her guests."

My face burned. "Just give me a minute to wash up, and I'll peel the potatoes."

"Already done." Mateo gripped my hand and three seconds later, he pressed me against my bedroom door, pushing my rain- coat off my shoulders as he kissed me, hot and needy.

"But." I gasped for air. "My family's going to be here in"—I checked my phone—"twenty-three minutes."

He plucked the phone out of my hand and set it on the dresser. "Then we don't have time for talking."

He unbuttoned my slacks and tunneled his hand inside. "Ah, Mimi, so wet for me."

I palmed the front of his—apron? A snarky comment rose to my lips, but as soon as he thrummed my clit, I forgot it. In fact, I forgot how to breathe. I became a pillar of pure pleasure. My ears buzzed.

Buzzed?

"Mateo, stop. I think someone's at the door."

"They can wait," he growled. "I can make you come in three minutes. Two if I—" He wedged a second hand into my pants, from the back this time.

"No, Mateo." I gripped his shoulders. All I wanted to do was hold on and let him guide me to my release, but I couldn't. Not while my guests—my flipping *early* guests—waited outside in the rain. "Stop."

He stopped, but when he pulled his hand out of my panties, he gave his fingers a thoroughly obscene lick.

"You're killing me." I adjusted my underwear and buttoned my pants.

"Two minutes?" He raised his eyebrows.

I rose on my toes and kissed him. "No. No matter how handsome you are and how good you are at that, we have guests." An ice storm zinged through me at that. *We* didn't have guests; *I* did. But that little word, *we*, kept creeping into my speech.

I didn't hate it.

Fluttering my hands over my blouse, I rushed out to the main room and pressed the intercom button. "Hey."

"I was about to get out my key and make sure you hadn't succumbed to the flames shooting out of your oven."

"Ha, ha, Benny. I should make you wait out there." But then I remembered he was bringing Cooper. Although he wasn't my boss anymore, I planned to hit him up for another donation to

Jackson's foundation before the end of the year. I hit the buzzer to let them in.

I opened the door a crack and ran back through to the bedroom to my bathroom, where Mateo was washing his hands.

He caught my gaze in the mirror. "Want to jump in the shower?"

"No time." I scanned my work-rumpled clothes. They'd have to do.

He lifted my hair, coiled it around his hand, and kissed the back of my neck. "We could be fast."

There was that *we* again. I spun in his arms and kissed his cheek. I wanted to linger there, sniffing his aftershave and exploring all my favorite places on his body. "We have guests. Go say hi to Ben and your cousin while I wash my hands and put on lipstick, 'kay?"

"Okay." He nuzzled into my neck, laying a kiss there, but a second later, he was gone.

I stared into the mirror at my huge pupils, my kiss-swollen lips. Fuck it. Let my family see how happy Mateo made me.

I washed my hands and slathered on some long-wearing lip stain that ought to stand up to a few more stolen kisses. I swapped my low heels for slippers and closed the bedroom door behind me.

Everyone squeezed into my tiny kitchen around Rosa. Ben arranged a bouquet of chrysanthemums in a vase while Cooper spoke quietly to his mother. Mateo stood at the stove, checking the potatoes.

"Hey, guys," I said.

"Hey, sis." Ben fluffed the flowers one last time and threaded through the others to hug me.

"Mimi," Cooper said. "Everything smells delicious."

"Thanks to your mother and Mateo."

"Hard day at work?" Ben asked.

"Great day. You'll never believe the donation I accepted."

"The amount or the donor?" he asked.

"Both. Plus the person being honored."

"Ooh. Do tell."

"So Jamila Jallow walked into the office today—"

"Mila?" Cooper's head snapped up. "How much?"

"Don't be jealous. She told me it's exactly what she gave to your foundation. One million."

Ben whistled.

"But wait. Here's the weird part. She said it was in honor of— get this—Natalie Jones." Natalie was helping me plan next year's gala. We weren't leaving it to the last minute like Larissa had done. She'd been showing me some brochures for venues when Jamila breezed in. And Natalie had gasped like Jamila carried a bloody ax and not a teeny designer bag with a thrillingly generous check inside.

Rosa clucked her tongue. "That Natalie Jones lights up like a marquee whenever Jamila is in the room."

"Really?" I scrunched my nose. Natalie was so naturally viva-cious I hadn't noticed anything different in front of Jamila. "You're right. She went red as Thor's cape. And then after Jamila said she was honoring *her* with the gift, she just ran out. And Jamila ran after her. Well, she didn't run. It was more like a fast glide. She moves like she's on ice skates."

"Interesting." Ben exchanged a look with Cooper.

"What? Is something going on there?"

Cooper shrugged. "Maybe you're right, babe."

"What?" I wailed. "She's never said anything to me, and we're *friends.*"

"Don't take it personally," Ben said. "That one hides a lot under all that fashion and poise. With her mother, and what Jackson would say—" He shook his head.

"You can ask her about it on Monday, mi amor."

Mateo's gentle words reminded me we were gossiping about my friend. "I will. It was so weird. And I've never accepted a donation that huge. Jackson was over the moon when I called him. Though I *didn't* mention the tribute. I figured Natalie would tell him."

"Family's weird," Ben said.

As if on cue, the intercom dinged.

"Why is everyone so damned prompt?" I muttered, turning toward the intercom.

In another *we* moment, Mateo stepped up beside me to welcome my parents inside. For a moment, I imagined having him here all the time. We already spent every night together when he wasn't on the night shift. The last night of his most recent string of nights on duty, I'd gone to his place even though he was working, just to sleep in sheets that smelled like him. To have him cuddle up behind me for an hour in the early morning before I got up for work.

But before I could say anything or even squeeze his hand, my parents appeared in my doorway. I hugged my dad while Mateo kissed my mother's cheek. Then he stepped behind me to shake Dad's hand while I hugged Mom.

"I smell something spicy," she said.

"The brisket's got a little Caribbean flair tonight. Rosa and Mateo made it."

Dad sniffed the air. "If it tastes as wonderful as it smells, I might have to steal the recipe."

"I'm sure it will," I said. "Rosa and Mateo are a dream team in the kitchen."

"I brought lemon cake." Dad raised the cake container.

I hummed. Dad's cakes were the best.

"Let me take your coats," Mateo said.

"No, I'll do it," I said. "I have to get the candles out of the closet, anyway."

"We'll both do it." He helped Mom out of her raincoat, then took Dad's. He followed me to the hall closet, but instead of waiting outside and passing me the coats, he crowded in with me and dropped them to the floor. He pulled the string to light the bulb. In the dim light, his eyes had gone dark with only the thinnest ring of blue.

"What are you doing?"

"Having an amuse-bouche." Avoiding my lipstick, he kissed down my neck to my collarbone. "The sound you made when your father mentioned the lemon cake…"

"You and your amuse-bouches." But I buried my hands in his hair and held on tight, letting desire spark to a flame in my center. Mateo's touch was so much better than even my dad's baked goods.

His hand smoothed over my breast, swirling lazily over my nipple. He couldn't feel it through my industrial-strength work bra, but my nipples pebbled with want.

"Two minutes?" he murmured into the valley between my breasts.

"Mimi?" My mother's voice came through the thin closet door. "Do you need help?"

I clenched my fingers in his hair and reluctantly tugged him away.

"No, Mom, Mateo's helping me." I gave him a fierce stare.

"Okay. Want me to open the wine we brought?"

"Yes, please. We'll be out in a minute."

I gave her a few seconds to walk away and then said, "Reach that box of candles on the shelf for me, please."

"Ah, my Mimi." Mateo clucked his tongue. "So serious. So businesslike."

"You love that about me."

He smiled. "I do. But what I like even better is turning you from serious to sex-drunk."

"I do not get sex-drunk," I lied.

"Don't you?" He turned, and his muscles bunched under his black T-shirt when he stretched to reach the box from the shelf. God, his ass was amazing. And it was all mine.

"See?" He winked at me over his shoulder.

Shit. I'd said it out loud. "So what if it is amazing? And mine?" I gave it a squeeze for good measure.

"Watch out, or you'll make me indecent." He tucked the box under his arm and adjusted his jeans.

"Can't have that, can we?" I quirked up one side of my mouth. "I'll set up the candles while you take a minute."

Before he could kiss me senseless again, I snatched the box and slipped out of the closet.

Mom had found my candle holders and set them on my table. I settled the candles inside and took a deep breath, letting go of thoughts of Mateo, work, and my stressful dinner guests. I scratched the match along the side of the box and watched the flame hiss to life. I held it to the candles until the flame caught and held, then I set the match on the tray, where it burned itself out.

Following the traditions Mom had taught me, I waved my hands over the candles to welcome in the Shabbat and then covered my eyes to recite the prayer. The candles burned brightly when I was done, and their warmth seemed to settle into my middle.

Mom hugged me. "Thank you for inviting us tonight. Do you think you'll keep up the traditions when you...?" She nodded at Mateo as he emerged from the hall, a smile spreading over his handsome face when our gazes connected.

"When I...?"

"It seems that the two of you"—she glanced at Mateo in the kitchen and picked her words carefully—"are getting serious. And he seems more religious than Cooper." The gold cross shone at his neck.

"Oh, but we're not—" But that seemed like a lie. We *were* serious. The same peaceful warmth as when I lighted the Shabbat candles filled me when I saw him at the end of the day. My brain had started associating him with happiness. Safety. Home.

Huh.

"He loves the Shabbat traditions. And I could go to Mass with him." Though I'd hate to give up a Sunday morning twined around him in bed.

"Your dad and I made it work. You can, too."

"Mimi, where's a serving bowl for these potatoes?" Ben called.

"Just a second," I called. Then I flung my arm around Mom. "You're right. Mateo's my person. I'm not giving up who I am. I'm adding him into my life. We'll work it out. Together."

The candlelight sparkled on Mom's glistening brown eyes. "A job you love and a good man. I'm so happy for you, sweetie."

Mateo walked out of the kitchen with the wine and met my gaze. The warmth spread through my center like butter on warm bread. "I'm happy for me, too."

———

Thank you so much for reading *Forget Me!* Please consider posting a review on your favorite retailer, BookBub, or Goodreads. Reviews help other readers find new authors like me.

Want to see Mimi and Mateo take the next step in their relationship? And read about Mateo lifting heavy objects and the…feelings…it gives Mimi? Join my newsletter at michellemccraw.com/Mateo or use your phone's camera to take a picture of the QR code below to download a bonus epilogue!

Want to see how it all began, before Jackson found his happily ever after with another prickly heroine and started his foundation? That story is *Work with Me,* a rivals-to-lovers romantic comedy set in Austin, Texas, and it's available on your favorite retailer. Read on for a sneak peek.

WORK WITH ME (SYNERGY BOOK 1)
CHAPTER 1

ALICIA

THE SKY WAS the color of pea soup. Angry pea soup.

Having lived in Texas all my life, I knew the sky turned that color and the clouds boiled only when they were brewing something especially violent.

I gauged the distance from the overhang of the parking garage to the building entrance across the cracked pavement of the four-lane street. There'd be no sprinting across in my four-inch heels.

"Trying too hard," I muttered. "Flats would've been fine. Or even boots." But I'd wanted to make a good impression at my first gig for my brand-new company. Serious. Capable. Flawless. Ready to use my pointy-toed shoes to kick ass and create a name for myself by turning around this troubled project.

This was my stick-it-to-em moment. To my old boss, Lowell, who'd said I was too "sensitive" to be management material. To Dr. Fletcher, who'd told our entire class—while I, the only woman in the room, sat there, too flummoxed to object—that women didn't have the drive to succeed in technology. To every coworker who'd ever talked over me, taken credit for my work, or tried to mansplain programming to me. I was walking into Synergy

Analytics, a Fortune 1000 company founded by two Stanford grads and now worth over six *billion* dollars, to use my smarts to help them succeed.

Not bad for a local girl who went to a state university. I brushed invisible dust off my shoulder.

My phone pinged. Thirty minutes until the meeting. Plenty of time to get through security, shake some hands, and take my seat at the head of the table. I drew myself up. For the first time in my life, I was my own boss. I was more than qualified to do this gig, and I could beat the rain, too.

As my shoe hit the sidewalk, I heard the first plink. *Ha! Missed me!* A good thing, since I was wearing a white blouse, my suit jacket folded over my messenger bag to keep cool in Austin's early-September heat. A see-through shirt at my first meeting would not be a good look. Another quick step, and I checked the street for cars. Clear, if I went fast.

I stepped off the curb, and a raindrop bounced in front of me. *Bounced?* Another one to my right. A blur of white zoomed in front of my nose. That wasn't rain; it was hail. Pea-sized. No sweat. Hail wouldn't even get my blouse wet.

Crossing the second lane of traffic, I kicked a hailstone. That one was bigger, about the size of a marble. An anomaly. *Still, better watch out.* If I stepped on one that size, I'd probably go down in the middle of Sixth Street. And then I'd get run over by a car. I couldn't let Noah lose another parent. Besides, I hadn't yet bought life insurance to replace the policy my old employer had provided. "If I get into this building safely," I murmured, "I promise I'll call the insurance company as soon as I get home."

Gritting my teeth against the pelting stones, I took two big steps to cross the last lane before hopping up onto the curb over the pile of white hailstones that had drifted against it. Two more steps took me under the building's sheltering overhang. I glanced up at the green clouds. "Thank—"

A flash of white, and pain seared my forehead right at my

hairline. "Ouch!" Cradling my face, I scuttled further under the awning. That'd teach me to practice gratitude.

"Are you all right?" A tall figure loomed up in my peripheral vision.

"Fine, I'm fine." But when I pulled my hand away, my fingertips were smeared with blood. I dug in my bag for a tissue.

"Scalp wounds bleed a lot. Hurt like a motherfucker, too. Hang on, I've got something." The man set down his duffel bag and rooted around inside. His faded black T-shirt with AC/DC's distinctive logo rode up on his back, revealing a vee of lean muscle that disappeared into his jeans. Between working a desk job and hanging out at soccer fields, I hadn't seen a lot of physiques like that. Not since Rick. I shook off the memory. I couldn't let Rick ruin my you-go-girl attitude.

The man turned, a heather-gray T-shirt in his hand. "It's clean, I promise. Mind if I—?"

Not sure whether my lost power of speech was due to his Greek-god bod or blood loss, I shook my head. Gently, he brushed away my hand holding the blood-soaked tissue and pressed the shirt to my face. The shirt smelled like fresh soap and something else. Leather. Like a boot shop. Or the inside of a luxury car. I inhaled, wishing I could wrap myself in that scent.

When he stepped closer, he kicked a hailstone. "What is this? It's not snow."

"It's hail." The shirt covered one eye, but I checked him out with the other. He was tall, a good three or four inches taller than me, even in my heels. Ah. It wasn't all his laundry soap. He was wearing some fancy cowboy boots; thus, the leather scent. Ostrich. Expensive. Faded, broken-in jeans that showcased narrow hips, and the shirt I'd already noted that stretched tight in all the right places. Dark hair, somewhere between brown and black. Dark eyes, too. Sharp. Assessing. But also kind. My cheeks heated under that stare.

"Hell? You mean, as in frozen over?" He spoke crisply, like the people on TV, not like anyone I'd ever met in real life.

"No. Hail. H-A-I-L. You're not from around here, are you?"

He smiled, the right side higher than the left. "Nope. Still trying to get used to some of these Texas accents."

"Just visiting, or do you live here now?"

That lush mouth tensed a little. "A little of both. I've been in Austin for three months, but I hope I can go home soon."

"You hope?" I flashed him an easy smile. "Clearly, you haven't had the full Austin experience. Most people never want to leave." Except me. After living my whole life here, my hometown had started to feel a little like a favorite shirt I'd outgrown. Soft and cozy, but a little too tight.

The tension disappeared, and his right cheek kicked up again. That smile should've been illegal. "Maybe I haven't had the right tour guide." His gaze started to trail down, and his eyes widened when they reached my chest. He blinked back up to my face. "You've, ah, you've got some blood on your blouse."

"Oh, shit." I put my hand over his on the T-shirt. His hand was warm and dry. Smooth skin, like he also worked at a desk. He slid it out from under mine so I could survey the damage. Dammit, two red drops right over my left boob. Holding one hand to the cut, I tried to unfold my jacket with the other.

"Let me help?"

I nodded, and he shook out my jacket. While he held it out behind me, I slid in one arm, swapped hands over my cut, and then slid into the other sleeve. When he pulled the sides together, we stood close, like we were dancing. That heavenly scent of his surrounded me, and the hail, my meeting, everything faded around me.

He looked familiar. I'd seen those full lips before, quirked to one side. The short, dark beard, thick on his chin and a little scraggly on his cheeks. The genuine smile seemed different, but I'd seen those eyes crinkled at the corners. How did I know him?

"Have we—"

He spoke at the same time. "You work around here? I don't think I've seen you before."

"It's my first day. I have a big meeting this morning." Clearly, I wasn't all that memorable if he didn't think he'd seen me before. Where had I met him?

"In there?" He tilted his chin toward the Synergy building behind me.

"Yes, I'm a consultant. I own my own business." Even bleeding there on the sidewalk, I felt my chest expand.

"Consultant." He stepped back, taking the glorious scent with him. The hailstones plinked outside the awning. "Let me get you a bandage. I've got one in my bag."

"No. Thank you, though." I couldn't walk into a meeting with Cooper Fallon with a bandage on my face.

"Would you rather have blood dripping down your forehead during your big meeting? That chunk of ice really got you." He rummaged in his bag and pulled out a small plastic first-aid kit.

"Are you a Boy Scout?" I carried a first-aid kit in my car for Noah, but I didn't know too many men who did.

He chuckled. "They kicked me out when I was nine. Marlee. My assistant. She takes care of me."

An assistant? My first-aider in jeans and a T-shirt didn't look like someone with that kind of power. But now that I thought about it, his voice did carry a slight imperious edge like he was used to giving orders. And having them followed.

He clicked open the kit and pulled out a bandage. When he peeled apart the wrapper, I caught a flash of red.

"What's that?"

"Oh. Lightning McQueen. You know, from *Cars?* She has a twisted sense of humor."

Of course I knew *Cars*. It had been Noah's favorite movie since he was three. "You're not putting Lightning McQueen on my face."

"Show me that smile. The one you gave me when you talked about your business. The one you'll show them in that meeting."

I couldn't help it. I smiled, big and broad, every time I thought about Weber Technology Consulting.

"That's it. No one will be looking at old Lightning McQueen here when you flash that gorgeous smile." He lifted the shirt away from my face, brushing my fingers. It wasn't blood loss that made them tingle.

"Thanks…" I raised my eyebrows.

"My friends call me Jay."

"I'm Alicia."

"Alicia." He rolled my name in his mouth. Then, with a light press of his warm fingers, he adhered the bandage to my head. "We match now, see?" He held up his arm, and, sure enough, across his elbow was a Lightning McQueen bandage.

"The hail didn't get you, too?" I'd been too focused on my own injury, my own problems, and I hadn't been paying attention. Jay's arm bulged with lean muscle, and a vein wrapped around his forearm. I'd only seen that on TV, too.

"Nah." He rubbed it. "Got too close to a tree on my run." He stepped closer again. "May I?"

I nodded, my throat too dry to speak. He tugged my jacket so the sides met in front. Then he slid a finger into my hair near the cut and smoothed it down. He scanned me from my head to my toes, and every spot his gaze hit tingled.

"Good as new." He stepped back. "Feel okay? Not too dizzy?"

Dizzy? Yeah. I blinked. Had I said that out loud? "I'm good."

"Good." He opened his mouth and then closed it again. Was he about to ask me out? He had to be feeling what I was. That thing he'd said about my smile was definitely flirty. An invisible tether kept either of us from moving toward the door or out onto the sidewalk.

My sister's words echoed back to me from years ago. *Life is short. Don't wait for what you want. Ask for it, and then take it.* She hadn't lived long enough to follow her own advice. But I'd taken her words to heart, and I knew what I wanted: more time with this guy's gentle fingers and bottomless eyes. "Hey, Jay, I've got that meeting now, but maybe you'd like to get a coffee sometime?"

He glanced again at the door behind me. "I'm sorry, I...can't."

My belly went tight and heavy, and my cheeks heated. "Oh, okay." Did he have a girlfriend? Was Marlee more than his assistant? Or maybe I was in shock and had hallucinated the signs of his attraction. Served me right for putting myself out there. For following Melissa's advice.

I needed to get out of there. Regroup and focus on my meeting. I hitched my bag higher on my shoulder. "I have to go. Thank you for your help."

When I held out the shirt to him, the gray fabric was smeared with blood. Gross. I snatched it back before he could touch it. "I'll wash this out tonight and bring it back tomorrow. I'll leave it here in the lobby in the morning?"

"Sure." He bent again, showing that tantalizing sliver of his back, and picked up a golf ball–sized hailstone. He pulled a sock from his duffel and wrapped it around the hunk of ice before dropping it back into his bag. I had to smile despite my embarrassment. If he was anything like Noah, Jay would stash it in the nearest freezer and pull it out to examine later. Scientific curiosity always melted my nerdy heart.

Though this scientist-slash-first-aider's heart didn't feel the same about me. My cheeks blazed again.

He opened the door and held it for me.

I walked through, careful not to brush against him. The heat had spread down my neck to my chest. I spotted a sign for the restrooms to the right and turned toward it without looking at him. "Thanks again."

"Anytime, Alicia."

A few minutes later, I clipped a visitor badge to my lapel, mentally donning my armor again. *Back on track. Kicking ass. No more distractions, no matter how sexy.*

Another tall man strode through the security sensors, extending his hand to me. "You must be Ms. Weber. I'm Cooper Fallon."

I sucked in a breath. Chiseled jaw, sandy-blond hair, eyes the color of bluebonnets. I'd seen photos of him—the CEO of Synergy Analytics had been on the cover of *Forbes* at least twice, plus I'd Googled him, of course—but photos hadn't prepared me for six-feet-something of tanned skin and trim physique accentuated by a crisp blue shirt, tailored slacks, and a creaseless sports coat. I passed my hand over my slim black skirt, wrinkled from the drive over.

Mentally giving myself a shake, I grasped his hand. "Pleasure to meet you, Mr. Fallon."

He didn't ask me to call him Cooper.

"Stairs okay?" he asked. "We're meeting on the second floor."

"Sure." A little cardio might settle out my nerves. Taking a deep breath, I followed him through the security sensors to a wide, open staircase. Climbing, I looked around me. Wide wooden planked floors, exposed ductwork in the ceiling, bright reds, oranges, and blues in colorful splashes on the walls that reminded me of the Hill Country in spring. "How long have you owned the building?"

"Not long. We bought it from a company that decided to move to a remote workforce. We're living in the space for a while before we decide to make any changes."

"But Synergy didn't go remote?" I almost smacked my fore-head. *Obviously, Alicia. They're here.*

He waited for me at the top of the stairs. "No, we take a collab-orative approach to software development. Jamila says that's what you prefer, too?"

I smiled at the mention of my mentor. I could almost feel her standing next to me, saying, *You got this.* "Absolutely," I said. "Teams can get so much more done when they're located together, when they don't have to rely on email or even instant messaging for communications."

"I'm glad you think so. I'm sure you'll fit right in with the team."

He pulled open a frosted-glass door to a conference room. Inside, most of the chairs were taken. A quick glance told me the meeting attendees were all men; no surprise there. And at the head of the table—

"Jay?" I lifted a hand to my forehead. Was he one of the developers I'd be working with?

"Alicia!" Jay stood, his smile quickly turning to a frown as he glanced from me to Cooper. "What's going on, Coop?"

Maybe that hailstone had done more damage than I'd thought. Or maybe I'd been too infatuated by a pair of sharp, dark eyes. But seeing the two men together, the puzzle pieces snapped into place. Cooper Fallon and my-friends-call-me-Jay *Jackson* Jones, cofounders of Synergy Analytics. The business brains and the programming muscle that'd started the company in their dorm room at Stanford and had grown it into a Fortune 1000 company in less than a dozen years.

Why the hell did Jackson Jones need *me* on a programming project?

Beside me, Fallon straightened. "Ms. Weber is here to help set direction and move the project forward."

Over the phone, he'd told me I was there to rescue a struggling project. Huh.

Jackson's stare went flinty. "As the project lead, it's my role to set direction."

Next to Jackson, a young programmer slumped into his seat like he was trying to melt into the polyester mesh. I wanted to do the same. These two were supposed to be best friends, and now they were arguing. Because of me. Actually, because Cooper Fallon hadn't told his business partner he was hiring a consultant. Me. And who the hell was in charge here? I eyed the seat at the head of the table, the one I'd planned to occupy. The one where Jackson Jones now presided.

Something that wasn't my fault had suddenly become my problem. Nothing for it but to woman up and solve it. I stiffened my spine. *Showtime.*

"Mr. Fallon, would you like to brief Mr. Jones while I get to know the team?" I said, with what I hoped was the smile Jay—Jackson—had admired and not a teeth-baring snarl.

"Great idea, Ms. Weber." Fallon tilted his head toward the hallway. Jackson circled the table and followed his cofounder out the door.

A second before the door swung shut, Jackson's low tone floated through. "This is bullshit, Coop—"

I spoke loud enough to drown him out. "While Mr. Jones and Mr. Fallon talk strategy, we'll get to know each other. I'm Alicia Weber of Weber Technology Consulting, and I'm here to help get this development project back on track so we can deliver on schedule. I'm looking forward to getting to know all of you.

"Would you like to start the introductions?" Waving at the young guy who'd been sitting next to Jackson, I circled around to the head of the table. I moved a Synergy mug of coffee out of the way and sat in the power seat, surreptitiously lowering it so my feet touched the floor.

As the guys took turns introducing themselves, the arguing on the other side of the door eventually quieted, and before we'd finished, Jackson and Fallon slipped back inside. Fallon took the empty chair across the table, his expression serene as he listened to the team provide status updates on their assignments. Jackson leaned against the wall, arms crossed, the color still bright on his high cheekbones. He said not another word, but heat seemed to radiate from him, and the programmers closest to him squirmed in their seats. But to me, at least, there was no mistaking the hurt in his eyes. What the hell was going on between those two? They needed a couples therapist more than a consultant.

"Now that everyone has met," Cooper said as he stood, "I'd like to review the project constraints. With Alicia joining the team, I'm confident you'll be able to complete development by November 15 as originally planned."

Two months. I had two months to turn the project around and deliver shippable code. I could do it. I knew I could. Unless...

"Alicia?" Cooper asked.

What had he asked me? Something about the date, I thought. "Absolutely, Mr. Fallon. We'll get it done."

Jackson snorted.

I narrowed my eyes at him. He wouldn't sabotage me, would he? It wouldn't be the first time someone had tried. I'd seen it all before: deliberate slowdowns, bugs introduced "accidentally," even calling in sick at a critical point on a project. All because a woman threatened their fragile egos. They'd closed ranks and manspread around the table until there was no room for me.

I couldn't let that happen here. If we succeeded, Cooper Fallon's recommendation would open doors for me in Austin, in Silicon Valley, wherever I wanted to work. I'd write my own ticket. If I failed, though, that'd be the end of Weber Technology Consulting. I'd head back into someone else's cubicle to churn out code, something I'd been trying to escape for the past five years.

So when Cooper Fallon shook my hand and said, "See you at eight tomorrow morning?" I said, "Absolutely. Can't wait to get started."

It's always good to start a new job lying your face off, right?

As if he could see the guilty thought race across my forehead like a marquee, Cooper narrowed his eyes at me. "Until tomorrow, then." He turned to talk to Jackson, who stared at me with an unreadable expression. Gone was the tenderness he'd shown when he'd pressed that ridiculous bandage to my forehead.

I stared right back. It didn't matter how nice he'd been. Or how famous a programmer he was. No way was I going to let Jackson Jones ruin this make-or-break opportunity for me.

———

Work with Me is available in paperback from your favorite retailer.

———

She's got a checklist for every occasion. He's never met a bad decision he didn't make. Can these rivals work out their differences and find love?

Alicia's the new programmer – and the only woman – assigned to turn around a failing project. The problem? It's Jackson's project, and he doesn't think it needs turning around.

Exiled to Austin after a massive mistake, Jackson must produce brilliant software to distract everyone from his personal failures. Programming is the one thing he's good at. That's why it's a special kind of torture when Alicia tries to tell him how to do it.

But when Alicia and Jackson partner up, they're unstoppable. And the office isn't the only place they find sizzling chemistry.

Alicia's not about to endanger her professional reputation by kissing a coworker. Jackson can't afford another screw-up. They can't be together, but working together means they can't be apart.

Work with Me is a steamy, slow-burn, opposites-attract romantic comedy featuring a straitlaced single mom, a tech genius who hides a secret under a playboy exterior, and way too much tequila. Set in up-and-coming Austin, it's the first book in the Synergy Software series.

ACKNOWLEDGMENTS

I'm not someone who sits around and reflects—Capricorn here!—but as I publish my fifth book, I figure it's time to look back before I turn my attention relentlessly forward to my next project. So I'd like to take a minute to thank all the people who encouraged me on my writing journey.

My elementary school teachers at Prestonwood Elementary in Dallas, Texas, who must have found me disruptive because they excused me from class to use the computers in the school library to write stories (yes, they had romance in them even then).

Susan Elizabeth Phillips, who, while I fangirled over her at a book signing, told the audience we could write, too. Thank you, Susan. Your encouragement came at the right time.

My indie elders, Coralie Moss and Meka James, who welcomed a newb like me and shared their experiences. Thank you for the times you talked me off the cliff.

My indie pub squad, Tiffany, Brandy, Liz, Carla, and Kristin, who are the best cheerleaders. Thanks for helping me work through my MANY questions and problems.

My beta readers, Caragh Leon, Carla Luna, Laura Luna, and Ofelia Martinez. Thanks for your thoughtful feedback and reassurance.

Melanie Rose Clarke gets up every morning with me to write. Thank you for being there every day, for your advice, accountability, and support.

And thanks to my ARC team who help get the word out about my books. Y'all are the best!

CREDITS

Edits and Proofreading

April Bennett, The Editing Soprano

Cover Design

Avery Kingston

ABOUT MICHELLE

I write steamy contemporary romance featuring characters who unashamedly love science, engineering, and technology and also lots of sex. My novels have been finalists in the RWA Vivian Contest, the Contemporary Romance Writers' Stiletto Contest, and the Windy City Romance Writers' Four Seasons Contest.

A native Texan, I now live where my family considers me a Yankee, but I'll never stop saying y'all.

For updates about my upcoming books and more free reads—plus guaranteed puppy pics—please subscribe to my newsletter at michellemccraw.com/joinme. You can also follow me on Facebook, Twitter, and Instagram.

facebook.com/MichelleMcCrawAuthor

twitter.com/MMOWriter

instagram.com/MMOWriter

amazon.com/author/michellemccraw

goodreads.com/MichelleMcCraw

bookbub.com/authors/michelle-mccraw

BOOKS IN THE SYNERGY SERIES
CAN BE READ IN ANY ORDER

Work with Me

She's got a checklist for every occasion. He's never met a bad decision he didn't make. Can straitlaced single mom Alicia find a way to work with billionaire tech genius Jackson and save her business—without falling for him first?

"Slow burn magic!" (5-star review)

Friend Me

Romance-obsessed executive assistant Marlee has a plan to woo her crush, icy and aloof San Francisco tech executive Cooper Fallon. But it all goes wrong when her fake date, instead of making her crush jealous, sparks more-than-friends feelings. Kissing the wrong guy? Not in her plan. Neither is falling for her best friend.

"Un-put-down-able" (5-star review)

Trip Me Up

Nerdy computer scientist Samantha Jones didn't mean to end up on a book tour trying to pass off her artificial intelligence-written novel as one written the old-fashioned way. And she certainly didn't mean to fall for her flannel-wearing, poetic tour partner. Opposites attract in this road-trip romance.

"This book had me hooked right from the start and up until the wee hours devouring their story!" (5-star review)

Boss Me

Frosty billionaire philanthropist Cooper Fallon would never start a fling with his off-limits assistant, Ben…or would he?

"OMG…If you like forbidden romance this is the book for you!!!" (5-star review)

Forget Me

She doesn't remember their night together. He can't forget it. When Mimi's prospective boss mistakes Mateo for her boyfriend, she's shocked when he rolls with it. But when their fake romance becomes real, will buttoned-up Mimi let down her guard for love?